Moment
of Truth

Moment of Truth

a novel by

Cheri Crane

Covenant Communications, Inc.

Cover image © Stockbyte/Getty Images.

Cover design copyrighted 2005 by Covenant Communications, Inc.

Published by Covenant Communications, Inc.
American Fork, Utah

Printed in Canada
First Printing: March 2005

11 10 09 08 07 06 05   10 9 8 7 6 5 4 3 2 1

ISBN 1-59156-727-0

Dedication

For my siblings—Tom, Heather, and Trudi—eternal family members and friends. Thanks for always being in my corner.

Acknowledgments

Several people aided in the completion of this novel. I would like to thank RaNae Roberts, Shelly Wallentine, and Michelle Humphreys for their continued willingness to proofread my manuscripts, with an added thanks to my oldest son, Kris, who pitched in to proofread during a revision deadline. I would also like to offer my appreciation to the rest of my family—Kennon, Derek, and Devin—for their encouraging support. Merci beaucoup to the "V." It has been an honor flying with you ladies.

Thanks also to everyone at Covenant, with a special note of appreciation for my editor, whose skills always make for a better book.

Chapter 1

The first mistake I made that night was to stand next to my mother. Under normal circumstances, Janell Clark is a fairly calm person, but that night, she was a bundle of nerves. My older brother, Reese, was taking his sweet time opening the large, white envelope the Church headquarters had mailed. My mother shrieked when she found it in our mailbox that morning. The sound carried through my open bedroom window, snapping me out of a cool dream I was having about Johnny Depp—he was just about to rescue me from a band of evil pirates. I'm sure everyone else who lives in Roy, Utah, heard her reaction, which is why I was initially hiding in the far corner of our family room that night. Then Mom decided I could hold my baby brother while she ran the video camera. The only way I could keep Joey from fussing was to stand next to Mom. I'd say my younger brother is spoiled, but that would be the understatement of the century.

So while my mother did her best to not shake the camera as she trembled with excitement, Reese assumed several exaggerated poses until both Joey and I were ready to scream. I just wanted to get this over with. Reese's white envelope had ruined my plans for the day, plans that had included important things like hanging out at the mall with my best friend, Roz. We both had the day off—that never happens. The summer was nearly over, and Roz and I hadn't had a chance to do any of the fun stuff we wanted to do. On this day, we were going to go shopping for school clothes. Instead, I got to tend Joey while Mom made a series of phone calls. Then she insisted that we clean the house from top to bottom, and when that was done to her specs, we spent the rest of the afternoon making a mound of cream puffs to feed our guests that evening. Not how I had envisioned spending my only day off that week. So, yeah, I was ready to get the whole thing over with.

As for Joey, he was too young to understand what was going on. At six months old, his main concern was that his beloved routine had been disrupted. So that night I jiggled him up and down, humming a stupid lullaby, hoping our ham of a big brother would hurry this torture along.

My oldest brother has a knack for basking in the limelight, and this was his finest hour. To be fair, it was something Reese had worked hard to make happen. Some of us were afraid it would never take place, considering my brother had botched up his life for a while.

I don't know everything he did after our younger sister died in a car accident four years ago—and I don't want to know. Reese didn't handle things very well. For the record, none of us did. Losing Allison ripped us apart. But gradually, we all found ways to move on. Reese did it through alcohol and drugs. My dad, Will Clark, retreated into his job with an accounting firm by taking on the role of supervisor of his department, a promotion he had avoided before because it cut into family time. Mom went to work part time at a local flower shop to keep her sanity.

As for me, I began writing everything I was feeling in a journal. It was a good release, but once in a while, I still allowed my emotions to get the best of me. We all did . . . except for Mom. She kept things buried pretty deep until one night when Dad and I really ticked her off. In our defense, having Reese around hadn't been very pleasant. His problems had led to several ugly arguments. Finally, one night he slammed out of the house and out of our lives.

After Reese had been missing for about a year and a half, Mom found him. Actually, Reese's girlfriend, Stacy Jardine, found him sitting on a bench in the Roy cemetery, where he was contemplating life, death—who knows? Stacy freaked and drove up to our house to tell Mom that Reese was back in town. Anyway, to make a long story short, Mom wanted to bring Reese home, and Dad and I sort of threw a fit. It was nothing compared to Mom's explosion. Wow, talk about major heat. She got her point across, and after acknowledging that we were scum, Dad and I joined her in welcoming Reese back home.

We were nervous about it at first, but surprisingly, Reese had changed. He seemed nicer and more mature. It took some time and a lot of effort on his part, but he eventually gave up the alcohol and drugs and tried hard to make things right. Life seemed to settle down until the night Reese did something to break Stacy's heart. I never have figured out what that was all about. Maybe my big brother had been seeing someone else. All I know is that for a while, Stacy wouldn't even speak to him. At least they're friends now, but that's about it. And maybe it's for the best, considering they both want to serve missions. Which brings us back to why I was standing beside my mother, bouncing Joey in my arms as he drooled down the front of one of my best shirts.

Reese sat on the couch, taking great delight in dragging things out. Finally Dad let him know he had carried on long enough, and our future missionary tore the envelope open. We all stared as he slowly pulled the letter from its casing.

"I'm going to serve in . . ."

We hung on his every word, mostly because some of us had placed bets on where he was going. Personally, I was hoping it was somewhere like Nome, Alaska, figuring it would humble him a bit.

"Salt Lake City!"

"Reese!" the combined chorus complained, a chorus made up of our immediate family, plus two sets of impatient grandparents who hadn't been sure they would live long enough to see my brother serve a mission, our bishop—a man who had done as much as my parents to prod Reese along—and Stacy.

"Reese, that's as lame as saying Boise, Idaho," I added, disgusted by his feeble attempt to be funny.

"Okay, fine. Try to have a little fun, see what happens," Reese said with a grin. Clearing his throat, he began to read, "Dear Elder Clark. You are hereby called to serve as a missionary of The Church of Jesus Christ of Latter-day Saints. You are assigned to labor in the Missouri St. Louis Mission."

To the side of me, our mother screamed again, scaring Joey and permanently damaging my hearing.

"It's stateside," Mom exclaimed further, reaching around me to give Stacy a high five.

See, this is the problem I have with Stacy. She has always been close to my mother. It got worse after Stacy's mother died last year. My mom can be a pretty neat lady, but she and I don't always see eye-to-eye on things—which is probably why she likes Stacy so much. Stacy tends to agree with her most of the time. Stacy's also prettier than me, more talented, and just joined the Church a few months ago, which gives her added brownie points in my mother's eyes. I'm convinced Mom thinks that someday Reese will make her a permanent part of our family.

I'm not sure how I feel about that. Truthfully, there are moments when I think she might make an okay sister-in-law. Stacy can be very nice and she has tried to be friends with me. And like my mom is always pointing out, Stacy is a great example. She had to overcome a lot to join the Church. Her father, a reformed alcoholic, abandoned Stacy's family a long time ago, and not only that, he hated Mormons. Stacy had to get past all of that before becoming a member of the Church. So in a way, I kind of look up to her. But then there are moments like tonight when I want to stick my foot out and watch her do a face-plant in front of everyone.

As Stacy and my mother moved in unison to congratulate my brother, I glared at both of them and carried Joey to the other side of the room to calm him down. "Hey, hey, it's all right. I care about you even if no one else does," I soothed, but Joey wouldn't quit crying. I think he resented Stacy right then too.

"Bring Joey here," Reese hollered above the noise in the room.

"Why?" I asked.

"He wants to congratulate me, and you're not letting him," he replied. "That's why he's crying. Bring him to me." I was only too happy to oblige. I made my way through the crowd that had gathered around Reese and handed the squealing package over, taking great delight in watching as Joey snuffled against Reese's new green button-down shirt. "Gross," Reese griped. "Oh, well," he sighed. "All part of being a big brother."

I rolled my eyes and tried to ignore the nausea that comment triggered. To my way of thinking, Reese hasn't always been such a great big brother.

"Hey, guy," Reese said, looking pleased with himself when Joey calmed down. "What do you think? Your brother is serving a mission in St. Louis, Missouri."

Joey responded by drooling down the front of Reese's shirt, making the original mess worse. I almost laughed out loud.

"Thanks, dude. I'll be sure to return the favor when you get your mission call," Reese promised as he handed Joey to our mother.

"That works. You'll be old and toothless by then," I quipped as Reese did his best to wipe his shirt clean with a couple of tissues from a nearby Kleenex box. That comment was my second mistake of the evening.

"Old and toothless like us, I suppose," Grandmother Clark said sullenly.

When I saw the look on my grandmother's face, I cringed. I can't help it—she affects me that way. Like my dad, she doesn't have much of a sense of humor, and I always manage to say the very worst thing to trigger a lengthy lecture. Overly sensitive, Grandma Clark is not much fun to be around, and I absolutely hate it when people tell me how alike we are.

"Laurie, you would think, now that you're seventeen, you would be a bit more considerate of others," Grandma Clark began.

"Laurie, why you don't you head upstairs and start dishing up those cream puffs we made earlier today," Mom said, coming to the rescue. For once, her timing was perfect. Not only did it save me from being chastised, but it gave me an excuse to avoid the mushy scene I could see was developing between Stacy and Reese. They may have cooled their relationship, but there were still enough sparks floating around in that room to indicate the fire still smoldered. Whirling around, I hurried upstairs before I lost my appetite.

Chapter 2

On my way to work the next day I reflected on Reese's party. I guess the effort was worth it—everyone seemed to have a good time. The worst part was cleaning up after it was over. Someone had smeared one of the cream puffs onto the couch in the family room. I'm suspecting the guilty party had handed a cream puff to Joey, and guess who got to clean it up. Yep, yours truly. The other downer was the family photo moment that went on forever. Dad took enough digital pictures to last us the next hundred years.

He bought a digital camera two months ago, and he has spent all summer taking the "perfect" shot. Most of them end up downloaded on our computer at home. From time to time, Dad likes to set the main wallpaper on our computer with one of his treasured images. So I shouldn't have been surprised to see what was plastered on our computer this morning. I'm assuming Dad is responsible for the bright, smiling faces of Reese and Stacy that now adorn our computer. Reese with his thick, black hair and blue eyes, standing beside Stacy who has brown hair and big brown eyes with long eyelashes I would die for. Mom had asked the two of them to pose together, so they made googly eyes at each other while Dad snapped shot after shot. I'm betting my parents are thinking that one of these pictures would make a great wedding announcement in a few years. Like that'll happen. Who knows? For now, Dad picked his favorite image to save as our computer wallpaper. So when I first moved the mouse this morning, anxious to check my e-mail, there it was, seventeen inches of hurl material.

I'm just glad I have my own login account on our computer. It was a relief to see a gorgeous sunset replace Reese and Stacy, a picture I had selected for my own settings earlier last week. I like to rotate the images, choosing mostly landscape scenes. I feel they inspire my creativity when I write.

This fall I'll be a senior in high school. Most of the kids my age don't have a clue about what they want to be. I decided last year that I want to become a journalist and work for a big-city newspaper. I've been told that I have a talent for writing and I love getting the scoop on things, so this seems like a natural career choice for me. I've seen Dad, Mom, and Reese get this smirk on their faces whenever I tell them about my plans. They all think I'll get married after one year of college and have a ton of kids. I can hardly wait to see the stunned expression on their faces when I receive my first Pulitzer prize for a world-changing story.

In the meantime, I spend some time every day on the computer writing out my thoughts, feelings, and anything else that comes to mind. I call it *Laurie's View*, a personal column I write in a file I've hidden on the computer. I figure it's good practice for my future career. For now, I have to settle for working at a local drive-in called Harold's Burgers. Yeah, don't even get me started on how Reese teases me about my job. Typical adolescent humor—and he thinks he's ready to serve a mission. The people in charge at the MTC will have their hands full polishing that guy.

The drive-in isn't the greatest place to work, but it pays okay compared to other jobs I've had in the past, like babysitting for the neighbors, mowing lawns, and washing my dad's car. Now that I think about it, Dad never has paid me for washing his car. But he has been pretty good about giving me spending money when I need it. At least he was until I got this job at Harold's. Now he brags to people that I'm financially independent. I know this much—it'll take more than a job as a waitress to get me through college, which is why I'm taking a couple of honors classes this year. If I can get good enough grades, hopefully I can snag a scholarship or two to help out with expenses. I'm sure my parents will help me if I need it, but I'd like to do as much as I can on my own.

The neat thing is, I'll be the first one of us kids to go to college. Reese never did bother with college after high school. He was too busy damaging his gray cells at wild parties. When he decided to clean up his act, he got a job at Wal-Mart in Layton. He's still working there, saving his money for his mission. As for Allison, Mom's convinced that she's busy doing missionary work in the spirit world with some of our wayward ancestors and that, in her spare time, she watches over us. Sometimes that's a comforting thought. It depends on what I'm doing. Then there's Joey, and obviously it will be a while before he'll be old enough to go to kindergarten let alone college.

That reminds me, do you know how embarrassing it is that my parents had a baby at their age? And not only that, but my mother decided to breast-feed him. Talk about gross. Mom just smiles and tells me that someday I'll want to do something similar with my own babies. Yeah, right! Getting married and having a family doesn't exactly fit in with my future plans. As a journalist, I'll be traveling the world, reporting on historic events as they happen. Maybe someone will recognize my talent and hire me to be a television reporter. I can see it all now, "Live from Switzerland, Laurie Clark reporting on the world peace conference . . ."

The piercing siren behind me was as loud as my mother's scream the day before. I glanced down at the speedometer and noted that I was going about 65 in a 40. I hoped Allison wasn't watching right now. She'd be laughing her head off.

Groaning, I slowed down and pulled off to the side of the road. So much for my perfect record. I've never had a ticket—something Reese can't say. I rolled down my window as the officer approached. Mom had told me that once, when she was in a similar predicament, she had burst into tears and the officer had taken pity on her and had just given her a warning. I did my best to appear distraught, which wasn't too hard considering that was how I really felt.

"Officer, I'm sorry. I've never done anything like this before," I began, forcing a tear from one eye as I gazed down in an attempt to look repentant. Surely the officer would let me go with a warning.

"I'll give you an incentive to keep this kind of thing from happening again," a decidedly female voice stated.

Stunned, I glanced up. A slender, attractive woman who appeared to be in her late twenties had no qualms at all about writing up a ticket. I'm betting she had pulled Mom's trick before herself and that she had no sympathy for women in distress. Instead, she ignored my tears—which were no longer forced—and asked to see my registration and insurance information. For a minute I panicked, unable to remember where Dad had stashed it for me in my little Honda Civic. I had bought this car earlier in the summer when it became apparent to all of us that I needed a reliable form of transportation. The Civic was nearly five years old, but it had low mileage and was in excellent condition. It was also candy apple red, a color my father had warned me about. He was right—candy apple red does attract attention.

"Is this vehicle registered?" the officer asked snidely, repeating her request.

"Yes . . . just a minute," I pleaded, trying to think. I wiped at my eyes and pulled down the visor to look in the tiny mirror that was attached, certain my mascara was totally ruined, and for nothing, I might add. And there they were, both the registration and the insurance papers, tucked under an elastic band that was attached to the visor. Offering a silent thank you, I pulled out the papers and handed them to Officer Friendly. She studied them for several long seconds and seemed disappointed when all was in order. Passing them back to me, she finished writing out the ticket and added it to the collection of papers in my hand.

"You can contest this if you feel it was given unfairly, but you should know that my radar clocked you going fifteen miles over the speed limit."

"I'll just pay it," I responded, setting the offending piece of paper on the seat next to me. I replaced the registration and insurance papers on the visor and grimaced at myself in the tiny mirror. How would I ever explain any of this to Dad? "Is it okay if I go now? I really need to get to work. I'm late enough as it is."

She smiled and got in a parting shot. "Go ahead. But watch your speed, even if you're late," she advised. I waited until she had walked back to her car before I called her a not-very-nice name. Then I signaled, glanced over my shoulder to check my blind spot as I had learned last year in driver's ed, and pulled back onto the road. I could tell this was going to be another in a series of very long days.

* * *

All hope of sneaking into Harold's Burgers unnoticed went out the window as I crept inside. Harold himself stood guard, waiting for me. Grimacing at the annoyed look on his face, I once again tried the pitiful girl routine. "Sorry. I got a ticket on the way to work."

"You're late. Don't let it happen again," Harold wheezed, shaking his chubby index finger at me. From the size of the man, I'm convinced Harold's diet has consisted of greasy hamburgers for a very long time. "Put on your apron and get to work. We're swamped. It's lunch rush and we needed you here twenty minutes ago," Harold continued to complain, following me as I threw on the ugly yellow apron and headed up front to the counter. As I greeted the customer who was first in my line, Harold backed off and went to harp on the kitchen help.

"How can I help you?" I politely asked.

"I've been standing here for fifteen minutes waiting to be served," the older woman exclaimed.

"I'm sorry. How can I help you?"

"Well . . . let me see . . ." she said, studying the menu that was posted along the back wall.

I shook my head. If she had been standing there for fifteen minutes, why hadn't she already made her selection?

"How big is the Harold's Special?" she asked.

I held up my hands to illustrate.

"What's on it?"

"Everything listed on the menu," I replied, gritting my teeth.

"I can't see," she said as she squinted at the menu in question.

"Pickles, onions, cheese, two beef patties, barbeque sauce—"

"I can't have barbeque sauce. It gives me heartburn," she confided.

"Our double cheeseburger doesn't have barbeque sauce," I suggested.

"Does it have tomatoes?"

"If you'd like it to," I said, trying to ignore the way the shaggy-looking guy behind Mrs. Finicky was leering at me. "We do charge ten cents extra for the slice of tomato."

"What?" she asked, looking appalled. "You charge extra for a little slice of tomato?"

"Most places do," I explained, my skin crawling as the creepy dude's eyes continued to explore my body. At least the apron covered my front, making his task more difficult.

"I can't imagine charging people for a little slice of tomato. Why, I have tomatoes at home, growing in my garden."

Then why don't you go home and eat one? I thought silently. Forcing a smile, I tried again. "We have a wonderful grilled ham-and-cheese sandwich."

"Does it come with tomatoes?" she asked, still offended.

"No, but it has a lot of tiny pieces of pickle mixed in the sauce—"

The woman shuddered. "Give me a chicken sandwich with a small order of fries and a small Sprite."

I knew better than to ask if she wanted a slice of tomato on her sandwich. Instead, I punched her order. "That will be three dollars and ninety-five cents," I said, handing the woman her receipt.

"What? Nearly four dollars for a little sandwich?"

"And a drink and an order of fries. I put it together as a combo meal to give you the best price," I replied, still trying to smile.

Grumbling, she slipped her purse from her shoulder, opened it, and gravely took out her wallet. I was starting to feel guilty about the price of that silly combo meal until she undid the wallet's fastener and pulled out a wad of twenties. Flipping through them, she finally located a five-dollar bill and handed it to me.

"Don't expect a tip," she told me.

"I never do," I said under my breath. I rang up the final sale and placed her five-dollar bill inside the till, picking up a nickel and a one-dollar bill to give her in return. As I handed her the change, she appeared horrified.

"I gave you a twenty," she exclaimed. "You're trying to cheat me!"

I stared at her in disbelief. No wonder she had a wallet full of twenties. This must be a scam she pulled quite often.

"Is there a problem?" Harold asked, wheezing over my shoulder.

"This . . . this girl overcharged me for a sandwich and then didn't give me back the right change," the woman accused.

"I charged her for a chicken combo," I said, holding up the other receipt. Suddenly, Grandma didn't look so smug—she had forgotten that I had a second copy.

"That is the price for a chicken combo," Harold said, gazing at the receipt.

"I gave her a twenty," the woman persisted. By this time, the other two cashiers were both staring at me in amusement, and the three lines of customers varied between curiosity, indifference, and outrage.

"We always leave the money on the till in plain sight until the transaction is completed, don't we, Laurie?" my boss emphasized.

Now I knew I was sunk. In my hurry to hustle the woman along, I had already placed the money inside the till. It was going to be her word against mine, and in Harold's world, the customer is always right. Then I thought of the receipt. "Look, it shows right there that she gave me a five-dollar bill."

Harold studied the receipt in his hand.

"That just shows the numbers she punched in," Grandma said, giving me a livid look.

"We'll give you back the change for a twenty," Harold said, shoving the receipt in my face as he smiled at the woman. "It's coming out of your next check," he added in a soft whisper that only I could hear.

"Order up," the cook hollered.

Harold took it upon himself to personally give the chicken combo to the little dear who had caused all of the trouble. He even walked with her, carrying her tray as he found her a nice place to sit.

Steaming, I glared at the next customer, Mr. Pervert. I hated the way he kept looking at me. My parents have both commented that I'm becoming a lovely young woman. Sometimes I don't trust their compliments. They're my parents and they're supposed to say nice things about me, but I've been hearing it from other people too. From pictures I've been shown, I look a lot like my mother did at my age—we both have the same blonde hair and vivid blue eyes. Her hair is shorter now, and mine was too until a few months ago. I decided to grow it out, and when it's down, it hangs almost to my shoulders.

"Can I help you?"

"Oh, yeah," he replied, grinning. "What time do you get off work?"

"Not interested. What would you like to order, sir?" I added that last word, hoping to accent the difference in our ages.

"One of you to go," he persisted.

What was this, pick on Laurie day?

"I believe the young lady isn't interested in what you have in mind," a voice said, coming to my rescue. "And if you're not here to order food, leave so the rest of us can."

I smiled at the middle-aged man who was standing behind the perv. It was good to know there were still nice people in the world.

"I'll take the bacon-burger combo," my admirer snapped. Upset as he was, he still managed to ogle me as I rang up his order and carefully took his change, this time placing it in clear sight on the till until the transaction was finished. I breathed a sigh of relief when he finally disappeared out of the drive-in. Thankfully, he had ordered his meal to go.

"Thank you for your help," I said to the man who was standing in front of me now. He wasn't bad for a man who was old enough to be my father. Unlike my father, he still had most of his hair.

"It makes me angry when I see young women, or women of any age, being treated like that. It's not right," he replied.

"Well, thanks again."

"No need to thank me. I have a daughter who is about your age, and I would like to think that when I'm not around to watch out for her, someone else is."

"Mark?" an attractive woman called out as she stepped inside the drive-in.

The man in front of me turned his head. "Over here," he motioned. "That's my wife," he said proudly. "We decided to meet here for lunch today. We used to come here all the time when we were first married."

"Sorry I'm late," his wife said, puffing slightly as she approached. "I got pulled over by a sweet young thing with an attitude problem. She claimed I was doing ten miles over the speed limit."

It had to be the same cop. I listened sympathetically as she described the snide way the officer had handed her a ticket.

"Are you going to fight it?" Mark asked.

"No, I was driving about that fast. But she didn't need to be such a snot about it."

"Yeah," I agreed, flushing when they both gave me a questioning look. "I got pulled over by the same cop on my way to work. She wasn't very nice."

"You've been having a bad day," Mark observed. "First you get picked up for speeding, then you get ripped off by a senior con artist—"

"What?" his wife asked, a bemused expression on her face.

"Oldest scam in the book. A sweet old lady handed this girl a five, then claimed it was a twenty."

"You saw that?" I asked.

He nodded. "I'm just sorry I didn't come forward. I figured the receipt would settle it."

"My boss took her side. He always does—the customer is always right, you know. So the extra money will come out of my check."

"That's terrible," they both agreed.

"That's just the way it is," I replied.

"Laurie, what's the hold up?" Harold asked, stepping forward. "Is there another problem?"

"No problems here," Mark said. "We're both very impressed with this young lady. She must be one of your best employees," he continued, smiling as he slipped his arm around his wife's waist. "She was answering all of our questions about your menu."

"Oh, I see," Harold said, still giving me the evil eye. Harold wasn't one to believe in complimenting his employees. I guess he figured it would spoil us. Uncomfortable with the positive comments that were being made about me, he retreated to the kitchen to harass the cooks.

"We'll both take the Harold's Special combo," Mark said, placing his order. "I'll have a lemonade to drink. What would you like, dear?"

"A root beer," she replied, smiling. These two were almost convincing me that married life could be bliss, something to consider later on in life—after I received my Pulitzer.

"Okay, that'll be eleven dollars and thirty cents," I said, punching in the order. He handed me fifteen dollars, and I gave him back the correct change. When his order was ready, I placed everything on a tray and called out his number. He smiled, slipped me a twenty-dollar bill, and then picked up his tray.

"You've already paid for your meal," I said as I tried to give the money back.

"Keep it. We'll call it your tip," he said, winking. "That should make up for what will be deducted from this week's check."

"But—"

"It's my good deed for the day," he said, turning to make his way to where his wife was waiting.

"Thank you," I called after him. "Wow," I said quietly as I pushed the twenty dollars into the front pocket of my jeans. "When I grow up, I want to meet someone just like him." Smiling, I greeted the next customer.

Chapter 3

"You were picked up for speeding?" my father exclaimed, looking like he was about to have a stroke.

I glanced at my mother, a told-you-so expression on my face. I had stressed to her earlier that we would be better off to keep my transgression between the two of us. That way Reese couldn't tease me about it and Dad wouldn't have a coronary over it. But Mom had pointed out my ticket would raise the amount Dad would have to pay for my car insurance. He would find out about it anyway, and keeping it from him would only make matters worse.

Dad stared in disbelief at the ticket I had shown him. "How could you go that fast and not realize it?"

"Honey, her mind was on other things," my mother said, trying to help me.

"It should've been on the road," he rebutted. "That's how accidents happen. What was so important that you couldn't focus on driving?"

Thanks, Mom, I mentally grumbled. "I was . . . uh . . . thinking about the future," I stammered. It was the truth. They didn't have to know that I was daydreaming about my future exploits.

"She has a lot of decisions to make this year," Mom said in my defense.

"She keeps driving like this, she won't have a future to worry about," Dad sputtered.

"Dad, I'm a good driver. I let the speed get away from me today. Trust me, I won't let it happen again."

"You'd better not, or you'll be paying for your own insurance," he threatened.

Dad and I had made a deal when he helped me buy my car this spring. I would make the payments on it and he would pay the insurance if I was a careful driver. It sounded like a good idea at the time. Now I wasn't so sure. I could see Dad holding this and other mishaps over my head forever. Every family gathering would start with, "Remember when Laurie shamed the family and got a ticket for speeding?"

"William, none of us is perfect," Mom stated firmly. She only uses Dad's full name when she thinks he has crossed a line somewhere. "I seem to remember someone else who tended to get a few tickets when he was a teenager."

I gazed with interest at my father. Somehow I couldn't picture him as a teen, let alone as a teen with a lurid past. Had there ever been a time when he was young and silly? Not that I was silly, but I was young enough to think my parents were too old for some things, like having babies, for instance.

"Janell, we aren't discussing the mistakes we made when we were younger. We're discussing—"

"We? As I recall, I've never had a ticket," Mom said defiantly, her blue eyes twinkling with mischief.

"Only because you talk your way out of them," Dad retorted.

Mom grinned and moved in to start tickling my father. Sensing my lecture was finished, and desiring to leave before they started pawing at each other, I left the room.

* * *

"I heard you got a ticket," Reese commented when he joined me in the family room two hours later. Home from work, he was no doubt here to torment me. He sat beside me on the couch and smiled.

"Don't go there, okay," I warned. "I've had a bad enough day without putting up with you."

"Hey, if that's the worst thing you ever do, count your blessings," he said, surprising me.

I remained silent, certain he was up to something. No way would he let this opportunity pass without making me miserable. It was an unwritten code for older brothers.

"Seriously, Laurie. Getting a ticket isn't the end of the world, even if Dad makes it sound that way."

Now I knew what he was up to. He'd wait for me to say something derogatory about our father, then he'd let Dad know about it. This was low, even for Reese.

"Hey, you in there tonight?" he asked, poking my side.

"Look, I messed up, okay? I'm sure it'll make the front page of the *Ogden Standard-Examiner* tomorrow morning. The heading will read, 'Laurie Clark Receives First Ticket of Her Pathetic Life. Causes Her Parents Untold Grief and Has Been Sent to Live in a Convent.'"

"Mormons don't have convents," Reese said, grinning.

I hate it when he grins—he looks just like Mom, only with black hair and a five o'clock shadow. "Whatever," I replied.

"All I'm trying to say is that sometimes Dad can be a little tough, especially if it's going to cost him extra money."

"I told him during dinner tonight that I'll pay for my own insurance."

"Laurie, you can't afford insurance and college. I'm wondering how you're going to afford a car payment and college."

"Haven't you heard? I work at Harold's Burgers. I'm rolling in the money."

Reese laughed. "You're a kick, you know that?" he said. "I'm going to miss your one-of-a-kind sense of humor when I leave."

"That reminds me, how soon will that be?" I shot back.

"Soon enough," he said, stretching out so that his feet were resting on Mom's antique coffee table, a big no-no when Mom was looking.

In silence, Reese and I watched a stupid commercial on the television across the room, one of those that advertises items that embarrass both of us. Reese picked up the remote and changed the channel to a commercial that was almost as bad. Sighing, he finally shut off the TV.

"Man, some of those commercials are disgusting," he muttered.

"So are a lot of the shows," I agreed, glad that we were steering into neutral territory. "Last Saturday, Roz and I rented a movie that was supposed to be pretty good. All of our friends had told us to see it. It was horrible. We turned it off halfway through."

"Good for you," Reese said, glancing at me.

I returned his gaze through narrowed eyes. Now what was he up to?

"Actually, I've been meaning to talk to you about that. I've noticed when Roz comes over, you two tend to watch a lot of videos."

"So? What else is there to do?"

Reese sat up to look at me. "That's not the point I'm trying to make, although there are a lot of other options in the world."

"What is your point?" I asked, not wanting another lecture on the evils of wasting my time in front of the TV, something I already endure on a regular basis from both of my parents. The thing is, I do have other interests, like reading, writing in my journal, stuff like that. Watching movies is a way to relax, a favorite pastime that Roz and I enjoy.

"I'm concerned. Sometimes you two rent movies that aren't very good."

"Hey, didn't I just tell you about what we did last Saturday?" I challenged.

"Yeah, and that's great. But I know there are other times when you overlook the content because it's a movie you really want to see."

"I don't watch movies that are R-rated," I said, glowering at my brother.

Reese nodded. "A lot of the PG-13 movies are about as bad."

Now I was mad. Who was he to criticize me?

"Laurie, you've always had high standards. I've admired you for that. But sometimes I think you don't understand how awful some of those things are."

"Like what?"

"Like some of the innuendos in the movies you watch. Maybe you don't get what some of those things mean, but they're disgusting."

"Oh, so not only am I a lowlife, but I'm also stupid?" I responded, cutting him off midsentence.

"No, Laurie. Don't pull a Grandma Clark on me."

Rising, I left the room before I said something I would not regret later. I was still fuming an hour later when Mom poked her head into my room.

"Laurie, could you come into the kitchen for a few minutes? Your dad and I have some special news to share."

My heart slipped down to my bare feet. Probably another pregnancy. People in our ward were grinning enough whenever they saw my parents toting Joey around. Gathering my courage, I followed my mother down the hall and into the kitchen where both my dad and Reese were waiting. I nodded at Dad and refused to even look at Reese. I walked around to my normal spot at the table and sat down.

"Your mother and I have been talking things over," Dad began.

I felt my right eye twitch. It only does that when I'm nervous or when I'm about to hear unappealing news.

"Reese, you'll be leaving on your mission in a couple of months," Dad continued.

I watched my parents' faces carefully for clues. Were they thinking that because another child was leaving home, it was time to repopulate the family again? But unlike Allison's departure, Reese would be coming back. Then he and Stacy, or some other poor girl, would get married and give our parents all of the grandchildren they could possibly want. There would be plenty of babies to play with and the best part was, we could send them home to their parents whenever they got messy or cried. I tried to send this silent message telepathically, but I don't think it was picked up on the receiving end. Dad had a silly grin on his face and Mom was practically beaming. That couldn't be good.

"So we were thinking that it's time for another—"

"No, it's not," I exclaimed, glancing around the table. "I mean, you'll still have Joey and me. True I'll be heading off to college in about a year, but I'll be coming home for visits. BYU-Idaho isn't that far away. And Reese will be home in two years. Then he'll get married and have lots of babies, won't you, Reese?" I pleaded.

My entire family stared at me like I had lost my mind.

"Laurie, what are you talking about?" my mother ventured.

"What are you guys talking about?" I replied, regretting my outburst. Reese and Dad were whispering something about hormones.

"We were about to announce that we think it's time to take a family trip," Mom said, lifting an eyebrow at me. "What's this about babies?"

"Janell, I think you and Laurie need to have a talk—after we're done here," Dad said, still looking at me funny. "We were thinking that before Reese heads off on his mission and before you start your senior year of high school, we should take a family trip."

There was a brief silence as everyone reflected on the fact that our last family vacation had taken place a few months before we lost Allison. Thanks to the drunk driver who had plowed into the van Allison had been riding in after a friend's birthday party, our family outings had come to a complete stop. For a long time, it hadn't seemed right to take a trip without Allison. Then there was that whole mess with Reese. During his absence, it would've been just Mom, Dad, and me. A lot of fun that would've been. Now we were pretty much a family again, with Joey to add to the excitement. Maybe it was time for another trip.

"So, what do you think?" Dad prompted.

"Sounds good. So where are we going?" Reese eagerly asked.

I didn't comment, relieved that our family population wasn't about to increase and concerned about the irritated look on my mother's face. Dad and Reese might've missed what I was getting at earlier, but Mom had probably figured it out. No doubt there would be a mother-daughter chat later on that night. Silently groaning, I folded my arms on the table and rested my suddenly aching head on top of them.

"We remembered that a few years ago you kids thought it would be neat to go to Sea World."

"In San Diego?" I asked, reviving quickly.

"Yep," Dad replied. "While we're there, we'll go through that live animal preserve, see the world-famous zoo, and maybe drop down into Tijuana."

"Awesome," Reese exclaimed.

"Laurie?" Dad prompted.

"Way cool," I responded. "But when will we go?" I asked, remembering that school started in three weeks.

"I figure it will take about a week for all of us to arrange for time off," Dad answered.

The smile on my face wilted. That meant I had to face the wrath of Harold. Asking my boss for time off was like asking him to remove body parts.

"We'll plan to leave a week from this coming Monday."

"How long will we be gone?" Reese asked.

"A week or so. Since your mother doesn't work anymore, it won't be a problem for her to get away. She'll just have to turn over the Relief Society reins to her two counselors."

My mother grimaced over that comment. She's always afraid the ward will fall apart in her absence.

Dad was still talking. "I have three weeks of vacation coming, but I know it will be harder for the two of you to get that many days off. So if you can arrange for at least a week, we'll make the most of our time."

Reese and I agreed to try our best to get time off, and the family council was over. I tried to sneak away to my room, but Mom intercepted me, inviting me into her scrapbooking room down the hall. It used to be Allison's bedroom. Now it serves as a combination guest room and scrapbook storage facility. A small table sits in front of the window. Mom can spend hours sitting there working on scrapbooks. Tonight I sensed she had a different project in mind.

"Have a seat," Mom invited as she closed the door to the room.

I took a deep breath and selected one of the separated bunk beds to sit on. She sat down on the opposite bed and frowned.

"Laurie," she began, using *that* tone of voice. "I'm concerned about your attitude lately. At first, you seemed excited when Joey was born. Now you act like you're being picked on when-ever I ask you to watch him."

"Mom, I'm sorry. I've had a lot on my mind," I said, trying to stop the tidal wave of guilt that was heading my way.

"Let me finish," she replied, giving me her no-nonsense look. "It's more than that. You act embarrassed to even be seen with me and Joey. And as for your squeamishness about nursing—"

"Do we have to talk about that?" I moaned.

"Laurie, it's a perfectly natural way to feed a baby. And it's not like I put myself on public display. I always find a secluded area and cover myself up, even here at home. I nursed every one of you kids. Why shouldn't Joey have that same advantage?"

I think the nausea I felt over that revelation was visible on my face. This was one conversation I didn't want to have. "Could we talk about something else?"

"Honestly! You're just being silly," my mother exclaimed.

"Maybe I am, but I'd really rather not talk about any of this."

"I see. Let me guess, you also don't want to discuss your fear that your dad and I might decide to have another baby. That was the trigger behind your little outburst this evening, right?"

I had to give the woman credit—she didn't miss a thing. She has this annoying habit of always zeroing in on what's going on with me. So naturally I deny anything she figures out. "No, it wasn't," I replied, ignoring the twinge of guilt I felt from lying.

"Uh-huh," she responded, indicating she didn't believe me.

Gazing down at the carpeted floor, I knew I had two options. I could try to argue my way out of this and make my mother even more upset than she already was, or I could do my best to change the subject. There was a third approach. I could confess, burst into tears, and throw myself on the mercy of my mother's tender heart. I only use that ploy as a last resort. Mom is pretty quick to pick up on insincere tears. Deliberating over my choices, I began leaning toward confession. Then I had another idea.

"Mom, I didn't tell you what happened at work today," I began, knowing she would forget all about being upset with me when I told her about the lowlife who had leered at me at the drive-in. Her worst fear is that someone will hurt me. I know this because of all the lectures she delivers on a regular basis about locking my car when I'm driving around by myself, and locking it when I park somewhere. I've lost count of how many times she has told me not to walk home by myself—ever. So I told her what had taken place, and it worked like a charm.

"Tell me the exact words he used," Mom coaxed, her blue eyes wide with concern.

I told her, and she stood up to pace the room. I smiled, pleased with myself. There would be no more discussion of embarrassing items. Instead I would be flooded with sympathy and given advice about being cautious.

"Why didn't you tell me this earlier when you first came home?"

I lowered my eyes. "I was too embarrassed."

"Thank heavens you weren't working the late shift. You hear about this kind of thing all the time. I'm just glad he wasn't hanging around the parking lot, waiting for you when you got off work."

I nodded. I hadn't even thought about that possibility. Shuddering, I tried to push the image of his face from my mind.

Mom sat down on the bed beside me. Gently turning my chin, she looked into my eyes. "From now on, whenever you work the late shift, one of us will come pick you up when you're through," she stated firmly, releasing my chin.

Whoa—where had that come from? That wasn't what I wanted. My newfound freedom was dissipating.

"When you work the day shift, call me before you leave the drive-in so I'll know when to expect you. And make sure you park as close as you can to the building, in plain sight, where everyone can see you walking to and from your car."

Nice. I should've taken the lecture she'd had in mind earlier. "Mom, I'll be okay," I tried to assure.

"Yes, you will," she returned. I hate it when she gets that stubborn look on her face. It means there is no discussion. Her word is law. "Now, about this other business—"

This time I groaned out loud. Thanks to my big mouth, I would not only be treated like a little kid who needs protection, but I still had to talk to Mom about . . . you know.

When it was over, I retreated to my room and closed the door. This had been worse than "the talk," that event we all suffer through when we reach a certain age. Since I started high school, I've gotten a version of that talk from Mom every year before school starts. I was afraid tonight's mother-daughter chat would lead to this, and it did. One minute Mom was ripping into me about how having Joey at her age was a blessing, not an embarrassment, then she jumped into the topic of how having a baby at my age isn't appropriate. That led to dating guidelines, a review of standards, a reminder of the importance of staying virtuous, and a brief synopsis of what certain things can lead to, ending this glorious day on a lovely note.

Lying on top of my bed, I pulled my pillow over my face and tried to block out the images Mom had planted in my head. Was it true that Mormons didn't have convents to run away to when life took a nasty turn? I wondered if there was a suggestion box at Church headquarters.

Chapter 4

"I can't believe your mom put you through that again," Roz sympathized.

Sipping at the Sprite in my cup, I glanced around the food court of the Layton Mall before nodding. The place was crowded, but I didn't see anyone else I knew. Most of the people sitting nearby were either young families or older couples.

Roz grinned, revealing her perfect smile. A beautiful girl, she has been my best friend since grade school. In a lot of ways, we're more like sisters than close friends. I knew only Roz would appreciate how awful the talk with my mother had been last night.

"You'd think she'd realize you're an adult now," Roz continued.

"She just worries," I replied.

Roz shook her head. "Over nothing," she said before drinking the last of her root beer.

"True," I agreed, swishing the ice around in my cup.

"In a year, we'll be heading off to college. Will she give you the chastity chat then too?"

"Probably." I sighed.

"At least she won't be coming with us to college." Roz's dark eyes searched my face. "Right?" she teased.

"No, she won't be coming with us," I replied.

"Good girl," Roz said, laughing. "Now hurry up and drink your pop so we can get in some good shopping time."

I guzzled the pop, then stood up and walked to the nearest trash dispenser to throw it away. Roz handed me her cup, and I threw it away as well. Then we set off in search of bargains that would be stylin' for our senior year.

* * *

"You're not buying that," I said, my eyes widening at the tight-fitting, low-cut blouse Roz was holding in her hands.

"What's wrong with it?" Roz asked, glancing down at the blouse.

"It doesn't look very modest," I said.

"What it looks is good on me," Roz replied, holding it up to herself. "And those pants will be a perfect match," she added, grabbing a pair of low-riding jeans. "These are so cool. And they're even on sale," she pointed out.

I gazed at the rack of jeans. They were a popular style, but not anything my mother would want me to wear. That almost made them more attractive than the price. Making a hasty decision, I picked out a pair to try on. As I glanced in the mirror on the door of the fitting-room stall, I noted that they were tighter than I was used to wearing. Shrugging, I figured I could always wear a longer shirt to hide how low they rode.

Still debating as I continued to study my reflection in the mirror, I decided this was one time I would choose fashion over the guidelines Mom has set for me since I was in junior high. My conscience pricked a bit, but I reminded myself of the unnecessary talk I'd had with my mother the night before. Roz was right—I was an adult, and it was time I started making decisions for myself.

I didn't find a blouse I liked, appeasing my now-nagging conscience with the thought that at least I wasn't buying revealing tops, like the two Roz had picked out. Walking up to the clerk, I set the low-riders on the counter and grabbed my wallet. Ignoring the unease I experienced as I paid for my selection, I tamped it down, rationalizing that this was the current style. Everyone was wearing pants like this.

Roz had already bought the clothes she had picked out, and after I made my purchase, we walked down the center of the mall, glancing at the varied shops that lined each side.

"Hey, let's look around in there," Roz suggested, pointing to a large bookstore.

"Why?"

"I've been reading a lot of books this summer. I want to see if they have anything new."

"There's an LDS bookstore just down there," I said, pointing in the opposite direction.

"Yeah, right. Like I want to read a sappy book from Mormonville," Roz retorted.

Lifting an eyebrow, I followed my friend inside the bookstore she preferred. I spotted a bargain bin and began sorting through to see if anything caught my eye. I could use a new book on our trip to San Diego. No doubt there would be plenty of time to lie on the beach, relax, and read.

"What are you looking for?" Roz asked, suddenly reappearing at my side.

"Something good to read," I murmured, picking up a biography of a well-known movie star. I thumbed through the pages, blushed, and quickly replaced the book inside the bin.

"You should take a couple of these with you on your trip," Roz said, showing me the two books she had picked out.

"Roz, these are romance novels," I exclaimed, appalled by the suggestive pictures on the covers.

"And they're wonderful," Roz replied. "I've been reading them all summer."

"You're kidding," I said, shaking my head. "Those are trash books."

"You're quoting your mother again," Roz chastised, giving me a disgusted look. "Read one for yourself and see. They're not bad—just educational."

She handed me one of the books. I turned it over in my hands and read the back cover. Then I rolled my eyes. This sounded like it was straight out of a soap opera, something else my mother has cautioned me to avoid, but something Roz and I had watched together once in a while at her house. There are scenes in those shows that make me uncomfortable, and I was certain these books would be similar. I handed the book back to Roz. "Sorry, I'm not interested in this type of book."

"Why not?" Roz asked, frowning.

I gazed at my friend and saw that she was seriously offended. Then again, Roz was an avid fan of several television programs I felt were inappropriate—most were prime-time shows that often depicted casual sex, something we'd had a huge argument over during girls' camp earlier this summer. When Roz had groaned about missing her favorite shows while we were camping, I had informed her that she needed to get a life. The argument had become fairly heated until our Laurel leader, Kaye Dunning, had thrown a large kettle of cold water on both of us, effectively ending the debate. For once, I had managed to take things in stride, but Roz had pouted the rest of the day, refusing to take part in the testimony meeting held later that night.

"Take this with you on your trip," Roz said now, replacing the book in my hands.

I gazed at the graphic cover. Once again I experienced an uneasy feeling. Was it a good idea to keep ignoring it? What was it Mom had told me a while back—if you continuously ignore the promptings you receive from the Holy Ghost, eventually those promptings stop?

Almost on cue, the negative feeling I was experiencing increased in its intensity. "Roz, I'm not comfortable with this kind of book," I said, giving it back to her.

"Oh, I see. You think it's evil to read harmless romance novels."

"What kinds of scenes are in those books?" I countered.

"Nothing you'll ever see in your lifetime," Roz said, scowling fiercely at me.

Now I was insulted. I walked out of the store before I said something that would make matters worse. I watched as Roz stomped up to the counter to buy both books she had selected. What was going on with her? Hadn't we both promised just last year to avoid anything that would go against the standards we had been taught our entire lives?

I glanced down at the colorful bag in my hands and felt consumed by guilt. What had I been thinking? Could I take the low-riders back and exchange them for something else in that store? Then it occurred to me that I hadn't seen anything else I would feel comfortable wearing. Shaking my head, I made myself a promise. I would never wear this new pair of jeans. They would hang in the back of my closet until I found a way to get rid of them.

When Roz walked out of the bookstore, she offered a smile. "Sorry," she said quietly.

An uneasy truce settled between us. I returned her smile, but worry filled my heart as I reflected on the changes I was seeing in my best friend. Uncertain of what to do about it, I followed her into another clothing store where she found more clothes I knew I could never wear.

Chapter 5

Reese and I were both able to arrange to have a week off for our family trip. Reese didn't have any trouble at all working out his schedule. His boss knew that he'd be leaving on a mission soon, and he was already dropping hints for Reese to check back with him when he returned. For some reason, he thinks Reese would be a prime candidate for manager training.

I didn't have things quite so easy. First Harold got this pained look on his face like I had mortally wounded him. Then he muttered something about young people not understanding what it was to work these days. From there he began sighing and glancing through his calendar, proclaiming from time to time that it wasn't possible to give me the time off I needed. When I told him my dad would be happy to talk to him about it, he grunted in response and made the schedule work. I've learned that Harold doesn't like dealing with our parents. I don't play that card very often, but it looked like the only way I would be able to get the days I needed for our trip.

Now here we were, waiting in the Salt Lake City airport for our flight to San Diego. My parents had decided that it would be easier to fly at night, hoping Joey would sleep during the short trip. When they finally called our flight, we gathered up our carry-ons and hurried toward the ramp that would lead us onto our plane.

I was glad we were finally on our way to San Diego. When I was younger, I used to dream about going to Sea World. It still sounded fun, even at my age. I had looked up some information on the internet and discovered there were all kinds of exhibits waiting to be explored: Polar Bear Plaza, Wild Arctic, Penguin Encounter, Shark Encounter, not to mention the feature attraction, Shamu the killer whale. Leaning back in my seat, I closed my eyes and imagined how great it would be to see all these sights in person.

I had almost fallen asleep when a piercing wail startled me awake. I wasn't surprised to learn it was Joey. Something about the air pressure hurting his ears. Naturally, he had caught a slight cold before we left, which made it all that much worse. He was in distress during our entire flight. So were all of the passengers.

To Mom's credit, she tried everything. First she dug out the baby Tylenol. After drugging Joey, she stood up and rocked him back and forth, singing silly songs. She even wandered back to the tiny bathroom stall to see if he needed a tire change, Dad's tactful way of saying Joey needed a new diaper. I suspect Mom also went back there to see if he was hungry. Nothing worked. Not even the pacifier he was so attached to. It went flying across the airplane, smacking a tall teenage boy in the head. At least the guy wasn't cute. I doubt I would've made a very good impression as sister to the whiny child.

It might have been my imagination, but I could have sworn I heard the other passengers applaud when our family left the plane after we landed in San Diego. Thirty minutes of nonstop crying tends to have that effect on people. Joey's vocal protest had my own ears ringing. But by the time we had picked up the white minivan Dad picked out at a nearby car rental booth, Joey had calmed down, and he fell asleep in the built-in car seat on the way to the hotel.

Always looking for bargains, Dad had booked us into a Days Inn that was fairly close to the airport. The hotel itself was actually pretty nice, the rooms were good-sized, and the place even had an outdoor pool. It was late enough when we arrived that the pool was closed, but I vowed to make good use of it during our stay.

Dad had reserved two rooms, figuring Reese and I could share one room, while he, Mom, and Joey stayed in the other. Mom had managed to pack a small portable playpen, thinking Joey would sleep in it. She soon learned that not only would Joey refuse to sleep inside it, but he seemed determined not to sleep at all. Dad said Joey was spoiled and wanted his own crib back home. I agreed and almost suggested that we give Joey his wish and send him on his way.

Poor Mom spent the night in a chair, holding Joey as he alternated between crying and hollering. Reese closed the door that linked our rooms, climbed into his bed, and pulled both pillows over his head. I attempted to do the same in my own bed, but it didn't quite block out Joey's fussing. Our family bonding adventure was off to a good start.

* * *

Mom looked like the last chapter the next morning. Her hair was sticking up in an interesting fashion thanks to the small naps she was able to take in the chair between Joey's fits. Bags hung under each eye, proof that the sleep she did get wasn't very much. At least Dad volunteered to take Joey while she got into the shower. Joey screamed until she stepped back in sight. I guess he was petrified that Mom would abandon him in this strange place. I wouldn't blame her if she did.

While Mom finished getting ready for the day, Reese picked Joey up and tried to get him to smile. He almost got a grin out of the kid before Joey decided Mom had taken a long enough break. By then she'd had a chance to blow-dry her hair and throw on some makeup. I didn't have the heart to tell her that she still looked exhausted and about ten years older than she was.

We took the elevator down to the lobby, and after Dad made small talk with the on-duty clerk, we left the hotel and walked down the sidewalk to enjoy a quick breakfast in a family restaurant that was on the corner. Food didn't appeal to any of us that morning, but we knew we had to keep up our strength, so we ordered four specials. Still in noise mode, Joey got a big kick out of banging his spoon on the table until Dad took it away from him and handed him a straw to play with instead. Mom had managed to tie him into a wooden high chair, and after whimpering for a few minutes, Joey decided he liked it and was all smiles and dimples. Now he tried to be cute and adorable. None of us bought his act. We knew we were very likely in for another sleepless night when bedtime rolled around.

Eating breakfast revived our spirits somewhat. From the restaurant, we drove out to see the ocean. I've only seen it one other time, and that was during the Oregon trip we had made about four years ago. I had been disappointed that the only seashells to be found on public beaches during that outing were broken clam or oyster shells. I had high hopes of discovering classier shells on this trip.

Driving across the Coronado Bay Bridge, we could see several large ships that were docked in what Dad told us was a naval station. On the right side of the bridge, I could see several fishing boats and a couple of sailboats. In the distance on that same side were a couple of aircraft carriers and what looked like a military airport. Dad proclaimed it the North Island Naval Airstrip, and he and Reese excitedly babbled on about how neat it was to be this close to a military base, but I found myself drawn to the sailboats, which, to me, looked very romantic against the bright blue horizon. I could picture myself sailing around the world in such a vessel, meeting people and exploring places very few ever see. I slipped into a daydream about my future life until Mom exclaimed that she could see the Hotel del Coronado.

We were exiting the lengthy bridge that links San Diego to Coronado Island. In the distance on the east side of the island, I caught a glimpse of a towering edifice that beckoned to the explorer/reporter side of myself—the famed Hotel del Coronado. Tall, white turrets capped by red shingles rose above the houses and trees that lined Orange Avenue. We passed several impressive homes as we drove on, but it was the mystical past of the hotel that called to me.

The Del was built in 1888, and it was the first electrically lit hotel in the world. Thomas Edison was given the honor of throwing the switch that bathed this grand facility in sparkling wonder. I wish I could have been there to see it. From what I had read, celebrities—including past presidents and movie stars—had flocked to the Del, enthralled by its elegant charm. Now, anyone who wanted to pay the price—unlike my father—could bask in this remodeled luxury. I made a note to myself to someday return to this island and spend adequate time enjoying the splendor of the Del.

As I continued to drool over the historical hotel, Dad drove around until he found a place to park. Earlier he had learned from the clerk at Days Inn that you could pay a small meter fee to park all day close to the shore on Coronado City Beach. So when he hopped out of the minivan and pushed the exact change into a meter, we eagerly vacated our rented mode of transportation and headed down to the ocean.

Reese and I raced each other to the salty water while our parents took a more leisurely stroll, Dad carrying Joey as they tried to get my baby brother excited about seeing the ocean for the first time. Personally, I don't think Joey cared much for any of it until they set him down on the sand. Then our six-month-old pride and joy stopped crying long enough to stick his hands in the squishy sand. Deciding this was a fascinating pastime, he cheered up for a while, a brief reprieve that gave the rest of us a chance to enjoy the crowded scenic view.

We quickly learned this spot was a popular tourist attraction, and we were surrounded by people of all shapes and sizes and varying degrees of undress. All I will say here is that there should be a law forbidding middle-aged men to wear Speedos. I'll add that the bikinis some of the women were wearing were just as bad. Underneath my T-shirt and tan khaki shorts, I was wearing a one-piece navy blue contraption my mother had picked out earlier this summer. She thought it was cute, pointing out that it had little white sailboats that ran in a horizontal line across my midriff. I know why she really bought it. She figured it was modest, a concept she has been preaching to me for years.

Aside from my recent purchase, I've always tried to dress modestly, although there are times when it's tempting to strut around the house wearing a plunging neckline just to see the look on my mother's face. It would almost be worth the lecture I know I would receive. I try to heed the things my parents and the prophet say. I wish he would come out with a statement against Speedos, though. That would be nice.

Turning our backs to the bathing beauties that lined the shore, my brother and I wiggled out of the clothes we had worn over our swimming suits and swam out into the ocean, enjoying the lukewarm water. In my opinion, San Diego would be a perfect place to live. The temperature stays practically the same year-round, averaging around 70 degrees, something I could live with indefinitely.

After Reese and I had taken a refreshing dip, we swam back to the shore where our parents had laid out the beach towels we had brought with us. Joey was still playing in the sand, my dad building him a sandcastle as fast as Joey was knocking it down. Both seemed to be entertained by this process. Mom was lying on one of the towels reading a book. After the night she had endured, she deserved a break.

Reese picked up his towel, ran it through his hair, and then wrapped it around his waist to cover his wet suit before he walked down the beach to explore. I dried off and decided to do a bit of exploration myself. I pulled my T-shirt back over my swimming suit, ran a hand over my ponytail, making sure it was still intact, then wrapped my beach towel around my waist, tying it into a knot. I glanced wistfully at the Del, then turned and walked the other way. We had already agreed as a family that we would wait and explore the hotel after playing in the ocean and sand.

As I wandered around, I was disappointed to find there weren't beautiful seashells lining the shore, waiting for me to discover them. I found pieces of driftwood, a broken clamshell, and what looked like a discarded beer can. Wrinkling my nose, I couldn't believe that people would litter in such a place. Desiring to become one with the waves again, I walked back to where my parents were still hanging out, pulled off my T-shirt, unwrapped myself from my beach towel, and headed for the water.

"Laurie, don't get out there above your head," Mom called out before I waded in.

Honestly, it's not like I'm six years old. Not only that, I endured swimming lessons for nearly five years of my life. I know how to swim. To prove my point, I swam out as far as I dared, then turned to see if my parents were jumping in the air over my rebellion. It didn't look like they were even paying attention. Instead, their focus appeared to be on a nearby beach volleyball game. I squinted to try to make out why they would find that so fascinating and found myself overpowered by a huge wave. Down I went into the water, swallowing a large portion of it. I came up sputtering and floundered around in a panic. Why hadn't I listened to Mom and stayed where I could reach the bottom? I had no idea how deep the water was, and the tide seemed to be pulling me out farther than I wanted to go.

Silently praying for help, I did my best to swim against the current. It had been much easier going out along with the tide than it was to fight my way back. I'm a fairly strong young woman, but this effort was wearing me out. I experimented and dropped down into the water, but I still couldn't reach the bottom. Close to tears, I fought my way back to the surface and continued trying to swim back to the shore. Discouraged, I felt like I was fighting a losing battle. As I tried to swim back toward my family, competing waves would push me away. Gulping for air as I tried to stay above the water, I prayed, asking that my life would be spared. I seriously doubted my parents could stand to lose another child, even if it was me.

Another wave hit, driving me deep into the water. This time it seemed to take forever before I could find the surface. My lungs felt like they were going to explode when I finally broke free from the ocean's grasp—and touched the bottom with my feet. Now I did cry, with gratitude that my life had been spared. Once again, my mother's advice had been right on the mark, something to ponder when my thoughts weren't in such a jumble. As I began making my way to the shore, a lifeguard grabbed me from behind, adding to my fright. Tunnel vision had blocked him from my view.

"Are you all right?" the attractive young man asked. I must have been in a state of shock or I would've enjoyed his attention. Instead, all I felt was embarrassment.

"I'm okay," I breathed, winded from fighting my way to the shore.

"I was trying to swim out to you, but you made it back in before I could get to you," he said, his brown hair dripping with salt water.

"Sorry. Thanks," I mumbled as he helped me walk out onto the beach.

"Be more careful out there," he advised as he let go of my waist.

I nodded as he made his way back to his perch.

I heard Mom calling my name and turned to see her and Reese pushing through the crowd to get to me. I tried to move in their direction, but my legs felt like they were weighted down with cement. Giving up, I stood where I was and waited, shivering, not so much from being cold, but from the turmoil of what had almost happened.

It didn't take long for Mom to reach me. Immediately, she scooped me into her arms and into the towel she was holding. "Don't ever do that to me again," she exclaimed, pulling me close as my teeth began chattering.

Grateful for her soft warmth, I closed my eyes and vowed I would never put either one of us through this kind of thing again.

Chapter 6

The rest of that morning was a blur for me. I was too dazed to enjoy our quick tour of the Del. The tour came after I had endured numerous scoldings from every member of the family. Their words bounced off as Mom helped me put my T-shirt and shorts back over my soggy swimming suit. She even cleaned the clinging sand from my feet and replaced my flip-flops. Still a bit shaky, I appreciated her help, and the fact that after her initial reaction, she didn't say another word of condemnation, unlike Dad, Reese, and even Joey, who seemed to get in on the act, warbling noisily from his vantage point in Dad's arms.

As they continued their exhortations, I learned that Reese had been involved in the beach volleyball game. That's why everyone's attention had been focused on it. Reese's side had been winning when I inadvertently ruined the game. When the lifeguard dove into the water, the game stopped as everyone gawked at my attempted rescue, which to hear Dad talk, cast much shame upon the family. I was grateful when Mom interrupted him to suggest that we head toward the Hotel del Coronado before it grew any later.

As for the tour, I vaguely remember red carpet, intricate woodcarvings, a central courtyard with a funky-looking gazebo, and that's about it. Mom kept reading tidbits out of a guidebook she had picked up somewhere. Through it all, my head pounded with a fury. It was almost a relief to make our way back to the minivan. Mom asked Reese to sit up front with Dad to play navigator while she stayed in the backseat with Joey and me. I guess she figured she had two babies to look after.

The built-in car seat—Joey's permanent seat during our stay in San Diego—was located in the middle of the first bench seat. Mom chose to sit next to him on the side that folded down out of the way if anyone wanted to sit on the small bench seat in the very back. That's where Reese had been riding earlier. After I climbed in to sit against the window on the left side of the middle seat, Mom fastened a squirming Joey in next to me then pushed her seat in place and climbed inside, shutting the sliding side door to the minivan. She snapped on her own seat belt, and I caught her glancing to see if I had done likewise.

Dad started up the engine while Reese searched the map of San Diego to find the best route to Old Town. Borrowing Mom's guidebook, Reese read to us that Old Town San Diego is considered to be the birthplace of California. A man named Father Serra arrived in this location 225 years ago to establish a mission, the first in a chain of twenty-one missions that began the colonization of California. We had decided during breakfast that we would have lunch in this historical place and then spend the rest of the afternoon exploring the numerous shops, historical buildings, and museums.

As Dad fought his way through traffic, I leaned my aching head against the window and closed my eyes. I silently berated myself for being so stupid, reliving every minute of my ocean humiliation. I jumped, startled when I felt Mom's light touch as she reached around Joey to gently massage the back of my neck. As she continued to caress those tight muscles, I relaxed, allowing her to undo the knots that were probably causing my headache. By the time we reached Old Town, I was feeling much better and had regained my appetite, something that became apparent as we enjoyed authentic Mexican cuisine in a colorful outdoor restaurant, complete with a mariachi band.

After lunch, Mom put Joey into the portable stroller, hoping he would drift off to sleep. This is when our party split up. Dad and Reese wanted to take in all of the historical sights in Old Town, which included watching a living history demonstration. Fearing the noise of the live show would keep Joey awake, Mom suggested that she and I take Joey around with us as we visited some of the quieter shops. We were all in favor of doing anything we could to get Joey back on a schedule we could live with, so everyone agreed to Mom's plan. Dad and Reese disappeared into the crowd, and Mom and I took our time walking around, hoping Joey would cooperate and nod off to sleep.

We wandered into a little shop that created homemade hand soap. I had noticed that most of the shops in Old Town took pride in manufacturing the wares they sold to tourists—something about preserving the skills of a long-ago era. I'm sure the homemade soap they sold in this store was nothing like the old lye variety I've read about in history books. These soaps might have been made from scratch, but their heavenly scents were enticing, not repulsive as I had read lye soap had been.

Mom and I took turns savoring the colors and aromas of several different bars of soap. Mom finally settled on buying a peach-scented set. I picked out a set of lavender-colored soaps that smelled like jasmine. Joey refused to let go of a small, transparent aquamarine soap he had filched from a lower basket. Thank heavens it was covered with cellophane—I doubt he would've enjoyed a mouthful of soap, even if his behavior lately was worthy of that treatment. He gummed the wrapping around the soap while Mom paid for his selection along with her own. She offered to buy mine, but I had brought along some of my own spending money on this trip, and I told her I would get it.

The next shop was also filled with wonderful delights, and I think Mom was relieved Joey was strapped in a stroller. It was a small glass blowing factory, and the shelves were lined with glass figurines and vases. Joey threw his soap on the floor and pointed in vain toward several works of art. Mom ignored his request and pulled his pacifier out of the diaper bag, sticking it in his mouth instead. Joey voiced his displeasure as he sucked on the pacifier. It's probably a good thing we couldn't understand his chuntering. I picked up his soap and pointed to it menacingly before I placed it in the diaper bag. Ignoring me, Joey continued his vocal tirade. I think he's caught on that my threats mean nothing.

Two people behind the counter were busy making colorful vases out of balls of fiery red glass. I watched in fascination as the two artisans blew their glass blowing pipes to form the shape of the vase. They rotated the pipes in their hands as the glass cooled, coaxing glass creations from the molten balls.

We stayed in that shop for quite a long time, watching with interest as the vases took form and were set aside to cool. Mom tapped me on my shoulder and pointed to Joey, who had finally fallen asleep. I grinned in response—our plan had worked. We quietly walked around the small shop and studied the glass artwork. It was a difficult choice to make, but I finally picked out a small sculpture of two dolphins made of clear glass tinged with bright blue. Delighted with the detail, I carefully removed the figurine from the shelf and went up front to make my purchase.

Mom found a beautiful red-and-white-swirled vase and carried it carefully to the counter. "Is there a way to wrap this so it won't break?" she asked the clerk.

My sculpture had already been secured in bubble wrap and was encased inside a small square box. I knew I could place it inside my suitcase and wrap it in my clothes to buffer it against the trip home. Mom's vase, on the other hand, was about a foot high and would require special care to keep it intact.

"We can wrap it and mail it to your home address," the clerk behind the counter told my mother. "That's what I would suggest."

Mom liked this option. After paying for the vase and the postage it would take to mail it home, she led the way out of the shop, pushing Joey's stroller in front of her while I carried the small packages we still had to tote around.

We wandered inside a few more stores, then headed into a quaint ice-cream parlor where we ordered malts. Mom wanted a caramel marshmallow concoction, while I settled for plain old chocolate—my all-time favorite flavor. We sat down at a table to let Joey finish his nap as we consumed our treats.

"You have more color in your face now," Mom observed.

"I feel better," I replied, wishing she hadn't brought up my morning disaster.

"You scared us all pretty good—probably yourself more than anyone."

I quietly nodded.

"That's why your dad and brother ripped into you when it was over."

Nodding again, I took another sip of my malt.

"But you know they love you," Mom pointed out.

"I know."

"We all do," she continued. "So try to take better care of yourself, okay?"

"Okay."

Smiling, she changed the subject, and we talked about some of the shops we had explored earlier in Old Town. Among other things, we discussed how fun it had been to watch a lady in a nearby shop make tortillas from scratch. We decided to try that sort of thing on our own after our return home. We were just getting into how cool it would be to try glassblowing when a roving band of Mexican musicians popped into the shop and began to play rather loudly, effectively ending Joey's nap. At least he'd dozed for a little over an hour. That had to help his mood. Mom bribed him out of crying with a bite of her malt. Big mistake on her part—Joey ate the rest of it.

A sudden insight hit me with a jolt as I thought about how much Mom sacrifices for our family. She did most of the packing and planning for this trip. She was the one who handled Joey's rebellion on the plane and later at the hotel. And even after getting less sleep than anyone else, she was the first one to reach my side after my near demise. She was the one who had made me feel better about things when everyone else had made me feel like a total loser.

As I watched her patiently feed Joey what was left of her malt, a lump formed in my throat. I haven't exactly been the easiest daughter to raise. I'm sure Mom endured several temperamental episodes when I was Joey's age, not to mention everything I've put her through since that time. Plagued with guilt, I decided that from that point on, I was going to be more of a help than a hindrance to her. It was the least I could do, all things considered.

* * *

We were tired after our adventures at Coronado and Old Town. Taking a vote, we returned to the hotel to relax for the rest of the day. It was too early for dinner, so we decided to enjoy the hotel's pool. Mom put Joey in a special swimming diaper, and we took the elevator back downstairs to the pool. We set our towels and the room card on a deserted table next to a set of lawn chairs, kicked off our flip-flops, and stepped down into the water.

While Mom and Dad entertained Joey in the shallow end, where they could also keep an eye on our belongings, Reese and I swam under the rope divider and headed into deeper waters. I watched as my brother powerfully swam from one end of the fair-sized pool to the other. I was content to bob in the water, staying where I could touch the bottom.

"Aren't you going to swim around?" Reese asked, swimming to where I was leaning against the side of the pool.

"Maybe later. I'm going to relax here for a minute."

Reese smiled ruefully. "Hey, I'm sorry about earlier . . . at the beach. We came down on you pretty hard."

"I deserved it. I messed up," I admitted.

"No one deserves to get scared like that," Reese countered as he ran a hand over his wet hair. "And I'm sure we didn't help."

"It's okay. Mom and I talked about it when we were wandering around Old Town. I've learned from it. Let's move on."

"Agreed," Reese said with a grin. With that, he splashed water at me. Then he dove down before I could retaliate and swam to the deepest part of the pool.

"Hi there. Would you and your friend like to join us?" a male voice queried.

Turning, I gazed into the most beautiful brown eyes I've ever seen. The eyes belonged to a young man who appeared to be about my age, and they matched his wavy, brown hair. His dark eyes were fringed by long, black eyelashes, and I was pleased to note that the rest of his face was just as attractive.

"We figured we'd get a round of water volleyball going with whoever's interested," he continued.

"I'll play," I volunteered. "But I'm not sure about my brother," I added, emphasizing my link to Reese.

"Go ask your brother, and I'll finish rounding up our teams."

Nodding, I turned to look for Reese. Dismayed, I noted that he was sticking to the deepest part of the pool. I wasn't sure I was ready for another swimming adventure. I glanced back at Mr. Volleyball and caught a glimpse of shoulder muscles that made me inhale sharply. That settled it. Gathering my courage, I plunged my face underwater and began to swim. It was tough at first, a sense of panic washing over me as I left my safety zone. But as I continued to swim, my former training took over, and I glided easily through the water to reach Reese.

"Good job," Reese congratulated me when I grabbed the side of the pool to pull myself up beside him. "I didn't think you'd make it out this far . . . at least not today."

"I'm a trooper," I said, still trying to catch my breath. "Are you interested in playing water volleyball?" I asked. I explained what was going on, and Reese followed me back to the rope that divided the pool in half. The boy had been busy—by then about a dozen people about our age had been sorted into two teams.

"You made it," Mr. Gorgeous observed, revealing a dazzling smile. "By the way, my name is Ed, short for Edward Thomas Thackery the Third." Then he added apologetically, "I'm named after my dad and grandpa."

I'd never liked the name Ed till now. Now it sounded wonderful. "Ed, I'm Laurie, and this is my brother Reese."

"Cool. Reese, you're on my sister's team, and Laurie, you'll be on mine."

Reese gazed at Ed's sister, a freckle-faced, redheaded girl who couldn't have been more than thirteen. She grinned flirtatiously at Reese, waving him over. Reese paused long enough to shoot me a dirty look. It wasn't my fault Ed got all the looks in the family. I smiled at my brother and gave him a shove into the rope.

"You're so dead," Reese mouthed as he held up the rope to swim to the rest of his team.

I ignored Reese and made my way to Ed's side as he introduced me to the rest of our team. "You got acquainted fast," I commented, impressed.

"I know better than half of these people. We're all from the same town in Illinois."

"Really?" I asked, intrigued.

"Yeah, we're here to build homeless huts in Mexico."

I must've had a blank look on my face.

"For the past four years, our Baptist youth group has come here to help the homeless down in Tijuana."

Two pieces of information nailed me in the gut. First, my prince wasn't LDS, kind of a downer. But on the plus side, he was here to help the homeless, something that tugged at my heartstrings. What a neat guy. I told him how great I thought it was that he and the other members of his youth group were here to do something so noble, and I earned another radiant smile. He promised to tell me more about what they were doing after the game—a signal that it was time for water volleyball to commence. And it did with a flurry.

We played for well over an hour, having such a good time that no one bothered to keep score. Proclaiming it a tied game, we promised to meet for another round the next night.

"I'm not sure what time we'll be through playing tourist tomorrow," I said reluctantly to Ed. "But I'll really try to be here at whatever time you say."

Ed grinned. "It's hard to say when we'll be back too. It depends on how much work we get done, and sometimes we lose track of the time." He must've noticed the crestfallen look on my face. "Why don't we wing it? Maybe aim for later tomorrow night, say around eight?"

That sounded good to me. Surely Mom and Dad would be willing to wrap things up by then—today we were finished by 4:30. I gave Ed my room number just in case he needed to leave me a message, and he hurried out of the pool to join his youth group. I found I couldn't keep my eyes from following him as he walked away.

"I'll really try to be here at whatever time you say," Reese mimicked into my ear.

"That's it," I exclaimed, managing to dunk him a good one under the water. Big mistake on my part. Reese practically dragged me down to the deepest end of the pool and tried to drown me. For the second time that day, I was in fear for my life. Finally he let me up. I sputtered revenge while he laughed.

"Chill, little girl. I figured you could use some cooling off."

"What do you mean?" I demanded.

"Edward Thomas Thackery the Third," Reese taunted. He moved close and began twisting my ears.

"Quit it! What are you doing?" I asked, moving away from him.

"Trying to fasten your eyes back inside your head," he teased.

"So I think he's kind of cute," I said, downplaying my true emotions as I hung onto the side of the pool for support. I was tired and didn't want to waste my limited energy treading water.

"I see," Reese said, grinning. "Word of advice—keep it on the friendship level. Remember, he's not LDS."

"That doesn't make him a bad person," I countered. "He's nicer than a lot of Mormon boys I could list."

"I agree. But our parents would have a fit if you married outside of the Church."

My frown deepened. "I just met the guy."

"Good point. Remember that. Sometimes first impressions are way off base."

"He's here to help the homeless," I said in Ed's defense.

"I know. My teammates were telling me all about it. Just be careful. Guys can appear to be one thing when they're really another. And that's all I'm going to say about that for now," he said, holding up a hand to block the stream of water I had splashed at him. "Race you back to the other side," he said, cheating as he leaped forward in the water.

Disgruntled by his advice, I took my time swimming to the shallow end. Reese had already wrapped himself in a towel and was talking to our parents, who had been sitting poolside for quite a while with Joey. Sitting on Dad's lap, my baby brother was contentedly banging his hands on the glass-topped table, squealing with glee.

I walked out of the pool and reached for my towel.

"It looked like you were having fun out there," Dad said, smiling up at me.

I nodded, wondering what Reese had been telling our parents.

"What would you and Reese think if we went back to our rooms, ordered pizza, and selected one of those in-room movies to watch?" Mom asked.

"Sounds good to me," Reese replied.

"Laurie?" Mom pressed.

"Sure. That's great," I said, holding out my hands to Joey. I carried him inside the hotel and into the bathroom in my parents' room. Mom wanted to give Joey a bath to clean him up like she normally did at home each night, again trying to get him back into a routine we could live with. As a whole, Joey had been a lot better-natured this afternoon, and we had hope that he would sleep through the night.

"Laurie, I can handle things from here if you want to go shower and change into dry clothes," Mom suggested. "I'm sure Reese has already been in and out of the shower in your room by now."

"Okay," I responded, thinking a shower would feel wonderful. A half hour later, when I returned to my parents' room, the pizza had already been delivered and everyone else had showered and changed. We spread out across the two queen-size beds to watch the movie Dad had decided was worthy of being watched, a recent Disney flick. Mom and I reclined on one bed together, sitting up against the headboard, using pillows as backrests. Joey sat between us, gumming the small piece of crust Mom figured he could suck on without choking. Dad and Reese were sitting cross-legged on the other bed, snarfing pizza as fast as I've ever seen. Shaking her head over their lack of manners, Mom ignored them and nibbled at the piece of pepperoni pizza in her hand. As I leaned back against the headboard, enjoying my own piece of pizza, I reflected on how much fun we were having as a family. This idea to take a trip together was turning into a wonderful adventure. Tomorrow would be even better. Not only were we going to Sea

World, but I would get another chance to spend time with Ed tomorrow night. Warmed by that thought, I missed the question my mother had asked.

"Earth to Laurie," Reese said, hitting me in the head with a wadded-up napkin.

"What?"

Mom lifted one of her eyebrows at me. "I asked which animal exhibit you wanted to see first tomorrow."

"That would be the Ed variety," Reese crowed, enjoying himself a little too much.

"Ed?" My dad repeated, glancing first at Reese, then at me. "Who's Ed?"

If looks could kill, we would be planning Reese's funeral about now. My brother merely chortled over the dark expression on my face and refocused on the movie.

"Is that the nice young man you met while you were playing volleyball in the pool?" Mom guessed.

Okay, maybe I was wrong. Maybe this was too much family togetherness rolled into one day. Vowing to get even with Reese, I slid off the bed and pretended I needed to use the bathroom. Once inside that small room, I sat down on the side of the tub and planned my revenge. All it would take was one or two well-placed comments to Stacy about the girls Reese had played beach volleyball with earlier today. That would take care of things.

When I rejoined the family about five minutes later, Reese didn't even look at me. In fact, no one did. Through the bathroom door, I had heard Mom telling Dad and Reese to back off, reminding them I had had a pretty rough day. It was good to know that she was currently in my corner. I smiled at her, then climbed back onto the bed beside Joey and reached for another piece of pizza. I glanced over at my older brother, who was still concentrating on the movie. It didn't matter that he was leaving me alone now. Reese had thrown down the gauntlet, and I had picked it up.

Chapter 7

As we had hoped, Joey did sleep better during the night. I only heard him fuss twice, and it was for just a few minutes each time. Evidently, he had decided that things weren't so bad, and as long as he could see our parents—mostly Mom—all was well. As a result, Mom looked a lot better the next morning. As we sat around the table at the family restaurant discussing our plans for the day, I forgot about my ongoing feud with Reese. Today we were going to Sea World, making one of my lifelong goals come true.

Following a quick breakfast, we loaded back into the minivan and, with Mom playing the role of navigator this time around, arrived at the parking lot of Sea World about twenty minutes later. After we unloaded Joey's stroller as well as the digital camera and the video camera, Dad locked the minivan. I glanced at the cameras we would be packing around that day and shook my head. I guess Dad figured today's adventure was the ultimate Kodak moment. Yesterday he had only used the digital camera. Good thing—I would've hated watching a rerun of me being escorted out of the ocean by a lifeguard.

Dad tucked the video camera bag into the front compartment of Joey's stroller. That's where Mom usually keeps the diaper bag. Amazingly both bags fit in there, as well as Mom's purse. Myself, I packed light. I had chosen to wear a pair of knee-length Levi shorts with a turquoise T-shirt and a pair of comfortable leather sandals. I shoved my small wallet into the front pocket of my shorts in case I found a treasure to buy while we were at Sea World. I'd left my purse back at the hotel, intent on being as comfortable as I could as we walked around today. Yesterday, I had hated the way the slender strap of my purse had dug into my right shoulder as we had explored Old Town. My purse isn't very big, but I usually manage to fill it to the brim with makeup, a brush and comb, a tiny mirror, and other necessities of life.

As Reese and I impatiently waited to explore Sea World, Dad examined his digital camera and Mom buckled a protesting Joey into his stroller. Sighing, she finally handed him his pacifier to settle him down. She stood up, looking pretty classy in her tan capris. After Joey was born, she started working out most mornings to a Pilates tape, and it shows. For a forty-two-year-old lady, she doesn't look too bad.

Dad was our fashion disaster. He was wearing baggy Levi shorts that hung well below his knees, a yellow polo shirt, black socks that reached above his ankles, and a pair of Nikes that had seen better days, not to mention an old, purple baseball cap with the Utah Jazz logo on the front. With that dopey digital camera bag hanging from his neck, he looked like the tourist you always see in those comedy sketches. All I can say is that it's a good thing Mom loves him. I noticed even Reese kept his distance from Dad as we entered the park.

At the gate, we showed the all-day passes Dad had purchased online before we left home, and we hurried into Sea World, entering a magical land. Everywhere we looked, there was something to do. In the center of the park, the Skytower Ride beckoned. That's where we made our first deal of the day. Reese and I wanted to ride to the top of the Skytower. Mom and Dad wanted to ride the Bayside Skyride across Mission Bay. We consulted with the schedule we had been given and noted that we would have time for both rides before the Shamu show took place. Later, we would take turns experiencing Sea World's newest ride, Journey to Atlantis, something that had just opened this past spring.

Reese and I were allowed to go first, with the understanding that we would babysit Joey while our parents enjoyed their ride. Hurrying to the Skytower, we showed our passes and climbed inside the rounded, glass elevator that would slowly climb a slender tower 320 feet high. As the elevator started to rise, Reese and I moved to the windows that looked out over the north end of Sea World. From this view, we could see the buildings that housed the sharks, manatees, penguins, sea lions, and—my favorite—the dolphins. We could also catch a glimpse of the Journey to Atlantis attraction. Along the west side, we could see the flamingos, the Haunted Lighthouse, the Bayside Skyride, an area where beached animals are kept, and a couple of large buildings that housed aquariums. To the south, we could see where the sea otters were kept, as well as Shipwreck Rapids and the outdoor amphitheater where we would later watch Shamu's show. Toward the east, we could see where we had parked and entered Sea World. As we began to drop down, we could make out people who were more than likely our parents waving. Dad's bright yellow shirt was a dead giveaway. When we reached the ground, Reese and I exited the ride and walked over to where our parents were waiting.

"How was it?" Dad asked.

"Pretty cool," Reese answered. "You can see the whole park from up there."

"And now it's our turn," Mom reminded, pointing to her watch. "The way I have it figured, if your dad and I hurry, I'll have time to feed Joey before Shamu's show starts. I noticed on our park map that there's a nursing mothers' facility over by the dolphins."

Joy, I thought silently. Oh, well. At least Joey's feeding ritual would be out of public view.

At first, Reese and I followed along behind our parents. Then Reese had a brainstorm. He decided that he and I would take Joey to see the aquatic life in the nearby aquariums while Mom and Dad rode the Bayside Skyride. Liking this idea, we made arrangements to meet our parents at Flamingo Cove when their ride was over. From there, it wasn't very far to the dolphin exhibit, something the rest of us could enjoy while Mom nursed Joey in the mothers' lounge.

We split up, and Reese and I hurried off to entertain our baby brother. On our short walk to the World of the Tide Pool Sea Aquarium, Reese decided to apologize for last night. I let him grovel, enjoying the fact that he was worried over any potential paybacks. He had a reason to be concerned.

When we entered the darkened interior of the aquarium, Joey started to fuss. I guess he caught on that our parents weren't walking by our side. Reese volunteered to pick him up, and I let him, remembering how heavy Joey is now. The kid weighs a ton, thanks to Mom and her dedication to feeding him every five minutes. So Reese bounced our brother in his arms, trying to get him interested in little crabs, mollusks, and starfish while I pushed the stroller along. Dad had switched the digital camera for the video camera, deciding we could all enjoy the view from their ride. Reese and I hadn't bothered taking pictures from the Skytower Ride, certain the tinted windows wouldn't make for very good shots.

I reached down and made sure Dad's digital camera was riding snug beside Joey's diaper bag. It wouldn't be good if either item came up missing. I continued to follow behind Reese and Joey, enjoying the sights of the aquarium, when a nasty smell assaulted my sensitive nose. I looked up at the guilty party and noted that Reese was pulling a face.

"Great," Reese exclaimed, holding Joey out away from him. "Man, you reek!"

I think Joey sensed he had just been insulted, and he burst into tears. "Nice, Reese," I chided, taking Joey from him. I instantly regretted that decision. Reese was right—Joey reeked.

"Do something with the kid. He's foul," Reese pleaded, holding his nose.

"I don't suppose you think it's possible for you to do the honors?" I asked, still trying to calm Joey down.

"You're better at it," he replied.

"Yes, but you just said that you owe me big time for dropping Ed's name in front of our parents last night, remember?" I reminded him.

Grimacing, Reese held out his hands for Joey.

Exultant over my victory, I reached into the diaper bag and pulled out a clean disposable diaper and a small package of baby wipes. "Here you go," I said, handing both items to Reese.

"On the map of Sea World I noticed there's a unisex diapering area right next door at the Marine Aquarium," I suggested.

Nodding, Reese left the building with Joey, and I followed behind pushing the stroller. We searched for the diapering facility and found it without too much trouble. Reese disappeared inside with Joey and I waited, enjoying every minute of Reese's misery. My Laurel leader was wrong—revenge was sweeter than turning the other cheek.

It took a lot longer than I would've guessed, but Reese finally reappeared with Joey, who looked and smelled much better.

"That was gross," Reese muttered, handing Joey to me. "I'm glad we're not eating lunch for a while. I'm not sure I could eat anything right now."

"Oh, it wasn't that bad," I said brightly, bouncing a gurgling Joey in my arms. He was a much happier baby.

"We are totally even," Reese said, giving me a pained look.

"Pretty much," I replied, grinning.

"What a cute baby," an older woman said, reaching to pat Joey's back. "Is it your first?" she asked, smiling at me.

"Uh . . . well . . ." I stammered, feeling the blush in my cheeks.

"It's actually our third," Reese said, the mischievous look on his face indicating he felt this was poetic justice.

"Your third," the woman said, studying my face more closely. "Goodness. You don't appear a day over fifteen." Appalled, she walked off to join two women about her age who had wandered out of the women's restroom. She pointed me out to them, and I could just imagine the things they were saying.

Turning to Reese, I smacked him a good one in the arm and walked off, leaving him to push the stroller.

* * *

I absolutely loved Shamu's show, aside from the fact that those three sweet old ladies had managed to sit in the section next to our family. My mother noticed how they were pointing our direction and whispering, but I didn't care. Ignoring them, I let Mom entertain Joey while I focused on watching Shamu. We had arrived early for the show, so we were able to sit right down front. At first it was great—we could see everything. Then the tables turned, and Shamu splashed the audience, drenching our family. Mom, Dad, Reese, and even Joey laughed it off. I was furious. I had spent nearly thirty minutes on my hair so it looked just right, and now I resembled a drowned rat. That's when I noticed the sign down in front that warned the audience to wear rain gear if they didn't want to get wet.

Dad's main concern was the cameras, but the digital camera had been well protected inside Joey's stroller, and he had managed to cover the video camera with his body when he saw that fish-propelled tidal wave heading our way. My concern was the fact that everything I needed to repair myself had been left in my purse back at the hotel. As we wandered out of the amphitheater a few minutes later, Mom caught up to me and handed me her purse.

"Here, I think you'll find everything you need inside," she said, pointing me in the direction of the nearest restroom.

Nodding, I entered the restroom and headed for a mirror. I opened Mom's purse and found that she was right. Not only did I find makeup—not the colors I prefer, but workable—but there was also a brush and a pick. I dug out what I needed and went to work repairing my face and hair. The makeup wasn't too bad, but my hair looked awful. Sighing, I kept digging in Mom's purse until I found a rubber band. Using it, I gathered my hair into a ponytail and called it good.

As I put everything I had used back into Mom's purse, a piece of paper floated out of it. I picked it up off the restroom floor and was about to put it back inside when I noticed my name on it. Curious, and figuring if it had my name on it the note was fair game, I read it, then wished I hadn't.

Janell,

I thought you'd want to know that I saw Laurie hanging around the other night with a rough-looking crowd. As your visiting teacher, I felt it was my duty to bring this to your attention. Young people seem to struggle so much these days. I'd hate to see your daughter follow in Reese's footsteps.

Sincerely,
Penny Rallison

There were several things that upset me as I read the note. For the record, I do not run around with a rough crowd. Not only that, but I am not my brother. I don't plan to make the same mistakes Reese did. And who was Penny to judge him anyway?

At the sight of Penny's spidery signature, I frowned. Penny Rallison, Mom's nosy visiting teacher. She's known for being the ward gossip, which is why my mother probably got saddled with her—Mom wouldn't have assigned the older woman to anyone else, figuring it was her duty as Relief Society president to tolerate the woman.

Penny is one of those meddling types who dresses in fancy clothes, drives a huge, old Cadillac, and figures it's her duty to save us all from ourselves by spreading everything she sees or hears to anyone who will listen. I hate how she uses most fast and testimony meetings to preach to the rest of us. To me, that's as wrong as the note that was in my hand. I almost wadded it into a ball and hurled it into the trash can—then I remembered it was Mom's property and something I wasn't supposed to see.

What rough crowd was Penny talking about? The only person I hang out with is Roz, and even if I don't agree with everything my best friend is doing these days, she was never a rough crowd.

Puzzled by Penny's accusation, I went over the events of the past week. Then it hit me—Roz had picked me up one night from work. We had gone to the Layton Mall to kill some time before we went to see a movie at a nearby Cineplex. While we were at the mall, a group of guys from our high school came over to where we were eating nachos in the food court and made general nuisances of themselves. Members of the football team, these guys think they're a gift to the world, and lately, they've been flirting with Roz and me whenever they see us. Personally, I think it's because we don't give them the time of day, so we present a challenge. Roz thinks they give us a bad time because they're attracted to us. Right! Regardless, contrary to what Penny Rallison thinks, I don't run around with these guys. But Penny must have seen us together at the food court that night. Great. That's what I needed—Penny bad-mouthing the Relief Society president's daughter all over town.

I stuck the note back inside Mom's purse and wondered what to do about it. Mom hadn't said anything to me. I hoped it was because she trusted me. I hoped she wasn't waiting for a time when we could have another mother-daughter chat. I shuddered, thinking about the last lecture I had endured. That one was painful enough.

"Laurie? Are you okay?" Mom asked, walking into the restroom. "You're taking forever."

"Yeah, I'm just trying to look like a person," I mumbled, handing her back her purse.

"Why are you scowling?"

I pointed to my hair. "This wasn't the look I was going for today."

Mom laughed. "You look fine. Much better than you did when you came in here. And if you're hungry, your father and Reese bought us some hamburgers."

Shrugging, I followed her to where the rest of our family was waiting. I didn't care that I had to eat a hamburger, something I get sick of seeing at Harold's Burgers. I had other, more important things on my mind, like realizing the attempt Mom had been making to get close to me on this trip was more than likely due to that note in her purse. The fact that she had kept it indicated she might think there was something to it. Feeling betrayed, I planned to keep my guard up. Maybe by the time she confronted me, I'd have a good story made up and confess to something outrageous just to see the look on her face. Simmering, I ate my hamburger in silence, plotting my revenge against Mom and Penny Rallison.

* * *

Our family spent most of the day at Sea World. After lunch, we wandered into a gift shop where I bought a sweatshirt with Shamu on the front—proof I had been to Sea World. Then we wandered around and looked at the animals and fish. Naturally, the dolphins were my favorite; I loved how playful they were and, for a brief moment, wished my life were as simple as theirs. Eat, sleep, and play in the water. It sounded pretty good at the moment.

After we had seen all the exhibits, we rode Journey to Atlantis. What a ride that turned out to be. I went with Dad, while Mom rode with Reese after. The ride began with Dad and me boarding an eight-passenger roller-coaster car shaped like a Greek fishing boat. After we took our seats, we experienced an exhilarating rush as we dashed around a seafoam green track, hitting periodic ponds of water that doused us with refreshing wetness. As with any roller-coaster ride, there were surprising twists and turns around every corner. At one point, we plunged sixty feet into a lake, causing me to scream and cling to my dad. He just laughed and put his arm around me, enjoying my reaction.

The ride was worth it, though, because we got to see a type of dolphin I've never seen before: Commerson's dolphins. Their bodies are white with black trim—beautiful mammals that were swimming around in a huge four-paneled acrylic tank. To my way of thinking, we had truly reached Atlantis, a city of wonders. I excitedly babbled to my dad that these sea creatures were the coolest things I'd ever seen. Then he said it, the one statement that ruined it all for me.

"Are they cooler than Ed?"

I sulked the rest of the afternoon over that comment, deciding I was through confiding in either parent. Both had proven that they couldn't be trusted.

Chapter 8

"How was Sea World?" Ed asked as I swam to where he was waiting near the dividing rope in the hotel pool.

"Awesome, even if I had to put up with my parents and brothers."

"It sounds like a hardship," Ed said, smiling.

"You just don't know," I responded, glancing back over my shoulder. I had left my family upstairs, unwilling to waste time waiting for them to get ready. I knew they would be down eventually. This way, I had a few minutes of privacy with Ed before they showed up to ruin everything.

As I continued to gaze around, I didn't see anyone else from Ed's youth group in the pool. "Where're your fellow carpenters?"

"They're pretty hammered tonight," he answered, laughing at the pun he had made. "Seriously, we did hammer together a lot of frames today. We're bushed. Some of them went right to their rooms to collapse and order in food." He pointed to the hot tub. "Some of them are over there soaking themselves, too sore to move."

"No volleyball game tonight," I guessed.

"Is that okay? I'm kind of tired myself."

"No problem. We can just swim around and talk," I suggested.

"I'd like that," he replied. We swam leisurely to the far end of the pool and held onto the side, water dripping from our faces as we bobbed in the water.

"What part of Illinois are you from?" I asked, curious. I've always wanted to explore Nauvoo, a destination my family has often discussed venturing to see.

"I'm from a town no one's heard of before," he answered. "A place called Quincy."

"Quincy, huh?" I repeated, trying to remember if I'd ever heard of it before. It sounded familiar, but nothing came to mind.

"It's on the west side of the state, right along the Mississippi River."

"Cool. Is the Mississippi as big as I've heard?"

"Yep, and probably twice as muddy," Ed laughed. "But it's still pretty neat." He shifted around, facing the other end of the pool. "Where are you from?"

"A little place called Roy."

Ed squinted at me. "Roy? That's the name of your town?"

"Uh-huh," I nodded. "I'm not sure how it got its name."

"Is it here in California?"

I shook my head. "No, it's in Utah." An alarmed expression appeared on his face, and I wondered if I'd said something wrong.

"Utah, huh? I don't suppose . . . nah . . . never mind. It doesn't matter."

"What doesn't matter?" I asked.

"Well, it's just . . . you know . . . you hear the word Utah, and you instantly think about Mormons."

Reese had been right—this guy was too good to be true. Crushed, I turned to face out toward the pool. "You have something against Mormons?" I couldn't bear to see the answer in Ed's face.

"Sort of," he admitted. "Are you a Mormon?"

"Yeah," I replied, hurt that my religion would be a barrier between us.

An uncomfortable silence settled in for several long seconds. Then Ed sighed and turned to look at me. "It's nothing personal, Laurie, but—"

"How can this not be personal?" I retorted, guessing what he was about to say. "You think that because I belong to the LDS Church, we can't even be friends," I said hotly, stung by his reaction. It suddenly came to mind where I'd heard about Quincy, Illinois—it had come up in seminary last year. We had been studying the Doctrine and Covenants, and as I recall, the residents of Quincy had befriended the Saints, only to turn around and persecute them, driving them from the state of Illinois after the martyrdom of Joseph Smith. Ed was no doubt a descendant of these people.

"I didn't say that," he responded, his eyes widening.

"Oh? What were you going to say?"

"That I've heard bad things about your church—"

"Big surprise," I interjected, still indignant.

"It doesn't mean I believe any of it. Unlike some people, I believe in giving others the benefit of the doubt."

Now I felt sheepish. "Oh. Sorry. Sometimes I get a little tired of hearing people bash my church."

"You've had this happen before?"

"Not to me personally. I live in an area that's predominantly LDS, so I haven't had to stick up for our religion much. But lately it seems like anytime a Mormon messes up, they parade it all over TV and the newspapers." I searched his face for understanding. "When the media reports a story about someone doing something wrong, they don't usually end with, 'And he was a Catholic!' or 'And she was a Baptist!'"

"Good point," he conceded.

"But boy, let a Mormon mess up, and they make sure everyone knows he's a member of the Church." I glanced at Ed and saw that he was smiling. "Sorry, I guess this is a sore spot with me."

"I've noticed," he relied. "Tell you what. Why don't we steer clear of religious discussions for now and enjoy spending time together?"

I liked that suggestion, my opinion of him rising to an even higher level. Ed was as awesome as I had first thought. A true gentleman, he helped me out of the pool, and together we walked to the hot tub to relax in the bubbling water with some of his other friends.

* * *

The next day, while Ed and his youth group headed to Mexico to work on the small houses they were building, my family went to see the San Diego Zoo. There we saw a ton of animals you don't often see in Utah, like an adorable baby panda bear named Mei Sheng. Dad snapped picture after picture with his camera, enthralled by the cub's playful antics.

Joey was entranced by the monkeys. I figured it was because his older brother acts just like them. It was hard for me to pick a favorite—I liked the entire zoo. But I felt guilty, thinking about how hard Ed and his friends were working down in Tijuana. Ed had described homes made from cardboard boxes and pieces of tin, meals cooked over open fires because that's the only thing they have to use. Children dressed so poorly it would make you cry to see them. My thoughts strayed to the haunting images Ed had planted inside my head as I walked among well-dressed tourists who were laughing, eating cotton candy and popcorn, and drinking pop. I finally silenced my conscience by promising to help Mom with the humanitarian projects she had encouraged our ward to complete by November. It was one way I could reach out to those who were less fortunate.

Deep in thought, I didn't add to the conversation that took place when we left the zoo around one P.M. It was decided without my vote that our late lunch would be another quick burger at a nearby fast-food drive-in. I could tell by the concerned look on her face that Mom wanted to talk to me, but I didn't want to talk to her just yet. So I tried to focus on what was being said and pretended to be as lighthearted as everyone else as we discussed our plans for the rest of the day.

After a quick lunch, we headed out to Escondido to the Wild Animal Park, where we enjoyed riding a monorail through the preserve. The park was a lot bigger than I thought it would be. The neat thing is, the animals in this location can romp around freely in their natural habitats. The monorail winds throughout the park, a five-mile excursion that lasts about 50 minutes. And because the monorail is not fully enclosed, you feel like you're a part of all that you see. I especially enjoyed watching the baby black rhino as he tagged along beside his protective mother. Our tour guide told us that because of organizations like the Zoological Society of San Diego, these amazing animals are being preserved.

As I marveled over this, I thought again of the people Ed had described. Because of neat guys like Ed, the poverty-stricken were being assisted. Shaking my head, I realized Ed was getting through to me, and it was more than just a physical attraction. He was inspiring me to think about things I'd never considered before. Here I was, a Mormon with a knowledge of gospel truths, and a Baptist boy from Quincy, Illinois, was having a bigger influence on me than I was on him. Ed was prompting me to quit taking life for granted, to be grateful for all that I had, and to be willing to share it with others. Thanks to Edward Thomas Thackery III, I would never be the same.

* * *

Mom finally cornered me later that afternoon at a pop machine down the hall from our hotel rooms. I didn't even see her coming. Then suddenly there she was, calling my name.

"Hi, Mom," I replied, trying to sound cheerful.

"Hi," she returned, leaning against the wall next to the pop machine. She shoved her hands into the pockets of her capri jeans and watched as I pretended to examine the variety of pop available in the vending machine. Uncomfortable with how she was gazing at me, I plastered a smile on my face, attempting to convey that all was well.

"Your dad and brothers are having a male-bonding moment watching sports on TV. Why don't we grab a pop and head down to the pool?"

It was all I could do to keep from wincing. Not another heart-to-heart. "I'm not wearing my swimming suit," I said gesturing to my white T-shirt and green khaki shorts, knowing she wouldn't buy that as an excuse.

She didn't. "Neither am I," she responded. "I'd like to talk to you, though, privately, before we drive over to Seaport Village for dinner."

Cringing inside, I selected a bottle of Sprite, then stepped back and watched as Mom bought a bottle of caffeine-free Diet Coke. Resigned to my fate, I followed her to the pool. She used her room card to unlock the gate and led me to a spot near the shallow end of the pool. I sat down on a lounge chair and watched as Mom dragged another lounge chair over to sit next to me. We both reclined in our chairs, sipping our pop in silence as we watched the people who were playing in the pool. Just as I was getting my hopes up that Mom would relax and fall asleep, she spoke.

"Laurie, you've seemed upset today. Actually, I think it started yesterday at Sea World," she began. "What's wrong?"

Where to start? The note in her purse? The way Dad and Reese kept giving me a bad time over Ed? The guilt I now felt over our family trip, thanks to Ed?

"Are you feeling all right?"

"Yeah . . . no. I don't know," I admitted, keeping my focus on the pool.

"Is it this boy you've become friends with?" she probed.

Turning, I gave her an irritated look.

"He seems like a nice young man."

"Mom, Ed's the best guy I've ever met," I blurted out before I could stop myself.

"Then why are you so down?"

I paused, knowing I would have to choose my next words more carefully. "Ed told me about the poor people who live in Tijuana—the people his youth group are trying to help. It makes me feel bad . . . like we have everything and they have nothing. I don't know how to explain it."

Mom gazed at me quietly for several long seconds. "You're feeling guilty because we've been blessed as a family?"

I nodded, glancing at my watch to see if it was time to head to Seaport Village. Disappointed that we weren't leaving for another hour, I sat back in my chair and fortified myself with a long drink of Sprite, hoping this conversation would eventually end.

"There are a lot of ways you can help those who are in need. You can donate money. There's a place on the tithing slips marked for humanitarian aid. Whatever you choose to donate goes directly toward helping the people who need it most."

"That's a great idea," I said, nodding eagerly. "I feel a lot better now."

Mom gave me one of those looks indicating we were far from finished with our talk. "You could also help me tie a baby quilt for the humanitarian effort our ward is making this year."

"Okay," I agreed. I must've been desperate to get this visit over with—I hate quilting. "I'm glad we had this talk. It's really helped."

"And this is the only thing bothering you?" Mom pressed.

"Yeah," I lied. No way would I tell her the other concerns that were making me miserable.

"Are you sure? You still seem upset. What else is wrong? You know you can tell me anything."

Do you ever get annoyed when your mother won't let something go? Do you ever say things you don't mean when this happens? Unfortunately, I have a talent in this department. Without warning, I erupted. "I'm feeling guilty over the wild parties I've been attending back home," I exclaimed.

"What?" Mom asked, looking mortified.

I only thought I had suffered from guilt earlier that day. Now it descended with a fury, letting me know I was being a royal jerk to my mother. My conscience never lets me get away with anything. "Mom, I'm sorry," I tried to backpedal, noticing we had drawn the unwanted attention of an older couple sitting on the other side of the table. Great, now we were providing free entertainment for the hotel guests.

"What wild parties?" she demanded, the hurt look on her face morphing into anger. Now I had her attention. She slid her legs off the lounge chair and swung around to face me.

"I wasn't serious," I stammered, lowering my voice so I couldn't be overheard by the older couple who were now frowning their disapproval my direction. "Sometimes I get sick of you and Dad always believing the worst about me."

"What do you mean?" Mom asked, looking hurt again.

"This conversation and others like it. It's pretty obvious you and Dad don't trust me—that you think I'm going to mess up my life."

"Laurie, we care about you, and we're concerned when we see you doing things that could lead to trouble."

"Like hanging out with Ed," I guessed.

"Maybe," she replied. "But before we get to Ed, explain your comment about wild parties," she insisted.

"It's that stupid note in your purse," I exclaimed. "It fell out when I was fixing my hair yesterday."

"What note?" Mom asked, looking confused.

"The one from Penny Rallison."

As the light dawned for my mother, it looked like she was trying to keep a straight face. Insulted by her reaction, I took another long sip of pop.

"Laurie, do you honestly think I pay attention to anything Penny says?"

"If it didn't mean anything, why did you keep the note?"

"She left it on the table in the Relief Society room this last Sunday, where I couldn't miss it. I read it, rolled my eyes, and stuffed it inside my purse so no one else could see it. I forgot about it until now." She tried to stifle a smile, but it leaked through anyway. "You've been sulking over Penny's note?"

I didn't acknowledge her question, sulking now because she thought this was funny.

"Honey, I know you better than you think I do, which is why I wasn't worried about that note. I know Penny twisted whatever she saw. Isn't that how it went?"

Still ticked, I nodded, and before Mom could drag it out of me, I told her exactly what had happened.

"That's why Penny thinks you're hanging out with a rough bunch," Mom concluded when I had finished.

"Yeah," I agreed.

"I'll set Penny straight the next time I see her," Mom promised, glancing at her watch. "Okay, in the twenty minutes we have left, tell me about Ed."

"Everything?"

"Everything. Where's he's from, this project he's working on, why you're so upset about it—everything."

Giving in, I spilled my guts. Without interrupting, she listened quietly and seemed to sympathize when I told her that I knew things would never work between Ed and me.

"Is that part of why you feel so sad today?"

"I guess it is," I replied, understanding now that part of my problem today had been just what Mom had figured out. "It's hard to think I'll never see him again. I feel this connection to him, like we've always known each other."

"I see," Mom said quietly. "And does he feel the same way?"

Blushing, I shrugged. "I don't know. We haven't really talked about it. We've talked about everything else . . . even religion. I mean, at first, when he found out I was a Mormon, he didn't seem very thrilled. But then he started asking questions about our church, and we had a really neat discussion last night in the hot tub."

"The hot tub, huh?" she responded, lifting an eyebrow.

Perturbed, I focused on the pop in my hands. No doubt I would now be hit with a ton of unwanted motherly advice—the evils of hot tubbing with the opposite sex.

"From my perspective, you're very attracted to this young man, right?"

"Maybe," I admitted.

"But like you said, he's not a member of the Church."

"I like Ed—that doesn't mean I'm going to marry the guy," I retorted.

Mom gave me a pointed look. "You marry who you date."

"What?"

"You develop feelings for the people you date. After a while that can lead to other things."

"Mom, Ed is leaving for home on Saturday, the same day we are. It's not like we'll have much of a chance to date. Besides, he comes back from Tijuana exhausted. He doesn't have the energy to date, let alone make out." I mostly said that last part to annoy Mom.

It worked—she frowned. "Okay, so maybe Ed won't be a problem. But I have had something come to mind quite strongly concerning you, and I've learned to follow through on those promptings."

Groaning, I slid down in my chair.

"Maybe you'll meet someone else this year . . . someone at school. Don't get me wrong. I want you to date and have fun your senior year, but please keep the guidelines in mind that you've been taught your entire life."

I rolled my eyes and waited for Mom to list those guidelines, items I could recite in my sleep, I've heard them so many times.

"Don't date the same person all the time. Go on group dates, so you're not alone. Don't stay out late . . ."

As Mom continued, I counted each item on my fingers, relieved when she finished reciting them all.

"Laurie, I can tell you're not taking any of this seriously. So I want you to think about something else. The other day, when you waded out into the ocean by yourself, I advised you to not get in over your head."

"Yeah, so?" I asked, irked by the reminder of that less-than-graceful moment in my life.

"It's pretty easy to get caught in a strong current, to get pulled out further than you ever intended to go."

I knew it! This was another disguised chastity chat. I rolled my eyes again.

"You can roll your eyes all you want to, but realize this—good kids make bad mistakes. It happens all the time. And if what you're telling me is true about what you're feeling for Ed and what he may be feeling for you, your emotions will be running a bit high the next couple of days. Just be careful, all right?"

"Yeah," I managed to say.

"And during school this year, be on your guard. Don't let yourself get dragged into a situation that can overwhelm and destroy you."

"Okay," I said, knowing that was the answer she was looking for. I looked pointedly at my watch. "Shouldn't we be getting back to our rooms to get ready for dinner?"

Mom sighed and ran a hand through the front of her hair. I think she knew I was not amused with her advice. She stood up, leaned down and said, "Remember always that I'm in your corner and that I love you." Then she planted a soft kiss on my forehead. "Now, let's go to dinner and have a good time. Deal?" She reached down to give me a hand up from my chair.

"Deal," I muttered, walking beside her as we left the pool area. I ignored the couple who had been eavesdropping on our conversation, wishing a bird would fly over their heads and leave a token of my esteem.

"And if Ed's around, do you want to invite him to come with us to Seaport?"

Was this another trap? On the other hand, it would give my parents a chance to meet him. Maybe they wouldn't think he was so bad then. Cheering up considerably, I agreed to Mom's idea and hurried into the hotel to see if Ed was back from Tijuana.

Chapter 9

I loved Seaport Village. It helped that Ed was able to come with us to dinner that night. Dad had called earlier to make reservations at the San Diego Pier Café. He called again before we left the hotel and added one more person to our party.

Seaport Village is located right along the coast, not far from the Coronado Bay Bridge. It's made up of a ton of cute shops that I could hardly wait to explore. But as everyone was starved and our reservation was for 6:30 P.M., we ate first.

Dad had done well. The restaurant he had picked out is at the end of a pier, right on the ocean. From where we were seated at our table, you could look out over the bay and enjoy the view. I watched as a beautiful sailboat slowly glided through the water, and I imagined again how wonderful it would be to travel the world on a craft that graceful.

"I tried sailing one of those once," Ed said next to me. "It's harder than it looks."

"I'll bet," Reese commented. Seated on the other side of Ed, I could tell my older brother was going to eavesdrop on our entire conversation. It was a relief when Mom took over and began asking Ed about Quincy. By the time Ed had answered all her questions, our food had arrived, and we eagerly consumed the fresh seafood set before us.

I'm a big shrimp fan, and, honestly, that shrimp was the best I've ever eaten in my life. I had ordered a combo platter with shrimp scampi, deep-fried shrimp in a spicy batter, and grilled shrimp kabobs intertwined with brightly colored vegetables. It was so delicious, for a moment I didn't care that I was sitting beside a young man I wanted to impress. I ate every bite, savoring the flavor of food I knew I wouldn't sample again for a very long time.

"It's good to see you've got your appetite back," Reese teased.

I didn't have to reach under the table to kick my older brother on the leg. Mom gave him a withering look, and he piped down immediately.

"I don't blame her," Ed said, coming to my rescue. "With food this good, it's a crime to let any of it go to waste."

Swallowing what was in my mouth, I gave Ed a warm smile. He nodded, then refocused on the captain's platter he had ordered.

I think we all felt stuffed when we walked out of the restaurant, but from the contented looks on everyone's faces, it was a good feeling. Even Joey seemed to be in good humor—he didn't complain when Mom fastened him into his stroller. Unlike the rest of us, Joey didn't partake of seafood delights, but Mom had fed him pieces of garlic bread that he had noisily sucked on, a sign that he had loved the taste.

For a while, Ed and I followed along behind my family as they wandered in and out of several shops and a couple of small art galleries. From time to time, I got the impression that Ed wanted to hold my hand. Dad always managed to be looking our way whenever that seemed to be a possibility, so it didn't happen. Just as I was starting to lose hope that Ed and I would have a moment alone, Joey started to fuss. This proved to be a good thing. Walking off with the stroller, Mom said she would find somewhere to feed him. Dad and Reese wanted to explore the Harley Davidson boutique, something I didn't really care to see. So Ed offered to take me around to a couple of shops I had pointed out a while back—Carousel Music Box Company and

A Few of My Favorite Things, two stores I knew Dad and Reese would hate. Our ploy worked. Dad grunted his assent, and after arranging to meet us near the Ben and Jerry's Ice Cream Parlor in an hour, he and Reese disappeared into the crowd. The minute they were out of sight, Ed reached for my hand. I felt a slight tingle at his touch, and I wished this night would never end.

We walked along the lighted path, oblivious to the tourists that surrounded us. On our way to find the Carousel Music Box Company, we stumbled onto Teddy Bear Stuffers. Grinning, Ed led me inside.

"I want to buy one of these for you," he offered.

"Ed, you don't have to do that," I said, hoping he would insist. He did, pointing out that my dad had refused to let him pay for his own dinner. This was his way of repaying Dad's generosity.

I glanced around at the possibilities, touched by Ed's offer. A sign on the wall caught my attention. *White Bears Say Love.* That settled it. I wanted a white bear, and I picked one that was smaller and less expensive. I was thrilled that Ed wanted to buy me something to remember him by, but I didn't want to go overboard on the price.

I picked out a red-felt heart pillow to be stuffed inside of my bear. If I had been braver, I would've asked to have Ed's name affixed to the heart, but I think Ed picked up on how I felt anyway from the silly grin on his face. Maybe that's how all guys look when they're inside a shop dedicated to the manufacturing of teddy bears.

It didn't take long to finish my bear. The salesclerk set it inside a bag and handed it to me. Then, holding hands, Ed and I left the shop and walked around until we found a tiny store that sold seashells. Here I returned Ed's favor and bought him the shell of his choice, a souvenir of San Diego and a little memento of me. Like my bear, this shell was also a white color with a pink-colored interior. Pleased by his choice, I also bought a small collection of shells, items I could show my friends and proclaim I had spent hours finding on the beach.

When we left the Seaport Village Shell Company, we wandered around until we found the antique carousel a store-owner had told us about earlier. Ed paid the four dollars for both of us to ride, and we climbed aboard. I quickly found a beautiful horse that beckoned to me. Ed settled for the lion located beside my horse. A few minutes later, the carousel started up and we rode around the circle, holding onto our trea-sures as we watched the scenery pass by. My gaze kept wandering to Ed's profile; he looked so handsome holding onto that lion. I wished I had Dad's camera to permanently record the image. Instead, I had to rely on the image in my head, one I hoped would imprint itself forever.

The ride ended too quickly. When it was finished, Ed climbed off the lion, then helped me down from my horse. For a minute, I thought he was going to kiss me as we stood, facing each other in this romantic setting. I waited, antici-pating a life-changing event. I had been kissed before, but those experiences were a far cry from what I'd been led to believe about kissing. My first kiss took place last year, after a formal dance I had attended with Rory Spalding, a boy from my ward. I hadn't planned on kissing Rory—Mom has drilled into my head repeatedly the evils of kissing on the first date. Evidently Rory hadn't heard that lecture. He forced the issue after he took me home. Less than pleasant, it reminded me of being attacked by a mushy washrag. I never agreed to go out with him again.

My second kiss went a bit better. This time it was after a second date I'd had with a guy from school, Bryan Smith. Bryan was in my journalism class last year, and we got to be pretty good friends. When Bryan kissed me it was more like an affec-tionate token of his appreciation, nothing too spectacular. Bryan hadn't dated much until I agreed to go out with him. After our second date, he became an aggressive dater, taking out a ton of different girls. I like to think I inspired him.

Now, here it was, kiss number three, and by a guy I actually liked. That had to top the other times. But instead of a kiss, Ed reached for my hand and led me off the wooden floor of the carousel. Disappointed, I tried not to let it show and pointed out several other shops we could explore. We still hadn't popped inside the two I had originally wanted to see. Shaking his head, Ed led me down next to the shore where we could watch the twinkling lights reflect off the ocean.

As I stood, enchanted by the beautiful scenery, Ed caught me off guard. This is where he chose to kiss me for the first time. It was soft and sweet and over before it began. Then, gathering his courage, he kissed me like I had read about in books. Shivers raced up and down my spine, and I knew Ed was the only guy for me.

When he pulled back—a bit breathless, I might add—he ruined the moment by apologizing.

"Laurie, I'm sorry. I shouldn't have done that."

"Why not?" I breathed, my heart still racing.

"Because it's not fair to you," he said, frowning. He found a pebble on the sand, picked it up, and threw it into the water.

"You mean because you'll be leaving for Illinois this weekend?" I weakly ventured.

"No . . . I have a girlfriend back home."

Closing my eyes, I tried very hard not to scream. The kiss had been perfect. The ending was not.

"Sarah and I have been dating since last year," he continued. "She usually comes to San Diego with our youth group. We've always known each other, but we grew close while we worked together building homes. She couldn't come this year because she plays on our high school volleyball team and their volleyball camp was this week."

Still reeling from the news about Sarah, I wondered if Ed realized he was rambling.

"You'd like Sarah . . ."

No I wouldn't, I silently exclaimed.

"You kind of remind me of her," he added, making things worse.

"I see," I mumbled, heartsick. I glanced down at the bag that contained my bear and was tempted to hurl it out into the water.

"But you're also very different," he continued, making no sense at all. I waited silently for an explanation. "See, like Sarah, you have high standards. I admire that in a girl."

"Good," I said numbly. Wouldn't Mom be proud?

"But you also have answers to questions I don't even know how to ask."

Now I was confused. "What do you mean?"

"Your beliefs. Last night when you told me how hard it was to lose your little sister—well, it hit me pretty hard. I lost my grandpa last year, and that hurt bad enough. I can't imagine losing one of my little sisters."

In addition to the redheaded thirteen year old who had developed a huge crush on Reese, Ed had two younger sisters at home. Ed was the only boy in his immediate family, aside from his dad who was a Baptist minister. That had come as a bit of a surprise. I wondered if Ed's father was the one who had planted negative thoughts about the Mormons in his son's head, but Ed quickly made it clear that his father had always taught tolerance of other people. In fact, it was Ed's father who had first organized their church's effort to build homes in Tijuana.

As my mind continued to bounce, it was difficult to focus on what Ed was saying. Forcing myself to pay attention, I tried to listen.

"Then you told me that you can handle losing your sister because you know you'll see her again," Ed continued, still staring out across the dark water. "I'd give anything to know that for myself."

I know, it was a perfect chance to share the gospel, and all I wanted to do is wring his neck. Why had he led me on if he already had a girlfriend?

"How do you know you'll see your sister again?" Ed asked, turning to look at me.

"Time out," I said, making a T with my hands. "You don't just jump from kissing me to telling me that you have a girlfriend and then end by asking about the plan of salvation."

"The plan of salvation?"

"No—one thing at a time. Right now, we're going to talk about that kiss."

"It shouldn't have happened. Sorry about that," he said, apologizing again.

"Ed, you can't stand there and tell me that you felt nothing."

He shoved his hands inside his pockets and stared down at the sand. "I could tell you that, but I'd be lying."

In the space of ten seconds, I felt my heart plummet and then soar. He had felt something too. I wanted to do one of those touchdown dances you always see on TV.

"But I'd also be lying if I said that I don't care about Sarah— and right now I feel like I've betrayed her."

It was back to plummet again.

"Dang it, Laurie . . . I didn't mean for this to happen. But since I've met you, I can't stop thinking about you."

Now I was soaring. So much for Sarah.

"You're one of the most fascinating girls I've ever met," Ed continued. "And yet, Sarah and I have a lot of history together."

I was beginning to think I hated Sarah.

"We grew up together . . . she's a Baptist like me."

I did hate Sarah. "But I can explain the things you're wondering about, like life after death," I sputtered, hating this ping-pong game we were playing with my heart.

"Maybe that's why we became friends," he said, gazing intently at me. "There are times when you tell me what you believe and I feel something here." He pointed to his chest. "I want to know more."

Was it true? Were we only meant to be friends because I was supposed to teach him about the gospel? Drowning in a sea of self-pity, I wasn't sure I was up to the task.

"There you two are," Reese said, startling both of us.

"What time is it?" Ed asked, trying to see his watch.

"About 8:45," Reese replied. "Everything all right?"

"Fine," I stammered, willing myself not to cry. This was the most wonderful and horrible night of my life.

"Good," Reese said, gesturing for us to follow him. "Everyone's ready for ice cream and this place closes down at 9:00."

"Serious?" Ed asked as he helped me back up onto the paved walkway. As soon as I was back on the path, he released my hand, a sign that he had cooled things between us.

Fighting tears, I followed Reese and Ed back to where the rest of my family was waiting near the Ben and Jerry's. I took several deep breaths and plastered a smile on my face, determined to get through the rest of the evening with my pride intact. Keeping a safe distance from Ed, I quietly ate my ice cream cone and wished the night were over.

Chapter 10

I cried myself to sleep that night, something Ed would never know about. I vowed that no one ever would. That's why I waited until I could hear Reese softly snore across the room before I gave in to the tears I had been fighting since my romantic debacle. Agonizing over everything that had been said, reliving everything that had taken place, I quietly sobbed into my pillow. How could I have let myself fall so hard for Ed? And why had he egged me on when he knew there was someone else involved? Then there was the whole gospel aspect. Was it fair of Heavenly Father to expect me to treat Ed like a brotherly friend when I felt something deeper for him? How could I possibly teach him about the gospel in this frame of mind?

Did You have to make me fall in love with him? I silently asked, turning to gaze heavenward. Then it hit me—I was the one who had fallen for Ed—no one had forced me into it. *But did You have to make him so cute? So wonderful? So . . . Ed?*

I'm not sure how late it was when I finally fell asleep. All I know is that morning came much too early. Reese threw a pillow at me, trying to rouse me. I used it to cover my pounding head. He finally gave up and turned me over to Mom.

I felt her sit down on the bed next to me, but I refused to open my eyes to look at her. I still had my head wedged between two pillows, hoping it would quit throbbing.

"Is it that bad?" she asked.

I nodded, still keeping my eyes closed. I was afraid that if I opened them, she would see how puffy they were from crying most of the night.

I felt Mom rise from the bed and heard her walk through the adjoining doorway into the room she shared with Dad and Joey. Voices murmured. I could hear bits and pieces of the conversation. Then I heard my family leave, locking the door behind them.

I felt relief, then alarm. My family had left me . . . alone? It took a lot of effort, but I lifted the top pillow from my head and forced myself to sit up.

"You look pretty rough this morning," Mom observed, startling me.

"I thought you had all left," I mumbled.

"Just the boys," she replied, sitting on the bed. "I sent them out to get some breakfast."

"Why didn't you go with them?"

"Because I figured someone else needed me more," she answered.

That's all it took. Hoover Dam burst all over again. Only this time, there was a floodgate that offered comforting control as Mom drew me into a much-needed hug.

* * *

"Feel better?"

I turned from the mirror to smile at my mother. "Yeah," I replied, rubbing a dab of lip gloss over my lips. I was now showered, dressed, and ready to go on a tour of Tijuana, the final adventure of our vacation. "Thanks . . . for this morning," I said, feeling a little awkward. I had sobbed like a baby in Mom's arms. And for once, she hadn't lectured, which is probably why I told her everything. Her advice had been short, sweet, and to the point. She recommended that I follow Ed's lead to cool things between us. She also suggested that, if it wasn't too painful, I get Ed's e-mail address and stay in touch as friends. If he was still interested in learning about the Church, she advised me to tell him how to contact the missionaries currently serving in his area. It was good counsel, and it sounded like a mature way to handle things, unlike my original plan, which was to purchase some overripe tomatoes and throw them at Ed when he returned to the hotel later today.

Rising from the chair she had been sitting in, Mom returned my smile. "That's what I'm here for," she said, standing next to me to glance at her hair in the mirror.

"Have you enjoyed any of this trip?" I asked. It seemed like she had spent most of the vacation taking care of Joey, Dad, Reese, and me.

"It's been wonderful," she said, turning to lean against the bathroom counter. "I'm glad we came. How about you?"

"Yeah." Even though my heart had been twisted into a pretzel, I had seen some pretty neat things in San Diego. I had also learned a lot. Like Mom had mentioned earlier, life is one continuous adventure. We can't always control what happens to us, but we can control how we react. It's part of the test. After surviving last night and this morning, I felt certain I could survive just about anything.

"We're baaaack," Reese called out as our manly crew returned to the hotel rooms. "Are you two lovely ladies ready to explore Mexico?"

I smiled at Mom. Thanks to her, I was.

"Did you bring us back breakfast croissants?" Mom asked.

"They're right here," Dad said, entering the room I shared with Reese. He held out a white paper bag that had a familiar logo on the front. "Anyone hungry?"

Mom always thought of everything. Nodding, I waited until Mom had chosen her croissant before I pulled mine out of the bag. Grinning, I noted that they had even brought us orange juice to drink. This day was definitely looking up.

* * *

For me, Tijuana was a blur of colorful images and haunting faces. We began by driving to a pay parking lot near the border of Mexico. Dad had decided he didn't want to try to drive in a foreign country, claiming it made him nervous enough driving around the United States. So we bought bus passes and climbed aboard a bright red Mexicoach bus that would take us across the border.

Earlier Reese had asked if we needed to exchange our money for Mexican currency, but Dad had found out that they actually like American money better in Tijuana, so we brought cash with us, intent on finding souvenirs.

At first, things didn't seem very different. There were tall buildings on the horizon like you see in most cities. While Dad held Joey and pointed out the bus window, Mom kept her nose buried inside a guidebook, scoping out the best places to see while we were exploring Tijuana. As I looked out my window, I could see that there were a lot of rundown buildings decorated with tons of graffiti, and things didn't seem as tidy as they were in San Diego.

It didn't take long (Tijuana is only about twenty miles away from downtown San Diego) to reach the tourist terminal, located in the middle of downtown Tijuana. We hurried off the bus and were immediately assaulted by the sights, sounds, and smells of Tijuana. A peddler selling T-shirts that sported sombrero-wearing frogs caught Mom right off the bat. He kept telling her, "See, pretty shirt. Good for 'Merican woman. Nice price. Only fifteen dollar."

Dad tried to get Mom's attention, but I could see that her heart went out to this man. I sided with her. I'm sure the guy was only trying to make a living for his family. I was proud of Mom when she gave the man a twenty-dollar bill and told him to keep the change. Elated, the guy disappeared, and Dad informed Mom that she could have talked him down to about five bucks.

"Janell, you don't just hand them money without trying to bargain for the goods. That's part of the trade system down here," Dad insisted. "They start high anticipating you'll bid under that."

Mom glanced over at me and winked. "We'll call it my good deed for the day," she retorted. "Now, let's find a booth that sells vanilla. I've heard you can buy real vanilla for dirt cheap down here," she said excitedly. "I've promised to bring back a few bottles for some of my friends back home."

"No, first, let's go inside the terminal and find a restroom," Dad countered.

Reese and I shared a grin. We had warned Dad not to drink the twenty-ounce bottle of pop on the way down here. No one has to make more potty runs than my father. It's become a family joke. But it was decided we would all be better off to use the restroom in the terminal before wandering down the famed Avenida Revolución, so we followed Dad inside. It was a surprise to learn that we had to pay for this pleasure, about a quarter per person. Not a huge amount, but different than what we're used to.

We rendezvoused a few minutes later near the doors of the terminal. There were several stores located inside the terminal, but Mom was antsy to head down the street, certain there were treasures to be found among the shops that lined Avenida Revolución. She figured we could always come back and look things over in the terminal before we boarded the bus to head back to San Diego. Eager to begin our shopping adventure, I agreed with Mom, and we all followed her out of the terminal.

As I walked out into the bright sunlight, I pulled my sunglasses out of my small purse. Slipping them on to cut the glare, I was startled by everything there was to see. I glanced down one direction and saw pottery displays, woven rugs, baskets of every shape and size, and figurines. Down the other side were competing fruit stands and booths offering blankets, clothing, hats, peppers, and spices. Across the street was a taco stand that beckoned. Mom quickly strapped Joey inside his stroller and off we went to explore.

While Mom and I looked at the silver necklaces inside one small shop, Dad and Reese went into another and came out with a hand-carved onyx chess set, something I'm sure Dad had picked out. He loves chess, and when he has the time, he's always challenging one of us to a game.

Mom and I decided to pass on the necklaces, but we both fell in love with the brightly striped serapes the next booth offered. We closely examined the long shawls as the proud shopkeeper used his broken English to point out the finer features of his wares. I selected a multi-striped serape in shades of purple, blue, black, and white. It would look good in my bedroom. Mom liked the one woven from shades of red, pink, and white. Joey tried to reach up and pull a stack of serapes off the table, but Reese caught him just in time and entertained our younger brother with a pen while Mom and I made our purchases.

Mom did better at bargaining this time around. I'm sure Dad was proud of her, but I couldn't help feeling guilty as I remembered everything Ed had told me about how poor some of these people were. Ed. Even the thought of his name triggered a sharp inner pain. Pushing his face from my mind, I focused on the sights of downtown Tijuana.

* * *

When it was close to one o'clock, we decided it was time for lunch. We had been warned by the hotel clerk to be selective about food and drinks while in Tijuana. He had recommended a restaurant in Zona Río on Avenida Paseo de los Héroes, the street where the Centro Cultural Tijuana complex, also know as the CECUT, is located.

The CECUT is a huge government-built complex that was easy to spot because part of it looks like a giant, sand-colored golf ball. It's supposed to represent the Earth emerging from a broken shell. Inside the sphere is an Omnimax theater, something Dad and Reese were looking forward to. There is also a museum in another section, art exhibits, a restaurant, a bookstore, and a shopping arcade that features Mexican arts and crafts. We figured it would probably take most of the afternoon to see everything available in the CECUT complex and decided that was where we would head after lunch.

Because we didn't know our way around very well, Dad paid for a taxi to drive us to La Cantina de Remedios, the restaurant recommended by the hotel clerk. Dad had served a Spanish-speaking mission, and his knowledge of the language was a plus when it came to dealing with the driver. They finally settled on a fee they could both live with, and we were on our way to lunch.

It turned out to be a great restaurant. Multileveled, it resembled a Mexican village, complete with balconies, street lamps, and the bright decor of central Mexico. I was impressed by the atmosphere and the food, which was wonderful. I ordered a chicken fajita and, aside from being a bit spicy for my taste, it was easily the best Mexican food I had ever tried.

Dad was reaching for the Tums in Mom's purse when we left about an hour later, but we all agreed it was worth coming to see. When we left the restaurant, Mom found a secluded spot to feed Joey, while the rest of us wandered around and tried to work off a few calories. Someone at the hotel pool had told Mom that the best shopping booths in Tijuana were located near the river in Zona Río. I'd have to agree with that. Not only was the area less crowded than Avenida Revolución, but it appeared to be somewhat more upscale.

I wished I had waited to buy souvenirs when I spotted a beautiful silver necklace at one booth. It was a braided silver strand intertwined with tiny bits of mother-of-pearl from an abalone shell. I fell in love with it instantly. The price was marked quite high compared to the silver jewelry I had seen earlier, but I decided the necklace was easily worth the price. I pulled out my wallet, but I already knew I wouldn't have enough. Not only had I spent quite a bit on the serape and a hand-woven basket I was using to tote things around, but I had given a good share of my money to the street urchins who were everywhere, selling tiny trinkets and gum and begging for money. I didn't have the heart to turn any of those kids away. Sighing, I stuck the wallet inside my purse and shook my head at the older woman who was running the booth. She tried to interest me in some of the cheaper jewelry, but I wasn't interested, and I finally smiled and walked away.

Mom returned a short time later with Joey, who was now taking a siesta in the stroller. We walked down to the CECUT and split up for the first time that day. Dad and Reese went into the spherical Space Theater to watch an omnimax flick, while Mom and I went into the center's Museum of Mexican Identities. This museum was filled with displays that represented the various Mexican ethnic groups. I found myself wondering if we were gazing at items similar to those used long ago by Lamanite or Nephite tribes who may have passed through the area.

Joey was still asleep when we left the museum, and we had about twenty minutes before we were supposed to meet Dad and Reese out front. So Mom and I decided to browse through the craft items that were in the shopping arcade. Mom found a painting of the Mexican desert that she really liked, but she was lacking in the funds department too. I figured I owed her one for this morning, so I gave her what was left in my wallet, and combined with what she had, it was enough to buy the small painting. She didn't want to take my money at first, but I told her how great that painting would look downstairs in our family room, and she reluctantly agreed, promising to pay me back when we returned home. I told her to not worry about it, that it would be my gift to her for being the family glue. Laughing over that comment, she asked me to watch Joey while she paid for the painting.

Dad and Reese were already out front waiting when we walked out of the center. They were excitedly discussing the movie they had seen, a documentary that touched on the history of Mexico. Like me, Reese had drawn quite a few comparisons between the Book of Mormon and some of the history that had been portrayed. As we talked, it made me curious about some of the ruins in Mexico and South America, something to check out for myself after I finish college.

We took another cab back to the bus terminal, figuring it was too far to walk. Joey was awake and wanted to be held, another reason to take a cab. (That kid is built like a tank.) By then, we were exhausted anyway, not to mention loaded down with souvenirs. What wouldn't fit in Joey's stroller had been stuffed inside the woven baskets Mom and I had purchased earlier. We had wrapped the bottles of vanilla in our serapes, hoping the bottles wouldn't break. Dad's chess set had fit nicely in the stroller. My basket was filled with the tiny trinkets I had bought from the children earlier in the day, plus the spices Mom had found. Reese had bought a shirt that we had also stuffed inside my basket. The T-shirt Mom had bought earlier was wrapped around the chess set to keep it from getting scratched. Dad planned to hold it on his lap in the cab and on the bus.

I think we had all enjoyed a pretty good day, one full of memories we would cherish for a long time. At least, I cherished them until our bus driver took a detour back to the border. He drove us past what had to be one of the poorest parts of town, a place where people were living in cardboard boxes and pieces of tin, just like Ed had described. Half-dressed children chased each other around in the dirt, and suddenly I wanted to cry. I wasn't the only one. I glanced around and every member of the family but Joey had been affected by what we had seen. We rode in silence back to the border.

Getting back into the States was more difficult than leaving. We had to exit the bus and walk through the customs office to certify that we were indeed United States citizens, something I've always taken for granted. We had to dig out our wallets and show our driver's licenses as proof. We had been told that we could each bring back up to $400 worth of merchandise duty free, and we were well below that amount. Mom did have an interesting time convincing the Mexican official that the dark liquid in the bottles was vanilla and not alcohol. Later, Dad claimed this man had given her a bad time because she was a beautiful American woman, pointing out that the labels were clearly marked in Spanish. Regardless, Mom was pretty flustered when we reentered the bus for the five-minute journey to the parking lot where we had left the rented minivan.

* * *

Dad had made reservations for dinner that night at a place in downtown San Diego. It was simply called Croce's. I had a difficult time pronouncing it, and to the best of my knowledge, I had no idea who the guy was who had inspired the restaurant. Somehow Reese knew all about Jim Croce, and he began singing snippets of songs he thought I would know. He was wrong until he began singing about bad, bad Leroy Brown. Then it clicked. Jim Croce is that singer Dad makes us listen to whenever we take long family trips in the car. I don't hate his music, but given the choice between Jim Croce and Josh Groban, I'd take Josh any day. Not only is the guy gorgeous, but he has a remarkable voice.

Back to Jim. Even though his music isn't my favorite, I had to admit his restaurant was impressive. The floor was made up of black and white tiles, the tables were covered by white table-cloths, and the chairs were black, making a nice contrast. The walls were covered with pictures of Jim and other assorted music memorabilia, including a couple of his gold records. I guess the guy wasn't all bad if he had earned some of those.

After we were seated and the menus had been passed around, we opened them and discovered things were quite pricey. Dad looked a little green at first, then forced a laugh and commented that it was only money. My dad actually said that? He then added that since this was our last splurge before Reese left on his mission, we should order whatever we wanted.

I glanced at the entrées again and noted that the cheapest item was linguine arrabiata with manila clams for $18.95. Everything else ranged from about $25 to $33. When the wait-ress came to take our order, we all waited for Dad to go first, figuring we would try to stay within the range he set.

Clearing his throat, he glanced at the menu and said, "I'll have the charbroiled filet mignon with passion fruit demi, Yukon mashed potatoes, and the seasoned vegetables."

The rest of us glanced at our menus and saw that he had ordered the most expensive thing on it. Mom grinned and ordered the wild salmon tournado with herb-crusted eggplant medallions, grilled asparagus, and seasoned vegetables, a mere $27.95. Reese ordered next, as I was still deciding. He settled on an entrée that to me was unpronounceable—orecchiette and broccoli rabe with roasted chicken, fresh tomatoes, broccoli, forest mushrooms, and caramelized garlic and basil. It was the same price as the linguine with clams, which is what I ordered. Joey had the cheapest thing by far, a couple of packages of soda crackers Mom had asked the waitress to bring for him to nibble on.

The food was excellent, but I kept thinking about the card-board shanties and half-starved children I had seen that day in

Tijuana. I guess it kind of ruined dinner for me. How could I ever eat another meal and not think about those who didn't know where their next one was coming from? Still, this was our final family hurrah before Reese left, so I tried to cheer up and joined in the conversation as we discussed our adventures that day.

Chapter 11

The next morning, Mom and Dad drove to the San Diego temple to hit a session before we flew back to Salt Lake that afternoon. Reese and I had volunteered to watch Joey while they were gone. We decided the easiest way to do that was to take him out to the pool to splash in the water. Joey loves that, so I dressed him in his swimming diaper and swimsuit, and I could've sworn the little guy clapped his hands together in excitement.

Reese had changed into his swimsuit while I was dressing Joey, then he entertained the kid while I changed. Joey seems to think Reese is his own personal clown, and he refused to come to me when I was ready to go. So Reese carried him down, and out we went to the pool.

Since it was morning, there weren't as many people using the pool, which was nice. Reese sat down and bounced Joey on his knee while I peeled out of my T-shirt and shorts. I used my towel to cover them up on a nearby table, then I took a protesting Joey while Reese pulled off his T-shirt. Earlier, we had both used generous amounts of waterproof sun block, and I had also rubbed it all over Joey to prevent him from getting sunburned, a sign of a good babysitter.

I told Reese to swim around while I played with Joey in the shallow end of the pool. We'd switch off in about thirty minutes—that way we could both enjoy a final swim. I sat down on the bottom of the pool and held Joey up so he could splash in the water to his heart's content.

"Think he'd like to play with this?"

Startled, I jumped, adding to Joey's entertainment. I glanced over my shoulder to see Ed. I hadn't seen him since Seaport Village. Yesterday, he had already departed for Tijuana by the time we headed out. Then we had stayed out later last night to have dinner. Plus, I had purposely avoided the pool when we returned to the hotel.

Ed slipped into the water beside me and tapped a medium-sized beach ball toward Joey. Joey gurgled his pleasure and batted at it, pushing it away. Thus a new game was born, and for about five minutes, Ed and Joey played bat the ball while I did my best to hold Joey in place and control my emotions.

"I was afraid your family had headed home," Ed finally said, handing Joey a neon green diving ring he had found on the bottom of the pool. He knelt in the water in front of me, trying to get me to look at him.

"We're flying out this afternoon," I replied as Joey banged the plastic ring into the water, splashing all three of us.

"Same here," Ed said, wiping the water from his face. "I was hoping to talk to you last night."

"We've been kind of busy."

"Are you avoiding me?"

I shrugged.

"I wouldn't blame you if you were. I was a real jerk."

He said it. Silently, I watched as Joey continued to bang the ring in the water.

"Why don't you two go for a swim and let me take Joey," Reese offered, suddenly surfacing by my side.

Not sure if this was a good idea, I handed Joey to Reese and followed Ed to the deep end. We swam to the far side, then pulled up out of the water to hang on the side of the pool.

"That felt good," Ed said, running a hand over his wet hair.

"Yeah," I said, wiping the water from my eyes.

There was an awkward silence, then Ed said, "So, tell me something. Do you hate me?"

I paused just long enough to give that indication, then shook my head. "No, I don't hate you. But it kind of hurts. Why didn't you tell me that you had a girlfriend?"

"I don't know," he admitted. "The thing is, we do date other people once in a while—mostly to keep our parents happy. They don't think it's a good idea to date the same person all the time."

"Same with my parents," I replied, realizing again that we had a lot of common ground.

"Do you think we could still be friends?" Ed asked, looking hopeful.

How could I say no to this guy? Despite everything, I really liked him, and having him as a friend was better than nothing. Besides, like Mom had said, maybe he would decide to check into the Church because of me. "Sure," I said, smiling. "Could I get your e-mail address before we leave? I'd like to keep in touch . . . if that's okay."

"It's better than okay," Ed said, grinning. "I was afraid you'd never want to speak to me again."

"Not true. It might've been yesterday, but not today."

"What changed?"

I thought about his question for several seconds and realized it was me. This may come as a surprise, but I have been kind of petty in the past, holding grudges over silly things, sometimes jumping to conclusions that weren't the best. But like my Laurel leader had taught in a lesson not long ago, we can grow from our experiences. It's up to us to decide who we're going to be, and right now, I was determined to be a much better person than I'd been. I would begin by forgiving Ed.

"Laurie?" Ed prompted.

"Sorry, I was thinking about your question."

"Which one?"

"You asked what changed. I think it's me. I've done some soul searching the past couple of days—"

"Thanks to me," he interjected, his eyes dark with regret.

"Maybe in part. But it hasn't been all bad. I've learned a lot from you—you've inspired me to look beyond myself to other people."

"Really?"

"Yeah," I replied, smiling. "And now it's my turn to apologize. Sometimes I go overboard on things. I shouldn't have gotten that upset the other night. Can you forgive me for how I acted?"

Ed gazed at me in total surprise. Then he grinned. "Why don't we just start over?"

"Good idea," I agreed.

"Hi, my name is Ed."

"I'm Laurie," I said, laughing.

"I'll bet I can beat you to the other side of the pool."

"You're on," I said, using Reese's trick to jump in the lead. When I thought about it later on the plane, I realized Ed had probably let me win—that guy could swim circles around me. It warmed my heart that he had let me win anyway.

* * *

Whoever said there's no place like home knew what he was talking about. Although we had had a lot of fun in San Diego, it was great to return to our own house late Saturday afternoon. We were so tired, it was all we could do to unload our car. Then we sat around and stared at each other until Mom suggested that we kick back and relax for an hour or two before trying to unpack. I liked that idea, so I retreated to my bedroom and lay down on my bed to take a nap. But before I fell asleep, I offered a quick prayer of gratitude for everything I've been blessed with. To some people, this bedroom would be a palace, something I would never take for granted again.

* * *

The next day during Sunday School, Roz pumped me for details of our trip. I gave her a few brief highlights as our teacher glared. Finally, I promised to give my best friend a full report that afternoon after church, and I focused on the lesson. We were studying the Book of Mormon this year, and I listened attentively, my interest rekindled after seeing a tiny portion of Mexico for myself.

Later, after we had both eaten dinner, Roz drove over to hear about the trip. I had bought her a gorgeous, tan-colored seashell with a pink interior, which she seemed to love. I also had a ton of postcards and all of the digital shots Dad had already downloaded on the computer to show her. As we sat at the computer and scrolled through the digital pictures, Roz gripped my shoulder and pointed to a shot I hadn't realized Dad had taken. It was one of me with Ed as we had reclined against the pool wall one night.

"Who is that?" Roz demanded.

"A guy I met," I said quietly. I hadn't brought up anything about Ed yet, keeping his memory to myself.

"Uh-huh," Roz replied, the look on her face implying that I was keeping something from her. "I want to know everything."

Rising, I closed the door to the computer room, sat back down beside Roz, and told her what had taken place between Ed and me.

"Wow," she said when I had finished.

"Yeah," I agreed, glancing at the picture on the computer screen. It was time to move on. I moved the mouse and closed the picture, bringing up one Dad had taken at the zoo. "Here's a cool shot," I said, pointing to the baby panda bear.

"Wait, I still have a dozen questions about Ed. I haven't decided which one to ask first."

"You can ask. That doesn't mean I'll tell you."

"Oh, you'll tell me," Roz exclaimed. "First—why didn't you kiss him again and make him forget about his silly girlfriend back home?"

I forced a smile at my friend. "I could tell he felt bad enough about things. I didn't want to make it worse. And we parted as friends."

"That's not very romantic," Roz complained.

"Maybe not, but it was the best way to end things."

"What do you mean end things? Didn't you say you'll be keeping in touch with him through e-mail?"

I nodded, not admitting Ed had already sent me an e-mail. It had shown up in my inbox earlier that morning. He had kept it simple, mostly questions about our trip home and comments about what was going on in Quincy. I had yet to reply, something I would do later when no one was looking over my shoulder.

Before Roz could ask any more questions, someone knocked softly at the study door.

"Come in," I said, grateful for the reprieve. Roz could be persistent when she wanted answers.

Mom poked her head inside. "Your dad has the tape ready to go if you two want to come downstairs and watch what he filmed in San Diego." Her gaze wandered to the computer screen, and I was glad I had changed the picture to the baby panda bear. I'm sure Mom would've had a few questions herself if she had seen us looking at the shot of Ed and me. Closing the program, Roz and I followed Mom out of the room and downstairs to the family room where a home movie and popcorn awaited.

* * *

That night, while Mom was putting Joey to bed and Dad and Reese were busy talking about who-knows-what down in the family room, I slipped back into Dad's study and sat down in front of the computer. I pulled up my settings and connected to the internet, eager to send an e-mail to Ed.

I reread what he had sent earlier that morning, then began to type a reply.

Hi Ed,

It was cool to hear from you. I'm glad you made it home okay. Again, I think it's neat that your youth group helped build four houses this past week down in Tijuana. I'm sure those people will always be grateful for what you have done for them.

I can't remember—did I tell you what our church does for the humanitarian effort? Mormons all over the world work together to build hygiene kits, first-aid kits, newborn kits, and school kits. Plus, they make quilts, blankets, hats, and donate all kinds of clothing. Some people even donate money, using tithing slips. That's something I did earlier today . . .

Chapter 12

On one of our last nights of freedom before the summer ended, Roz invited me over to her house to hang out and watch a movie. I didn't have anything else planned, so I headed over after I loaded the dishwasher. I pulled up in the driveway and noticed that both of the cars belonging to Roz's parents were gone. The Whitings are busy people, always on the go. Roz's dad is a bank manager in Salt Lake and he puts in long hours. He's the type of dad who always makes sure his family has the best of everything. I also admire Roz's mother, Regina. A successful lawyer, she's a beautiful lady and a power to be reckoned with. Roz and I hope to be like her one day. But there were times when I felt bad for my best friend. Regina was so busy, she didn't have much time to spend with Roz or Tyrone, Roz's younger brother. Tyrone is in junior high, and he's not around much either, usually hanging out at a friend's house.

I knew Roz hated being by herself, so I was glad I had been able to come over.

As I climbed out of my car, I gazed at the Whiting home. Our brick home is nice—not overly fancy, but comfortable. Compared to the Whiting abode, it's a shack. I've never asked Roz how much her parents paid for their house, but I'm sure it's more money than I could envision. I tried not to think about how many people in the world were living in poverty as I reached to ring the doorbell.

"You made it," Roz sang out, inviting me inside.

I stepped into the entryway and, as always, gazed around in wonder at my best friend's house. Everywhere you look, it speaks of luxury, from the furniture to the paintings on the walls. It is beautiful, but I'm always afraid I'll end up breaking something.

Roz led me into what her family calls the TV room. A big-screen TV fills an entire wall. It's hooked to a surround-sound system that could blow your eardrums without even trying. A comfortable leather couch sits in front of the huge television, and this is where Roz and I chose to relax. It's a recliner couch, so we could both put our feet up and watch the movie.

My friend had been busy. She had already fixed a large bowl of microwave popcorn and had selected pop for both of us to drink.

"What are we watching tonight?" I asked.

"I thought we'd see what's on pay-per-view," Roz replied, expertly using a remote to locate the proper screen. "Okay, it's what—7:30? Let's see what pulls up."

Together we looked the list over. I noticed that most of the movies were either rated R or PG-13. "Hey, there's one that's PG," I said, pointing to the screen.

"Get real," Roz responded. "I'm not watching a Disney flick. We're too old for that."

"But I watched it in San Diego, and it's funny. I wouldn't mind seeing it again."

"Not interested," Roz replied, pulling up the information on one that appealed to her. "This sounds good."

I read through the information and shook my head. "Roz, it says right there that this movie is full of sexual content."

"They all are. You just block that stuff out."

"No, you don't watch it," I countered, sounding uncomfortably like my mom. Pondering that thought, I missed the selection Roz made. "Which one did you pick?" I asked as the opening scene began.

"Shh," Roz replied, "it's starting." She watched in fascination as a young couple began to undress each other.

"Roz," I exclaimed, glancing away from the screen. With a TV that size, it's not easy to do.

"Give it a minute. I watched this one the other night. It gets better. See, it switched to a different scene."

I glanced at Roz. "Are there any more like that first one?"

"Maybe one or two. It's no big deal, Laurie."

"You used to think it was," I returned. "What gives?"

Roz gave me an irritated look. "There are a lot of good movies that we haven't seen because of the rating. Maybe I'm getting tired of it."

"They have those ratings for a reason," I said, again sounding too much like my mother.

"Laurie, we've reached an age where we have to start thinking for ourselves. It's not right that we allow others to dictate everything we do or see or say. That's for little kids, not us."

"Uh-huh," I said, not liking what I was hearing.

"We start school next week, right?" Roz continued. "It's our senior year, and I'm tired of never getting invited to parties or dances. That's going to change. This is going to be our year. We're going to snap out of sappy mode and have some fun."

Unsure of what to say, I remained silent. I thought Roz and I had always had fun. True, we weren't exactly the most popular girls in school, but we weren't social outcasts either.

"Do you realize that in one year we'll be on our own, away at college? We'll be making our own choices. Our parents won't be looking over our shoulders telling us what to do and how to do it. We get to decide that for ourselves. We might as well start now."

"BYU-Idaho still has standards we have to maintain," I said.

"Which is why I'm not going there. I've heard it's nothing more than a glorified high school. I want no part of it."

I gaped at my friend. "But . . . we've been planning for years to go to Rexburg—"

"No, you've been planning that for years. I've decided I'm going somewhere else. If you want to come along with me, great. But if you head off to Rexburg, you'll be going alone."

Stunned by this revelation, I sipped at my pop. Another one of those torrid love scenes popped up in front of us, and I looked down at the floor. If this was what Roz considered freedom, maybe we weren't cut out to be college roommates.

Regina showed up about halfway through the movie, and I noticed Roz quickly shut off the TV when her mother walked into the house.

"Why did you shut it off?" I asked, curious about her answer.

"I still live here. I have to heed the house rules," Roz hissed.

"I see, only when your parents are home."

Roz gave me a threatening look as her mother walked into the TV room.

"What are you girls doing tonight?" Regina asked, slipping out of her dress shoes.

"We're trying to find a good movie to watch," I replied.

Regina rubbed at her feet. "That sounds good. Do you mind if I watch it with you? I could use some unwinding after this day."

"Sure, Mama," Roz said, still giving me the evil eye.

Regina took off the beige, tailored suit coat that matched her skirt, pulled the blouse out over the skirt, and stretched. "That's better. Now, did you rent videos or are we watching pay-per-view?"

"We could see what's on pay-per-view," I said, reaching for the remote. Roz beat me to it. Somehow she flipped on the TV and switched it to the movie selection screen before her mother saw what was already playing. My ploy didn't work.

"There's nothing good on, is there?" Regina commented as she sat down on the other side of Roz. "Let me see that control, baby." Roz handed her mother the control. We both watched in silence as Regina scrolled down through the list. "I've heard that Disney movie is pretty cute," she finally said, highlighting it.

It was all I could do to keep a straight face as Regina selected the movie I had picked out earlier that night. When her mother wasn't looking, Roz pinched me a good one in the side. I yelped and then had to come up with a story about having spontaneous muscle spasms as Regina gave me a look of disbelief. Then it was Roz's turn to hide her smile.

Regina and I enjoyed the movie. I'm not sure if Roz liked any of it. She made up a couple of excuses to leave the room but eventually came back each time and sat between her mother and me to stare at the screen. When it ended, Regina decided it was time for ice-cream sundaes, and we walked into the huge kitchen where we helped Roz's mother prepare our dessert. About the time we had dished up three big bowls of icy temptation, Roz's dad sauntered into the house. He gave Regina a big kiss and Roz a quick peck on the cheek.

"How are my girls tonight?" he asked.

"Tired," Regina replied.

"But not too tired to dish me up a huge bowl of ice cream, I see," Steve Whiting teased as he took Regina's bowl.

I watched as Roz's parents chased each other around the kitchen. In some respects, they were a lot like my own parents. They loved their kids and each other, as I could plainly see. Active members of the Church, the Whitings seemed to have it all. Maybe. As I stuffed another bite of ice cream in my mouth, I glanced at Roz. We had both changed this summer.

Chapter 13

School started much too soon. Between the homework from my honors classes and working two nights a week after school plus most Saturdays, I was swamped. To top it off, I was asked by my journalism teacher to write the editorials for our high school newspaper. I was flattered that he would entrust me with this responsibility, knowing there were other seniors in that same class who would've done a great job with it. It would be a lot of extra work on my part, but I felt certain it was a stepping-stone on my way to becoming a professional reporter.

After I told him I would tackle his request, Mr. Geyer stressed that he wanted me to touch on timely issues, items that would catch the attention of most of the students. Suggesting that I select topics that would spark controversy, he confided that he hoped my column would increase an interest in our paper. I know, it was probably a pride thing, but I couldn't help but make one request. At first, Mr. Geyer didn't seem very pleased by the idea. Frowning, he mulled it over, his gray, bushy eyebrows expressing agitation. It's rumored that because he's bald, Mr. Geyer allows his eyebrows to grow out of control. The only thing I know for sure is that they often reveal his mood. After several long seconds of menacing twitching, both eyebrows relaxed in place, and I knew I had won. Shrugging, he gave me permission to use the same title I had given my musings at home, Laurie's View. Thrilled by his concession, I silently vowed to prove my worth to him, anxious to write columns the entire school would want to read.

I was given a week to write my first column. As it turned out, I only had to think about it for a short time before something came to mind. Avoiding religion in general, as Mr. Geyer had advised, I could still get away with a Mormon slant on some issues, like my first editorial. Drawing on what I had learned in Tijuana, I began my illustrious career with a fiery epistle on how spoiled we are as a society in comparison with those who are less fortunate.

LAURIE'S VIEW

The car of my choice. Stylish clothes. A variety of popular CDs by my favorite artists. Tickets to a concert. Perfect hair. Perfect complexion. Perfect life.

Let me share another wish list with you: Food. Clean water. A roof over my head. Clean clothes that aren't ragged. Shoes for my feet. A safe, warm place to live.

The first list could be composed by any student in our high school. The second would be the silent plea of thousands of people who struggle to survive each day. It is the wish list of those who have nothing, those who hope that someone, someday will make a difference in their lives.

"But this doesn't affect me," you may say to yourself. It isn't true. When one person suffers in this world, we all suffer. We all bear a responsibility to do what we can to make a difference, to cease being self-centered, to look beyond ourselves to those who need our help. And they're everywhere—not just in third-world countries, but also in our own backyards. How many of you can say that you have never seen a homeless person out walking the streets?

At this point you may be asking, "How can I make a difference?" In this editor's opinion, there are a lot of ways to help those who are less fortunate. Many churches offer humanitarian aid in some form. Find out how you can help with this effort. Donate time or money to worthy causes, like the Salvation Army or the United Way. Maybe you don't feel like your donations will help much. Trust me—a little bit can go a long way, especially if we all pitch in.

People often get sentimental about helping others during the Christmas season. Wouldn't it be great if we could feel that way all year? Maybe we could turn this troubled world around. It can start simply, but small acts of goodwill can have a lasting impact that can change lives forever. I challenge each one of you to contemplate how you can help. You will find that you will gain much more than what you ever give away. I believe Robert Browning said it best: "Live in all things outside yourself in love and you will have joy."

Mr. Geyer was surprised by my first editorial, but he ran it anyway, and sure enough, we sparked a controversy. It turned out that several students were insulted by the inference that they were self-centered. Figures. But at least we were making people think about helping others. It was a start. I realized that not everyone would capture the vision I had tried to share, but it made me feel good to know that I had found a way to use my talents for a noble cause. Eagerly I began making plans for my next editorial, realizing I had been entrusted with a rare opportunity and determined to make the most of it.

* * *

During the second week of school when Mom put a baby quilt on her quilting frames downstairs, I tried to help her with it whenever I could work it in. In the past, I'd avoided this sort of thing, so I didn't know what I was doing. But Mom patiently taught me how to tie the quilt, and once I got the hang of it, I was hooked. It was actually kind of fun. Not only was I learning a skill, but it gave Mom and me a chance to talk about important things, like who was going to get stuck cooking dinner that night. The best part was knowing that our efforts would help keep a baby warm somewhere in the world.

It didn't take us long to finish the first quilt, so Mom put another one on. We decided to see how many we could finish by November. Now that I was seeing my mother through a more mature perspective, I was amazed by all that woman could do in a day: take care of Joey, manage any crisis that came up in the ward, keep our home looking spiffy, not to mention all she was doing to get Reese ready for his mission. His departure date was highlighted in red marker on the calendar in the kitchen, a day that would soon be upon us.

Reese wanted to go through the temple early enough so he could attend sessions in as many different temples as possible before he entered the MTC, so he picked a date toward the end of September, and everyone made plans to attend. It would require another family feast, but Mom decided to keep it simple—we would have a picnic at a nearby park and call it good.

When the day arrived, Stacy and I were nominated to take care of Joey in the waiting room of the Ogden temple while the people who had been invited to go through Reese's endowment session went and did their thing. I kind of felt sorry for Stacy. I'm sure she wanted to go through with Reese, but Mom explained to me that it wasn't possible. Stacy couldn't receive her own endowment until a year after her baptism. So on the Saturday afternoon that Reese went through to receive his endowment, Stacy and I sat in the waiting room and entertained Joey for nearly two hours. It gave us a chance to visit, which turned out to be a good thing.

"What are your plans when you graduate?" Stacy asked as she played peek-a-boo with my baby brother.

"First, I'll try to find a better job for the summer," I replied, determined to leave Harold's Burgers by spring, "and then head up to Rexburg next fall." I frowned as I thought about how much fun Roz and I would have had. She was still stubbornly insisting that she was going somewhere else.

"That's right. Reese said you were going to attend BYU-Idaho. You and Roz."

"No, just me," I replied.

"Really?"

I nodded. "Roz thinks BYU-Idaho is a waste of time."

"Hmm. That surprises me. You two have always been so close."

"Things change," I murmured. I could tell by the look on her face that Stacy wanted to ask about what was going on with Roz. I was relieved when she let it go.

"But you're still planning to go to Rexburg?"

"If I get accepted. I've still got to send in my application."

"This early?" Stacy asked, looking surprised.

I nodded. "There are so many people who apply, not everybody gets in."

"Serious?"

"Yeah. That's why I want to have everything sent in before December."

"Wow, you do have to think ahead. I didn't even have a clue where I wanted to go when I graduated."

"You've done well, though," I pointed out. Stacy was a successful interior decorator. She had attended college for a couple of years to earn a specialized degree, and now she worked for a prestigious company that decorated several offices and fancy homes all over Salt Lake Valley.

"I'm lucky. I've been able to work into a career I enjoy."

"That's my plan too," I informed her.

"You still want to be a journalist?"

"Yeah," I replied, smiling. Since our San Diego trip, my focus had changed. Now I wanted to report on man's inhumanity to man, doing poignant stories that would alter how people treat each other, something I was already attempting through the high school newspaper. When I explained my new goals to Stacy, I think I impressed her.

"You'll be doing some good things," she complimented. "What made you change your mind about the kind of stories you want to write?"

I told her about meeting Ed and what his youth group had set out to do in Tijuana. Then I told her about the poverty I had seen and how it had affected me.

Stacy smiled warmly at me when I finished. "I can see you making a difference. I think it's important to try to change this world for the better."

I glanced at my brother's beautiful "special friend," as he called her. It dawned on me that we had something in common besides caring about Reese. "That's why you want to serve a mission, huh?"

Stacy nodded, handing Joey to me when he held out his little arms and began to fuss. I gave Joey a hug then dug inside the diaper bag to locate his pacifier. Settling down, he reclined in my arms, his eyes growing heavy. Hoping he would sleep for the next forty minutes, I sang him a soft lullaby. It worked. He fell asleep, killing my arm. Stacy came to my rescue. She picked up a nearby sofa pillow and wedged it underneath my arm, giving me added support.

"Thanks," I said quietly.

"You're welcome," Stacy replied. She sat down on a couch across from me, picked up a recent Church magazine, and began thumbing through it.

I watched her for a minute, then glanced down at my arm. Mom was right. Stacy was an awesome young woman, and if Reese had any sense at all, he would make her a permanent part of this family—after they both served their missions.

* * *

September flew by, and October arrived with gusto. One minute we were scrambling around to get Reese ready for his mission, and then it was time to leave him at the MTC—easily one of the most difficult experiences I'd been through.

After eating a quick bite at a nearby Olive Garden restaurant in Provo, Dad drove us into a crowded parking lot where other families were going through the same ordeal. We climbed out of our blue minivan, and while Mom tackled the chore of strapping Joey into his stroller, Dad and I each grabbed one of Reese's suitcases, leaving the biggest one for Reese to handle. I think Stacy felt left out until Mom handed her the diaper bag to carry.

As we walked toward the large brick complex that would be Reese's new home for the next couple of weeks, Dad spotted a place along the brick wall that said in bold lettering, *Missionary Training Center*. Naturally Dad insisted this was a Kodak moment, and he made us pose by the side of it. He asked a man who had just taken a similar picture with his own family to take the shot of all of us, including Stacy. Then Dad took a single shot of Reese.

Because we only had about fifteen minutes before Reese was to enter the famed MTC, we hurried to the front doors. There we were separated from my brother, and for a moment, I thought that was it. He went in one door, and we entered through another. As Reese stood in line in a roped-off area, my heart lurched into my throat. Couldn't we even give him a hug and say good-bye? Mom leaned over to let me know we would be reunited with Reese after he had checked in.

After Reese signed in, he asked Dad to come with him to stash his luggage. The rest of us walked down the hall to find the large room where most of the families were gathering. Mom pushed Joey's stroller into the room, and Stacy and I followed behind her. There were rows and rows of plastic chairs, some already filled with anxious family members. We found a row of empty seats as close to the front of the room as possible and sat down, saving a seat for Dad and one for Reese. About ten minutes later, they joined us. Dad sat on the other side of Mom and Reese sat down between Stacy and me. Mom had pulled Joey out of the stroller and was trying to keep him on her lap. A couple of his favorite toys from the diaper bag settled him down for a few minutes.

As we waited for the meeting to begin, Reese reached into his new black suit coat and pulled out two small packages. He handed one to Stacy and one to me. Surprised, I watched as Stacy unwrapped her gift. Inside was a silver necklace that had a tiny, heart-shaped mother-of-pearl pendant in the center. I stared at the slender package in my own hand. Certain I already knew what it was, I still couldn't believe it when I opened it and found the necklace I had fallen in love with in Tijuana, the silver one intertwined with bits of mother-of-pearl. I glanced over at Stacy and saw that she looked as stunned as I felt. She gave Reese a watery grin, and he reached to give her hand a squeeze. They must've communicated telepathically, because nothing was said out loud.

"Reese . . . How . . . Why . . . ?" I tried to ask.

"Shh, they're starting the meeting," my brother replied, giving me a wink. Leaning toward my ear he whispered, "I knew I had to buy it for you when I saw how much you liked it. Maybe it will remind you of me while I'm gone."

Tearing up, I gave him a quick hug, then focused on what was taking place at the front of the room. After an opening song and prayer, the president of the MTC spoke for a few minutes, followed by his wife. Then we watched a short video that tugged at my tender heart. When I saw the scene depicting the empty mailbox for a disappointed elder, I vowed that no matter how busy I was, I would faithfully write to Reese.

Despite the emotional upheaval, there was a special feeling in that room, especially when we were asked to stand to sing "Called to Serve." We cried happy tears, as Mom described it later to her mother. The Spirit was there, but so was a tremendous sense of loss. It's hard to explain unless you've been through it.

All too soon, it was over and time for Reese to walk through one door as we walked out another. Mom and Dad tearfully hugged the stuffings out of Reese. Then Reese reached for Joey and gave him a squeeze, something that made all of us cry; Joey would change so much while Reese was gone. It was my turn, and as Reese embraced me, I thanked him again for the beautiful necklace.

"You deserve it. It's my way of saying thanks for putting up with me," he said, doing his best to keep things light. Pulling back, he smiled at me. "Take good care of Mom and Dad while I'm gone. They're not as tough as they try to make us think."

I nodded and stepped out of the way as Stacy reached for a final hug. I noticed she was wearing the necklace he had given her. Following her example, I fastened mine around my neck and waved a final time before Reese disappeared from sight. Unlike us, he had a huge smile on his face like he could hardly wait to begin this new adventure.

"Well, I think we'd better go find some ice cream," Mom said, forcing a smile.

Agreeing, we walked quietly out of the room and made our way back to the car.

Chapter 14

We received our first letter from Reese about a week later. He sounded so excited about everything he was doing, we couldn't help but be happy for him. We still missed him, but we knew he was where he was supposed to be . . . finally. It was funny to see the change in him. In one week he had transformed from being a teasing older brother to a preacher of the good word. He listed several scriptures that he wanted us to read as a family during next week's family home evening. There was even a paragraph in his letter cautioning me to make wise decisions and to avoid anything that would prevent me from making it to the temple. I shook my head when Mom read that part of Reese's letter. As if there were any danger of me not staying temple worthy. What was Reese thinking?

Later that same week, I had another surprise. Someone filled my school locker with balloons of all shapes, sizes, and colors. "Okay, who did this and why?" Turning, I glanced at Roz. She was continuously doing strange things these days. I wouldn't have put it past her.

"I didn't have anything to do with it," Roz replied. "But if you ask me, I'll bet it has something to do with next week's homecoming dance."

"Yeah, right," I rebuffed as I reached inside to pull out one of the balloons. Selecting one in the middle, I yanked it out of my locker. It had the desired effect—the other balloons cascaded onto the tiled floor of the busy high school hallway. Several students kicked them out of the way as they hurried to leave the building.

"I'll bet I'm right. Look, there are pieces of paper inside some of these balloons," Roz scolded as she began scurrying around to gather the balloons that were floating down the hall, helped on their journey by a group of senior boys. "Would you guys knock it off?" she said sharply as the boys laughed and kicked another set of balloons. "Laurie, help me pick these up."

"Let's just stuff them into the garbage," I said, still convinced this was someone's idea of a joke. I was getting tired of the harassment I'd endured since junior high for being a Molly Mormon. I figured my senior year would be different, but it wasn't. I'd already had my fill of being made fun of for trying to have high standards. Several recent letters to the editor had been directed toward me and my column. Even though I had tried to steer clear of anything that hinted too strongly about LDS beliefs, I was still being criticized over the values I supported. Last week I had written about how disgusting some television shows and movies are today, challenging my readers to send letters of protest, thinking it would help inspire some changes. Letters of protest were written—fiery attacks against my view-point. It didn't help that Roz, my so-called best friend, was being less than supportive. In fact, I suspected one anonymous letter had been sent by her. It had contained some of her favorite phrases that she directed toward me lately: "snobbish prude, control freak, arrogant loser." I think you get the idea. It wasn't any worse than the other letters, but it hurt more, knowing Roz had more than likely sent it in.

You'd think living in a predominantly LDS area, you wouldn't have this problem. Hah! Sometimes I think it's worse. The most popular students seem to be those who break all the rules. They're supposed to know better, but they don't act that way. It's become a pet peeve of mine since I met Ed. If Ed had met some of these kids I go to school with, he would believe every bad thing ever written about Mormons.

I glanced at the inside of my locker door, relieved to see that the picture of the Savior was still there, as were the favorite quotes I had fastened underneath. One of my favorite quotes popped out at me. *No one would have crossed the ocean if they could have gotten off the ship in a storm.* I felt a twinge of apprehension. What kind of a storm was I facing now? Shuddering, I stared down at the balloons around my feet.

Roz tapped me on the shoulder. "Someone went to a lot of trouble to do this. The least you can do is check it out," she said, gesturing to the balloons.

"Roz, it's probably someone trying to be funny. Again."

"What if you're wrong?"

I hesitated.

"Here, I'll help you." Roz took out one of her earrings and popped one of the balloons that contained a piece of paper. "See, there're words inside some of these," she said, handing me the first piece of paper she had rescued.

I shrugged. "So it says my name. That doesn't mean anything."

"Yet," Roz replied as she handed me another word. "Take a look at this one."

"Homecoming," I read out loud. "Roz—it says homecoming," I exclaimed.

"Duh! Now will you help me?"

Nodding, I reached for the nearest balloon and used one of my sharp fingernails to pop it.

* * *

"Oh, and while Joey is sleeping, I need you to throw a batch of towels in the washer," Mom said as she wiggled into her suede jacket. I saw her out of the corner of my eye, but I didn't respond, still sitting at the dining room table in a brain fog. "Earth to Laurie."

"Huh . . . what?" I said, glancing at my mother.

"You haven't heard anything I've said since you came home from school," Mom chided, stepping closer to the table.

"Were you talking to me?"

"Trying to." That's when Mom saw the slender vase that was sitting on the other side of my backpack. "Flowers? Who sent you those?"

I glanced at the beautiful red rose that was centered between two white carnations, shadowed by bright green sprigs of fern. "I was asked to the homecoming dance."

Mom grinned her delight and leaned down to give me an intense squeeze. "That's great!"

I remained silent, half-heartedly returning the hug.

Straightening, Mom glanced at the flowers again. "Is there a problem?"

"I seem to be the only one who thinks there is," I mumbled.

Mom sank down into a chair beside me. "What's going on?"

"After school let out, I went to my locker and it was filled with balloons."

"And . . ." Mom prompted.

"Some of the balloons had words inside them. Roz helped me pop the message balloons, and when we put the words together, it said, *Laurie, will you go to the homecoming dance with me?*"

"That's all it said?"

"At first. Then down the hall we found two more balloons with words inside. They'd been kicked out of the way after they fell out of my locker. We popped them and found four more words: *Go to the office.*"

"So you went to the office—is that where these flowers were?"

I nodded.

"And you still don't know who asked you?"

"I know," I replied. "That's the problem." Picking up a small envelope, I handed it to her. "This was attached to the flowers."

Taking the envelope, Mom removed a small card and read the brief message it contained:

Laurie, be my date for the homecoming dance.
We'll have a lot of fun.

Jared M.

"Who's Jared M.?"

"Only the best receiver on our high school football team," I answered. "Mom, Jared Moulton has shoulders like this," I said, holding my hands far apart, "and he's hot . . . I mean—"

"I think I know what 'hot' means," Mom said as I turned a deep shade of red. "He must be a very attractive young man."

"And popular. He's on the student council."

"So what's wrong?"

"Do you know how long I've waited to date someone like this? Someone as popular as Jared doesn't usually know I exist."

"What about Ed? He's a good-looking young man, and he certainly is aware that you exist," Mom teased.

I sighed. "I wish Ed was the one who asked me. Then there wouldn't be a problem."

"Sweetheart, you are a very pretty young woman," Mom assured, still not understanding what I was trying to say. "I can see why someone like Jared would ask you out."

"No, you don't get it," I replied. "I tried explaining it to Roz, and she didn't get it either. She thinks I'm worrying over nothing."

Mom slipped out of her jacket and set it on a nearby chair. She then turned and gave me a long, searching look. "Help me understand, Laurie," she said, sliding her chair closer to mine.

"I thought you had to go somewhere."

"I can get groceries later. I'll make you help me," she added, jabbing me in the ribs.

"Something to look forward to," I said, slumping down in my chair. I hate grocery shopping. Mom always heaps the cart, making it look like she's feeding total pigs.

"Now tell me what's going on," Mom insisted.

"All right. Sometimes I hear things at school. I know a lot of it is rumor, but sometimes I wonder if some of it *is* true."

"What kind of rumors are we talking about?"

"Jared's reputation with girls."

"Oh," Mom replied, looking alarmed. "He has a reputation?" she repeated. "This doesn't sound good."

"Yeah, well . . . Roz thinks I'm being silly. She says it will ruin me socially if I refuse to go out with Jared—that I'll never have another chance to date anyone this cool again. But Mom, what if the stories about Jared are true?"

"Is this boy LDS?"

"Oh, yeah—his dad even serves on the high council of his stake, not that any of that seems to matter to Jared."

"So Jared's not in our stake?"

I shook my head.

"Does he take seminary?"

"He's in my class this term. Everyone thinks he's wonderful because he's so funny. But some of his jokes are pretty crude. Our seminary teacher, Brother Baker, came down on him last week, but Jared shrugged it off like it didn't mean anything. After class, he told everyone that Brother Baker was a total loser. Then he imitated the way Brother Baker talks and everyone laughed. Everyone but me," I explained. "No one dares to stand up to Jared because they're afraid of what he'll say about them."

Mom's frown deepened. "Are the stories about Jared bad?"

"I've heard that he tries to see how far he can get with each girl—that it's like a game to him." I stared down at my hands.

"Mom, what do I do? Give him a chance and hope the rumors are just that, rumors?"

"You don't know for certain that they're true?"

"No," I replied.

"There were a lot of rumors going around about your brother a while back. Most were worse than what had really happened."

"I know."

"And you know how upset you were when Penny wrote that note and left it for me in Relief Society. Thank heavens I was able to squelch the gossip she tried to start, or there would be stories going around about you," Mom reminded me.

I nodded. "So you think I should give Jared the benefit of the doubt and go out with him."

"No, I'm saying that you shouldn't believe everything you hear." Mom looked at the flowers Jared had given me. "What does your heart tell you?"

"My heart feels very confused," I responded.

"Do you think any guy will ever measure up to Ed?" Mom asked softly.

I didn't answer, irritated by what she was saying.

"But on the other hand, if you have a bad feeling about going out with Jared, don't go. You know how to recognize promptings when they come."

I thought I did. Right now I wasn't sure. I was feeling so many things, I couldn't sort it all out, which explained the headache that had developed since I had dropped Roz off at her house.

"Take some time and think about it."

"That's the problem. I need to give him an answer by tomorrow."

"Why so quick?" Mom asked.

"Roz set a deadline."

"Why did she do that?"

"Because she got asked out too—by one of Jared's friends. Roz found balloons in her locker after we found the ones in mine."

"And she wants to go?"

I nodded. "But Jared's friend has the same kind of reputation as Jared. When I tried to talk to Roz about it, she got mad and told me to mind my own business. She said there weren't that many good-looking guys in our high school and that Terrence was cool and she wasn't going to let me ruin her senior year."

Mom winced. "Ouch."

"Yeah. We had a huge argument over it when I drove her home. I'm not even sure she's still speaking to me."

"Why don't you put some prayer time in on this? Joey should sleep for about thirty more minutes. That'll give you some time alone to think things through. While you're doing that, I'll hurry to the store and pick up a few groceries. We'll have dinner, then maybe you should drive over and talk things out with Roz."

"Okay," I said, feeling a little better. "Why does everything have to be so complicated?"

"Welcome to life," Mom replied, reaching for her jacket. "I'll have the cell phone with me if you need anything." She grabbed her purse and headed out the door, making her escape.

I knew she needed a break once in a while. And it wasn't like she hadn't tried to help me with my current crisis. The problem was there wasn't an easy answer. Either the rumors about Jared were true or they weren't. Regardless, Roz had made me feel like I was being a total prude.

"You kissed a guy you barely knew this summer," she had pointed out when I had driven her home. "You know Jared. What's the problem?"

I glared at the flowers Jared had left for me. Roz was wrong—knowing Jared *was* the problem.

Chapter 15

Roz talked me into going to the dance with Jared using a combination of guilt and threats if I didn't cooperate. The guilt came from statements like, "You're ruining my chance to be popular." The threats were more like, "If you don't go, I'll tell everyone about the time you wet your pants in the third grade." My best friend also accused me of being pathetic sludge who was afraid of her own shadow. That hurt. To prove to Roz that I wasn't sludge, I told Jared I would go with him to the homecoming dance. Then I wondered if I had temporarily lost my mind. An uneasy feeling nagged at me the entire week. Mom was excited about helping me buy a new fancy dress and doing weird things with my hair, but I found that I wasn't looking forward to any of it.

Mom took me dress shopping the Saturday before homecoming week. We left Dad home to babysit Joey. Like I already said, Mom was really excited, until she started looking at the dresses. Then I heard her mutter words like, "low-cut," "sleeveless," "plunging neckline," "where the heck is the back on this thing?" and a complete sentence that went something like, "My daughter is not going to dress like a sleaze."

I agreed with her. Going out with Jared was scary enough. I didn't want to dress in any way that would encourage him to live up to those rumors that were floating around. Finally, after searching through about four different stores, Mom and I settled on a dress she would have to fix. It was sleeveless, but Mom said she could insert sleeves and take care of that problem. There was a decent back to this dress, so that part was okay. But the front was too low for my comfort, something else Mom said she would fix. It was a pretty pastel blue color, and Mom thought it would look great on me after it was remodeled.

We found some shoes to match, high-heeled white sandals that had a fake blue gemstone on the instep, and we called it good. On the way home, Mom was still fuming over the dress styles she had seen that day.

"No wonder the prophet is worried about the youth. Did you see those dresses today?" she asked, not waiting for a reply. It was a relief to finally pull in our driveway.

When Mom handed me my dress to carry inside the house, I wondered how successful Roz and her mother had been with their shopping last night. We had invited Roz and Regina to come with us today, but Regina had to work. Big surprise there.

Roz came over not long after we returned home from our shopping adventure to show me the dress she had picked out. Hers was still inside of a plastic cover the store had draped over it. Mom had already taken mine out the plastic cover, intent on making changes to it as soon as possible. It was lying over one of the kitchen chairs, so I led Roz in to where it was and held it up for her to see.

"Oh, Laurie, you'll look great in that," Roz exclaimed, running her fingers over the blue fabric.

"I will once Mom overhauls it," I replied.

Roz looked puzzled. "Overhauls it?"

"Yeah, she's adding sleeves and an insert in the front so it won't be so immodest."

Lifting an eyebrow at me, Roz shook her head. "There's nothing wrong with that dress. It's sleeveless like mine." She uncovered her dress to show me. It was a beautiful maroon dress made out of a silky material that seemed to glisten. But it was sleeveless, and it was one of those with the missing back and a rather low neck.

"It's gorgeous," I began.

"I know. I can hardly wait to wear it next week."

"But . . . I know your mom probably doesn't have time . . . Would you like my mom to fix it for you?"

"Fix what? This dress is fine the way it is."

"Don't you think the back is a little low?" I asked, moving closer for a better look.

"My mom didn't have a problem with it," Roz retorted. "She told me I look like a model with this on."

"I'm sure you do," I soothed, realizing Roz was upset with me. "And it would still look great if Mom changed a couple of—"

"Your mother's not touching this dress," Roz snapped, slipping the plastic cover back over her dress. "I should've known better than to bring it over here for you to see. You're just jealous, that's all," she said before walking out of the house and slamming the door behind her.

"What was that all about?" Mom asked, stepping into view with Joey on her hip.

"You can't believe the dress Roz is wearing to this dance," I sputtered, just as angry as Roz had been. Roselyn Whiting had sat there beside me during every lesson we had ever endured about modesty in Young Women. But in keeping with her new "independent" attitude, she was wearing clothes to school this year that weren't the greatest. Belly shirts, low-cut jeans, and tight-fitting shorts that, in my opinion, were too short. The sad thing is, I had been with her when she had bought most of those clothes. Twice as sad was the fact that I had bought that stupid pair of low-riders that she now held over my head whenever I said anything about what she was wearing. I wasn't proud that they were still hanging in the back of my closet with the tags attached, an item I would never wear. Roz mocked me continuously about it, but at least I didn't feel uncomfortable about my clothes, unlike my best friend who was constantly adjusting her outfits when they were too revealing. Why she thought that maroon dress was okay was beyond me. I told Mom about the dress Roz and her mother had picked out, describing the obvious flaws.

Mom shook her head. "What is Regina thinking? Why would she send her daughter to a dance dressed like that? Honestly, sometimes I wonder about mothers who care more for fashion than they do about what's best for their daughters." She went off down the hall muttering as she had done earlier that day as we had left each dress shop.

Sighing, I picked up my dress and looked it over. Despite what Roz had said, I wouldn't want to wear it without the alter-ations—I wouldn't feel comfortable in it. Roz shouldn't feel comfortable either. She had never worn anything like that maroon dress before. I had a hard time believing she would wear it to the dance. But then, Roz was doing a lot of things lately that I didn't agree with, like flirting after the football games with boys from our school as well as the opposing team. She had been trying to drag me with her, but I had a curfew, something that came in handy these days. Mom had told me once that I could use her to wiggle out of situations that weren't good. All I had to say was, "Yeah, well, my mom won't let me." I knew Roz's mom wouldn't let her either, but I doubted Regina knew what was going on. There were days when I was tempted to point it out to her. Then I would feel guilty over even thinking about betraying Roz. But on the other hand, wasn't she betraying everything we had formerly stood for? Hurt and confused, I wasn't sure what to do, and I wasn't looking forward to Homecoming at all.

* * *

Hi Laurie,

How are things in Roy? Things here in Quincy are good. But our homecoming celebration won't be for a while. Are you excited for the dance? You didn't say much about it in your last e-mail. What's this guy like who asked you? Knowing you, he's probably pretty cool. I know you wouldn't go out with anyone who wasn't.

You mentioned that you're concerned about your friend, Roz. I'm sure with your example and friend-ship, she'll work through things okay. Some people just have to struggle with figuring out who they are. Like me. I've been thinking a lot about the challenge you gave me last week to read the Book of Mormon. And thanks for the copy you sent. I noticed that you highlighted several scriptures for me. As soon as things slow down, I'll try to read through it and let you know what I think. Right now, football and some of my classes are keeping me busy. Not to mention my grandmother's farm. It seems like there're always chores to do.

How does your brother like serving a mission for your church? That would be pretty scary, trying to teach strangers about what you believe. Then again, this is your family we're talking about. You don't seem to have any problem sharing what you believe. I'm glad you took the time to share it with me.

Have a great day and keep in touch.

Ed

Chapter 16

As she had promised, Mom altered my dress, making it as modest as it was pretty. On the day of the dance, she invited Stacy over to help do my hair, and by the time Jared was supposed to arrive to pick me up, I was ready to go. Stacy had pinned my hair up, and I had to admit she has the same knack with hair that she does with designing the interiors of fancy homes and offices.

The final touch was the necklace Reese had given me. It looked great with my dress, and as I modeled in the full-length mirror in my parents' bedroom, I was amazed by my reflection. Was that really me?

"You look so much like your mother," Stacy commented as Mom beamed.

"Thanks," Mom and I said at the same time.

The doorbell rang, ending my preening session.

"Laurie, your date's here," Dad called out from the entryway.

"I guess this is it," I said, suddenly feeling nervous.

"Good luck," Stacy said, stepping away from the door.

"Have fun, and remember, I'm only a phone call away if things get out of hand," Mom whispered when she leaned close to kiss my forehead.

"Hopefully they won't," I breathed, suddenly wishing I were staying here with Mom and Stacy. They were going to work on another baby quilt tonight and catch each other up on the news they had received from Reese.

"Laurie," Dad hollered again, increasing in volume. I could just picture what he must be putting Jared through. Taking a deep breath, I began moving down the hall.

When I reached the living room, Jared stood up from where he had been sitting on the couch.

"It's about time," Dad teased when he turned and saw me.

"Wow," Jared exclaimed.

"Perfection takes time," Mom said, stepping in behind me. I knew she wanted a good look at my date for the evening. To his credit, Jared was immaculately dressed. He was wearing a nice, dark blue suit with a shimmering silk tie in shades of gray and blue. His curly blond hair had been tamed with gel—the guy looked sharp.

"You two make a nice couple," Stacy complimented.

"Thanks," Jared said. I hated how his eyes widened at the sight of Stacy. "Is this your sister?" he asked.

"She's a close family friend," my mother answered.

Jared grinned. "Want to come along with us?" he asked, still assessing my "sister." Just as I was getting ready to call the whole thing off, Jared laughed like he was joking. A part of me sensed he wasn't.

"Actually, no," Stacy replied. "Going to a high school dance at my age doesn't sound very tempting," she said, putting Jared in his place. Now it was my turn to grin.

"I'd like to get a picture of you two," Dad said, waving his camera. He made us pose in front of the white brick fireplace before he would let us leave. Then Jared stated firmly that there were people out waiting for us in his car, and he escorted me out of the house.

"Man, I thought we'd never get out of there," Jared said, loosening his tie as we walked to where he had parked his silver Mustang.

"Wait, I forgot your boutonniere," I said, turning to walk back inside my house.

"Forget it. I didn't get you a flower," Jared said with a smile. "I figured I spent enough on the one I already sent you, plus when you figure the cost of tonight's dinner, the tickets to get into the dance, and the pictures—"

"Okay," I interrupted, feeling like an idiot. I had always assumed that when you went to a formal dance, you bought each other flowers to wear.

"Hey, no worries. I figure you come from an old-fashioned family. It'll be up to me to educate you on current trends," he said, walking around to let himself into his car.

I stood by the door on my side and wondered what Jared had meant by that comment. Then I opened the door myself and tried to gracefully climb inside. Jared was already in the car, telling Terrence and Roz how silly my parents had been.

"It was a riot. Her dad actually sat me down and told me how he expected me to treat his little girl," Jared crowed as he started the engine.

Suddenly I didn't want to go anywhere with this jerk. My parents might be old-fashioned, but I was starting to realize this was a good thing.

"Hey, you think that was funny? You should've heard how Laurie's mom wanted to alter this dress," Roz laughed, sitting, in my opinion, too close to Terrence in the backseat.

"Your dress is perfect the way it is," Terrence said, rubbing Roz's bare back. And Roz let him. She didn't pull away or try to stop him.

Turning around before I hurled, I fastened my seat belt. Why had I agreed to this torture? Fingering my purse, I was grateful I had brought Mom's cell phone. I might be making a call much sooner than any of us had anticipated.

* * *

Instead of making reservations somewhere close, like at one of the nice restaurants in Layton, Terrence and Jared had made arrangements for us to eat in Salt Lake City at the Mayan. Jared explained this gave us more time to visit and get acquainted as we drove down and back. I think it actually gave Terrence more time to play touchy-feely with my best friend in the backseat. Thank heavens the freeway traffic kept Jared busy. He did set his hand on my knee once as we approached Salt Lake City. When I brushed it away, he just laughed and tried it again a few minutes later, creeping up my thigh until I slapped his hand soundly. Giving me a dirty look, he focused on the road.

It was a relief to finally arrive at the restaurant. Knowing I was out with a cretin, I pulled myself out of the car, then moved my seat out of the way for Roz. Terrence had already let her out of the car on his side and, holding hands, they were walking toward the restaurant.

"Hurry up," Jared said as he waited on the other side of his car.

I didn't answer but took great satisfaction in slamming his car door shut.

"Hey, watch it," he cautioned.

"You too," I muttered under my breath.

* * *

The Mayan was impressive. A huge adobe building housed the restaurant and gift shop. A long line of people stood waiting in the foyer and throughout the gift shop, but our party was taken in as soon as we arrived, thanks to the reservations Jared had set up earlier that week. As I walked into the restaurant beside Jared, I studied the junglelike atmosphere. Artificial plants and colorful mechanical birds gave it a tropical flair.

When the waitress led us out of the foyer, it was like entering a giant replica of the tree house in a movie I had watched when I was younger, *Swiss Family Robinson,* only this tree house was situated on the branches of four huge artificial trees. As I gazed around the restaurant, Jared managed to slide his arm around my lower waist, making me very uncomfortable. I tolerated it until we reached the elevator, then I pulled away, keeping my back against the safety of the elevator wall. Jared grinned and stood close beside me, a reminder that I would have to deal with him all night.

Our waitress took us to the third level of the restaurant. I noticed Jared's fascination with the way the young woman walked when the doors opened and she led the way into the third level. Disgusted, I made myself a promise that no matter what, I would never go out with this guy again. It was obvious Jared would never measure up to Ed. Sweet Ed who had opened doors for me and treated me with respect. Sighing, I glanced at Roz and Terrence. What would our Laurel leader say if she could see how these two were behaving?

We were escorted to a wooden table that gave us a clear view of a thirty-six-foot cliff complete with waterfalls that stood in the center of the restaurant. On varied locations along the cliff were mechanical iguanas and parrots that sang and told silly jokes.

I watched them for several seconds, then seated myself at the table—I knew better than to wait for Jared to assist me with my chair. After I sat down, I gasped, spotting three scantily clad divers who had appeared on the cliff. Stunned, I gaped down at the pool of water that waited below. "They're not going to dive down into—" My question was interrupted by one of the divers doing just that. I watched, amazed that anyone would dare dive into a pool that seemed so small.

"I told you this was a great place," Jared said, winking at me. Reaching across the table, he grabbed my hand and squeezed it until it hurt.

Embarrassed over the way the divers were dressed, I ignored Jared's comment, pulled my hand away, and slid my chair as far away from him as I dared. I didn't want a repeat of what had happened on the way here.

"It's no big thing. That pool is about fifteen feet deep," Terrence said, grinning across the table at me. "And the divers know what they're doing. Enjoy the show. That's why we brought you here," he added, sliding his arm around Roz's slender shoulders. He gave her a squeeze. "We figured it was a good way to get your engines running."

I felt horrible, knowing exactly what Terrence meant. Is that what Jared was thinking too? He had a rude awakening in store if that's what he thought.

"You've been here before," Roz said to Terrence. She smiled as he whispered something in her ear.

Sick at heart, I turned away, watching as three other divers somersaulted off the cliff into the water.

"Yeah, baby," two women exclaimed from a nearby table. Rising from their chairs, they clapped their hands and whistled.

"Oh, please. Those divers aren't nearly as good looking as other people I could mention," Jared said, gesturing to himself. "What do you think about this place, Laurie?"

Not wanting to answer, I reached for my glass of ice water and took a long drink. I gazed across the table at Roz. We had been as close as sisters ever were, but tonight, I didn't know her. She wouldn't even look at me, too intent on what Terrence was whispering in her ear. Then I watched, horrified, as he began nibbling on her ear and then her neck.

"Roz, let's find a restroom," I suggested, anxious to get her away from Terrence for a little heart-to-heart.

"Can't you find one yourself?" Terrence replied, giving me an irritated look.

I returned Terrence's look of disdain with one of my own. Who did he think he was? "No, I can't. My sense of direction is bad."

"So's your timing," Roz said, shaking her head at me. "Look, they're bringing us chips and salsa." She glanced around. "But where are the menus?"

"I knew it would take a while to drive down here, so I already ordered dinner," Jared replied. "We'll be eating Cliff Diver Fajitas made with beef."

"We'll be enjoying all kinds of good things tonight—" Terrence said, mostly to Roz.

"Including the entertainment," Jared interrupted, gesturing to the female diver who had just appeared.

"Oh, yeah, that's what I'm talkin' about," Terrence exclaimed as he watched the female diver launch herself from the cliff. I found myself wondering how she managed to keep her revealing bikini in place when she hit the water.

"Dang, the show's over for now," Jared said, pointing down to the divers who were retreating behind the man-made cliff. "We'll have about thirty minutes before they come back out again," he added, glancing at his watch. "Hopefully we'll be through eating by then, and we can go down to watch things up close." He reached for a homemade tortilla chip and took a generous helping of salsa with it. Offering it to me first, he ate it when I refused. What little appetite I'd had was gone.

"Dude, what kind of drinks did you order?"

Jared grinned at Terrence. "Tropical smoothies," he responded.

"With or without the alcohol?" Terrence laughed.

"You know what I'd prefer, but I'd better keep it clean for now," Jared replied. "Besides, I'm the designated driver."

Terrence squeezed Roz's shoulders again. "The rest of us shouldn't have to suffer."

"You know it," Jared said as he reached to do a series of hand gestures with his friend. I'd noticed that some of the other members of the football team had been doing the same thing lately in the halls at school, usually after a girl walked past. My eyes narrowed as it dawned on me what it probably signified.

"What does that mean?" Roz asked.

Terrence grinned at Jared, then winked at Roz. "I'll tell you later," he said, "in private."

That did it. I was taking Roz for a restroom chat now if I had to drag her by her hair. "Roz, let's go," I said, pointing to the restroom I had spotted around the corner from where our table was located.

"Something wrong?" Jared asked before stuffing another chip inside his mouth.

"Yeah, something I need Roz to help me with," I said, giving Roz a pointed look.

"Fine," Roz said, slowly standing up. I noticed she at least had the decency to cover the front of her dress with her hand as she leaned forward.

"Hurry back," Terrence said as we walked away.

Roz followed me in silence into the restroom. Fuming, I wondered how I could tactfully alert her to the danger she was in. I didn't realize she was just as upset as I was.

"What is your problem tonight?" she angrily demanded when we stood in front of the bathroom mirror.

"My problem?" I retorted. "You're the one with a problem."

"Me? You're the one acting like a refrigerator. You're one cold woman. How normal is that?"

Insulted by that comment, I decided to try a different approach. "Don't you see what these guys are all about?" I asked, searching her face for understanding. "Terrence can't keep his hands off you."

"And?"

"And that should bother you," I replied. "Roz, don't you remember anything we've learned from our Young Women leaders?"

"What do they know? They're old-fashioned, like your parents."

Now Roz was hitting below the belt. "My parents happen to care about me. They care about you too, and right now I know what they'd both tell you. Probably the same thing your own parents would say."

"Not interested," Roz said, moving past me to leave the restroom. "For once, a neat guy is attracted to me, and I'm not going to let you spoil it."

"Roz, you know where this is going to lead," I warned.

"You always blow things out of proportion," Roz said hotly. "Laurie, I've been your friend a long time, but I swear, if you ruin things for me tonight, I'll never forgive you. Try having fun for once in your life. Like my mom said when I told her what you wanted to do to my dress—you're critical about everything, and you never let yourself enjoy life. Well, if you're determined to be miserable, don't drag me down with you." She gave me a livid glare, then left the room.

Shaken by her response, I leaned against a sink for support. Roz's words hurt, but Regina's accusation was devastating. Regina was one of my heroes. Closing my eyes, I offered a prayer. Was I wrong? Several seconds later, I gazed at my reflection in the mirror. The answer had come, calming my heart. This wasn't a good situation, and I never should've agreed to this date. As soon as we drove back to Roy, I would ask Jared to drop me off at my house. They could all go the dance without me.

Gathering my courage, I walked out of the restroom and back to the table.

* * *

Do you ever get an impression from the look on someone's face that they're up to something? I had that sensation when we walked away from our table about a half hour later. I had seen the way Roz had giggled over a whispered conversation with Terrence just before the waitress had appeared with our check. Then as we entered the elevator, I caught Roz winking at Jared. Obviously something had been arranged during the time I had spent composing myself in the restroom. Certain I wouldn't like whatever it was, I had my guard up.

"Hey, Terrence, it's almost time for the divers to do their thing again," Jared said, his wide smile revealing his white teeth.

"You up for more divers?" Terrence asked, giving Roz a teasing look.

"Oh, yeah," Roz replied as the elevator doors opened to the ground floor of the restaurant. "Come on, Laurie, you have to see this close up," she said, following Terrence out of the elevator.

"After you," Jared said politely, motioning for me to exit the elevator ahead of him.

Suspicious about his motive, I kept a close eye on him.

Jared held out his arm to me. "No lady should walk through a jungle unescorted," he said as I rolled my eyes. He'd been such a gentleman all evening, I knew this was an act. But I didn't want to be accused of being a refrigerator again, so I took his arm.

"Hey you two, hurry up—you're going to miss the best part," Terrence called back to us.

Jared led me into the area directly in front of the pool. He glanced up at the divers who were assembling on the cliff above. "Stand here for the best view," he advised as he pushed me close to the fenced pool of water.

"We can't have you missing any of the fun," Terrence said.

The three of them moved back, and before I could ask what was going on, a diver sprang from the cliff and hit the water with gusto. He hit so hard, water splashed up out of the pool and all over me, thoroughly soaking my dress. People throughout the restaurant laughed, clapped, and cheered as I backed away, dripping.

"Awesome! You didn't tell us you were part of the performance," Jared said, laughing.

"You rotten—" I sputtered, wiping at my face.

"Temper, temper," Terrence said, waving his finger in front of my face. He and Jared continued to laugh, holding their sides, which I hoped ached severely.

"This is better than a wet T-shirt contest," Jared hooted.

"A revealing experience," Terrence added, pointing at the front of my dress.

I glanced down, mortified that my wet dress was clinging to me. Covering my front with one arm, I used the other to brush at my hair, which now hung down, dripping water on the floor.

"Laurie—I'm sorry. I didn't think you'd get that wet," Roz apologized. "The way Jared talked, it would just be a few drops of water. I thought it would cool you down. I didn't think it would ruin your dress."

"I'll bet," I said, furious. I pointed to a sign. A caution sign, it warned that anyone standing in that particular area could get wet. "Let me guess, you and Terrence hid this?" I asked as another diver hit the water. This time the splash missed me, but it did inspire me to leave the area.

"Laurie, I didn't know you'd get saturated," Roz said, following behind me.

I paused long enough to glare at my former best friend. "Look," I said, as my teeth started to chatter, "wh-wh-whether you meant it or not, it happened. I'm going into that restroom over there and c-c-calling my parents to c-c-come get me. You c-c-can either c-c-come with me, or f-f-finish this lovely evening on your own."

"Laurie, come back," Jared said, getting on his knees like he was begging. He and Terrence were still having a hard time keeping a straight face, and for a moment, I wished for extremely bad and horrific things to happen to them, like being hit with bolts of lightning for starters.

"Maybe we can dry you off," Roz said hopefully.

"R-r-roz, l-l-look-k at m-m-me," I replied. "There's n-n-no way t-too f-fix this," I said before turning away to run into the restroom. I vowed I wouldn't cry in front of those imbeciles and took several deep breaths to control myself. I looked in the mirror and saw that I resembled a drowned cat.

"Laurie . . . I really am sorry," Roz said, appearing behind me in the mirror.

I turned around to glower at her. That's when I saw the towel in her hands.

"One of the divers said to bring this to you. He said to apologize for nearly drowning you."

"Thanks," I managed to say as I took the towel she held out to me.

"Did you call your mom yet?"

I shook my head.

"I wish you wouldn't. Jared said he'd buy you a T-shirt from the gift shop out front. You could wear it over your dress until we get back to Roy. We could go to my house and find something else for you to wear. Then we could still go to the dance."

"No, I'm done," I said, trying to dry off as best I could. I was afraid one towel wouldn't do it. But it was better than nothing. After wiping the water from my face and hair, I draped the towel around the front of my dress.

"Are you sure?" Roz pleaded.

Shivering, I knew this was a pivotal crossroad. If Roz went home with me, I would still be ticked over the night's events, but I would get over it, and it would get her away from Terrence's roaming hands. If she went with Jared and Terrence, she was turning her back on the person I had always believed her to be.

"Roz," I said, trying to control the tremor in my voice. "Roz," I tried again, "this isn't good."

"Okay, it was a mean trick, but . . . well, everyone had had it with how you were acting."

"How I was acting?" Roz was missing the point. Did she honestly not get where this was heading? And she said I was naive. "Terrence is—"

"He's the best thing that's ever happened to me," Roz exclaimed. "He's a great guy. Why can't you accept that? A true friend would be happy and supportive."

I stared at Roz in disbelief. In my opinion, a true friend would stop her from crashing into a brick wall.

"Look, I'm sorry about what happened," she said, pointing to my dress and hair, "but maybe this is for the best. Call your parents and go home. The rest of us are going to the dance." Whirling around, she walked out of the restroom.

"Roz," I called after her, but she didn't come back. And the tears I had been fighting made their appearance, ruining what was left of my mascara.

Chapter 17

After I called home and told Mom about my predicament, she told me to sit tight, assuring me help was on its way. I clicked off the phone and paced around the restroom, trying to keep warm. Now, despite what Roz might think, I'm not an eternal pessimist. For a while, I clung to the mistaken notion that my best friend would come back for me. But she never did. I peeked out of the restroom once, and there was no sign of Roz, Jared, or Terrence. True to what Roz had threatened, they had left me behind.

A couple of customers stepped into the room, took one look at me, and left. One of them must have alerted the staff to my plight. A short time later, a waitress came into the restroom and handed me a complimentary Mayan T-shirt to put over my wet dress. It didn't change the fact that I was wet and chilled to the bone, but it freed up the towel, which I then wrapped around my hair.

I was taken to a nearby office to wait for my parents. Someone rustled up an old blanket, and I wrapped up in it while I shivered in a vinyl chair. I got the impression the staff was trying to make me as comfortable as possible, figuring they were liable for what had happened.

Nearly an hour later, Mom and Stacy came to my rescue. Dad had stayed home with Joey. I think Mom arranged it that way on purpose, afraid Dad would follow through on the threats he had made against Jared and end up in jail.

When Mom and Stacy hurried into the office, Mom gave me a huge hug, despite my waterlogged condition. Stacy smiled her sympathy and held out more towels and an old fleece sweat suit Mom must have dug out of the bottom drawer of my dresser. I didn't care—it was a warm alternative to my current outfit.

After ascertaining that my body temperature rivaled that of an ice cube, Mom led me back to the restroom, pushed me inside an extra-large stall, and helped me change out of my wet clothes. She handed everything over the stall door to Stacy, who stuffed it into a plastic garbage bag she had brought with her. If you ever want to experience total humility, try having your mother dress you when you're practically an adult. Not cool, but under the current circumstances, necessary. I was so cold I could hardly bend the formerly flexible parts of my body.

When Mom decided I was properly clothed, down to the thick socks and the old pair of gym shoes she had brought with her, she helped me pull on a jacket. Then she and Stacy led me out of the restaurant and guided me through the parking lot to Stacy's car.

Mom opened the back door of Stacy's red Jetta and helped me inside, then climbed in beside me, reached over, and fastened my seat belt. For a moment, I felt like I was five years old. Stacy started the car, cranked up the heat, and then leaned over the backseat to explain that before we returned to Roy, we would swing by her apartment nearby. Mom had talked Stacy into spending the night at our house, and she needed to get a few things. By the time we returned to Roy, it would be late, and Mom was insisting that Stacy stay with us and head back to her apartment in the morning.

True to her word, it didn't take Stacy long to drive to her apartment, round up some personal items, and return to the car. She handed back a fleece blanket, which Mom draped around me. Then Mom slipped an arm around me, pulling me close as Stacy drove us home. As I leaned against my mother, I closed my eyes and wished I had just stayed home that night. This date had turned into a nightmare of enormous proportions, and I knew it was far from over. With someone like Jared, it's never over. It would be spread all through the school, the story growing each time it was told. I was going to be the laughing-stock of the entire high school. It hurt to know that Roz would be among those who laughed.

Stacy popped in a CD that was soothing. I don't know what it was, but between it and the warmth I was starting to feel, I fought to stay awake. Somewhere between Bountiful and Roy, I lost the battle. Mom gently woke me when Stacy pulled into our driveway. I didn't want to wake up. Waking up meant I had to face everything that had happened. It meant I had to move from this feeling of warm security and listen to Dad's angry tirade.

In a daze, I allowed myself to be led inside our house, where Dad was busy pacing the kitchen floor. He opened his mouth to speak to me, gaped at the shape I was in, and looked to Mom for guidance. I'm not sure what kind of signal she gave him, but he didn't say a word. That's when I knew how bad I really looked.

Somehow Mom and Stacy managed to get me back to my bedroom and sat me on my bed. Stacy went into the bathroom down the hall and brought back my blow dryer. It took both of them to pull the pins out of my hair and to untangle the mess it had become. Then Stacy dried my hair with a brush and the blow dryer while Mom removed the shoes from my feet. When it was decided my hair was finally dry, I was tucked into bed, and Mom stayed with me until I fell asleep.

You can imagine the dreams I suffered all night. Images of Jared and Terrence laughing, taunting me about my ruined dress. Roz was in my face, yelling obscene threats. All around me, scantily clad divers jumped into ponds of blue Jell-O. The Jell-O bounced out of the ponds and covered my soggy dress, filling my veins with ice, and I knew I would never be warm again.

* * *

The homecoming dance at our school is always held on Saturday night, the night after the big game. Then on Sunday, the fortunate few who attended the dance come to church wearing the fancy clothes from the night before. I broke tradition. I didn't go to church at all.

I think Mom would've let me stay home anyway, considering what I'd been through. But I woke up with a raw throat, a stuffy nose, and a horrible headache. So I was allowed to stay in bed. Stacy tiptoed in to say good-bye before she left for Sandy that morning. Not only did she have to teach a Primary class in her ward, but she also had to cook dinner for her dad and brother that afternoon.

I tried to nod, but I could feel my pulse radiate through my aching head. Stacy gave my shoulder a soft squeeze, told me how sorry she was for how things had turned out last night, then commented that Jared was a perverted moron and I was better off without him. I silently agreed with her. I just wished I hadn't lost my best friend too.

I croaked out a thank you to Stacy before she left my room. She smiled, told me she'd call later to see how I was doing, and then walked out the door.

Dad left shortly after Stacy. He poked his head in my room just long enough to let me know he had to sing with the ward choir during sacrament meeting. He must have been desperate to leave the house—Dad hates singing with the choir. After he left, Mom walked into my room to tell me that she would stick around until it was time for Relief Society. Apologizing, she explained she would have to leave then because she was giving the lesson today for a teacher who had to be out of town. It didn't bother me—I wanted some time alone to reflect on how my life was ruined.

Mom tried to get me to eat something for breakfast, but nothing sounded good. She finally talked me into sipping some warm apple cider, which made my throat feel slightly better. I doubted anything would ease my heart. I relived every part of the previous night and agonized over how I could've changed things. Should I have ignored the vulgar jokes Terrence and Jared had shared while we had tried to eat dinner? Had I come down on Roz too hard over how Terrence had fondled her? Maybe I had deserved to be drowned in the middle of the restaurant. It was my fault Roz had left the restaurant with Terrence and Jared.

"Were you able to drink the cider?" Mom asked, reentering my room, this time carrying Joey on her hip.

I nodded, hoping Mom wouldn't notice I had been crying. She noticed. She set Joey down on the floor of my bedroom, handed him my fuzzy pink slippers to play with, and after pulling the chair away from my desk, sat down next to my bed.

"Want to talk about it yet?"

I shook my head.

She brushed the hair away from my eyes. "I can't believe Roz hasn't called to see if you're okay."

"I don't think Roz cares," I sniffed.

"I'm sure she does," Mom countered.

That's when I told Mom everything that had happened the night before. I had told her bits and pieces when I had called from the restaurant, but I had left out some parts, too cold and embarrassed to explain. Now she quietly listened, lifting an eyebrow over how Terrence had been treating Roz.

"And Roz didn't tell him to back off?"

"No, that's what she told me."

I won't share everything Mom said during the next thirty or forty minutes. A lot of it had to do with the inappropriate behavior of Jared, Terrence, and Roz. When she finished, I found myself rethinking things. "So last night wasn't my fault?"

"Heavens, no," Mom exclaimed. "Why would you think that?"

"Roz said—"

"I don't care what Roz said. At the moment, that girl is obviously a runaway hormone."

I blinked, surprised by my mother's comment. "So I'm not the one who messed up?"

"Laurie, quit beating yourself up over this. You were the only one trying to do the right thing. I'm proud of you . . . more than I can say." Looking a little teary-eyed, she forced a smile. "When Stacy was driving us home last night, I thought about something I went through when I was about your age. It's similar to what happened to you."

"Really?"

Mom nodded. "Want to hear it?"

"Yeah." She had my undivided attention. Somehow I couldn't believe my mother had ever been totally humiliated in public.

"When I was a junior in high school, there was a young man who was the star of our basketball team. Mike was tall, handsome, and very funny. Everyone liked him, including one of my closest friends, Gwen. The problem was, he wanted to go out with me."

"He did?"

Mom laughed. "Don't act so surprised. I've turned a few heads in my day," she said, patting her short, blonde hair.

"You still look pretty good—for a woman your age," I teased, attempting a smile.

"Thanks," Mom said, wadding up a Kleenex to throw at me. "Back to my story. I didn't want to do anything that would hurt Gwen, so I kept refusing to go out with Mike. Besides, I had heard a few things about Mike that didn't sound very good, but like you, I wasn't sure what to believe."

"So did Mike give up on you?"

"No." Mom shook her head. "One morning, the summer before our senior year, he called to tell me that some kids were getting together up a nearby canyon for a party later that night.

He said we'd roast hot dogs and marshmallows and then play a few games. It sounded like harmless fun."

"Did you go?"

"First, I asked Mike who was going to be there. When he told me that Gwen and some of my other friends had been invited and were planning to go, I finally gave in. I figured it wasn't really a date because so many people were invited. Later I called to make sure these friends of mine were going."

"And were they?" I asked.

"Some of them were, including Gwen. I made arrangements to ride up with those girls. Then Mike called again and said that he and one of his friends would be picking up Gwen and me."

"So it was more like a date."

Mom's eyes had a faraway look. "Yes, it was. Mike had quite a plan in mind, and he drove over to pick me up first. His friend was sitting in the backseat, and I had no idea where I was supposed to sit. Then I had an uneasy feeling, and I almost turned around and ran back inside of my house."

"But you didn't."

"No, I ignored that soft voice of warning. I'd looked forward to going to that party all day. I rationalized that it wasn't like we would be alone, and when Mike motioned for me to sit up front with him, I finally did just that."

"I'll bet Gwen was mad," I commented.

"She was. I could've sworn steam was coming out both of her ears when she climbed into the backseat a few minutes later. I turned to smile at her, but she wouldn't even look at me."

I picked up the Kleenex Mom had thrown at me a few minutes ago and wiped at my stuffy nose. "Did you try to explain things to her?"

"Yes, but she wouldn't listen. She knew Mike had been after me for months. Gwen figured I'd finally given in and had agreed to be his date for the evening. Everyone else thought the same thing when we arrived together at the campground."

"What did you do?"

Mom smiled sadly. "I had a miserable time. That party was a farce. Oh, sure, they had a fire going and some kids were roasting hot dogs and marshmallows, but there was also plenty of beer—"

"Beer?" I stammered, an incredulous look on my face. I had a hard time imagining my mother at a kegger.

"Beer," Mom confirmed. "And a few couples were wandering off for some quiet time alone, if you catch my meaning." She gazed intently at me.

"Hey, at least they didn't make out in front of you," I replied, thinking of the public display of affection I had suffered through last night.

Mom must have caught my train of thought. She smiled sadly at me, then said, "I still have a hard time believing Roz would let Terrence . . ." She paused, embarrassed. Evidently her train of thought had gone further than mine. "What has gotten into that girl?" she exclaimed.

I silently debated telling Mom the truth—Roz had been heading this direction for quite a while. But I couldn't go there just yet. Instead I shrugged and asked Mom to finish her story.

Mom gave me a probing look, like she knew I wasn't telling her everything. Then she sighed and continued. "It soon became obvious why Mike had tricked me into going that night. As soon as we arrived at the campground, he tried to get me to drink some beer. I think he believed that if he could get me drunk, he could get me to do things I wouldn't normally do." Mom's cheeks turned an interesting color.

"How did you handle it?"

"I threw the beer on the ground and told Mike to take me home. I also told him that he was a jerk and I never wanted to see him again. He was so mad, he refused to take me anywhere, so I found someone else who had driven up that night, someone like me who had discovered he didn't want to be there."

"Who?"

"Your dad," Mom said, smiling at the surprised look on my face.

"That's when you two started dating?"

"Shortly after that, yes. I was impressed by your father's standards, plus he always treated me with respect. He still does," Mom added.

"What happened to Mike?"

"He went after Gwen, who unfortunately made some poor choices that night. I tried to talk her into leaving with your dad and me, but she wouldn't listen. Even after that night, whenever I tried to talk to her about Mike, she acted like I didn't exist. It wasn't until later on, after Mike had all but ruined her life, that she realized how I'd tried to help her."

"Just like Roz last night," I said softly.

"Exactly like Roz last night," Mom agreed. "You were only trying to help her. But she may never see it that way." Rising, Mom leaned down to kiss my cheek. "Take it easy, maybe try to take a nap while I'm gone," she suggested. Turning, she picked up Joey and left to get ready for Relief Society.

When Mom left the house with Joey a few minutes later, I mulled over the story she had shared. It had been interesting to learn how my parents had met, and it helped to know that I wasn't alone in taking a strong stand. However, a piercing pain still cut through my heart. Aching over a friendship I feared was ruined, I was worried about Roz. She had changed so much during the past few months. What could I have done to stop things from getting out of control? How far had Roz let things go last night? How could I help her now?

Plagued by these and other thoughts, I fell into a fitful sleep until everyone returned home from church.

Chapter 18

Mom let me stay home from school on Monday, but by Tuesday I was well enough to go. I didn't want to, but I knew I would be struggling to catch up in my classes as it was. So I went through the motions of getting ready, choosing something bland to wear, hoping people wouldn't notice I was there.

Despite my efforts, they noticed—Jared saw to that. I don't know if he was watching for me or what, but soon after I walked inside the school, he made an announcement over the intercom, welcoming me back. Jared works in the office during first hour, and he gets away with all kinds of things. I ducked my head and tried to ignore the laughter that followed his smart-aleck remarks as he publicly thanked me for showing him a good time Saturday night.

If that wasn't bad enough, there were obscene posters plastered all over inside my locker, items I tore off and shredded the minute I saw them. I wasn't sure who was to blame for their appearance. The porn images had been printed off the internet—the internet addresses were along the bottom of each page. Who had done this and why? Jared would have had access to my locker combination from the office. But Roz knew it by heart, information we had always exchanged. Either way, I sensed it would be a losing battle to complain.

I kept looking for Roz, but we aren't in any classes together until after lunch, and she was keeping her distance, unlike some of Jared's football friends. Whenever I had the misfortune of walking down the hallways, boys from the football team winked at me, nodding and grinning like they were in on a big secret that we shared.

During lunch, I'd had enough. I spotted Roz hanging out with Terrence near the gym. Enraged, I marched over to where they were standing. Still hurting over the fact that Roz hadn't even bothered to call to see if I was okay over the weekend, it didn't help when she pointed at me and laughed as I approached.

"Terrence, look who showed up. I guess she realized she couldn't hide forever."

"Roz, we need to talk," I exclaimed, anger tamping down the pain in my heart.

"No, I don't think so," Roz retorted. "I have better things to do now." Turning, she walked off down the hall holding Terrence's hand.

"Hey, Laurie, I'll have to give you a call," a loud male voice hollered behind me.

I whirled around to see the grin on the football player's face and I wanted to hurt someone. Instead, I ignored him and disappeared inside the girls' restroom to calm down. Big mistake. Standing near the mirrors were two cheerleaders. One was a girl my age, Kathleen Tracy. I've never really cared for Kathleen. The feeling was mutual.

Keeping their backs to me, I thought at first they were going to snub me as usual, something I appreciated. However, these two made it a point to talk loud enough so I could overhear their conversation.

"Don't you hate hypochondriacs?" the perky blonde said to Kathleen.

"Hypocrites, idiot," Kathleen hissed.

"Yeah, that." The younger girl giggled. "People who say one thing and do another. I really hate people like that."

"Me too," Kathleen confirmed. "Like Laurie Clark over there. She goes around, acting like she's such a goodie-goodie."

"Yeah, she's not so sweet after all," the blonde laughed. "She's like . . . really sour."

If I didn't know better, I would've thought this was a badly rehearsed scene from a play. Rolling my eyes, I was about to leave the restroom when Kathleen exclaimed, "Jared was so disgusted by how Laurie threw herself at him, he had to dump her during their date the other night. The poor guy had to go to the dance alone."

I froze in place. That was the story going around the high school? Furious, I could feel my hair standing on end.

The blonde struggled to remember her next line. "Yeah . . . she was, like, out of control or something. Jared should've taken you to the dance instead, huh?"

At least that partially explained Kathleen's intensity. She had obviously felt slighted by Jared. Well, as far as I was concerned, she could have him. But first I had to make a few things clear. Turning around, I marched over to where the redheaded cheerleader was wearing a smug smile. "Let's get something straight," I told Kathleen. "I dumped Jared. He's a Neanderthal, and if you want him, you can have him. But understand, he lies through his teeth if he doesn't get what he wants. He's making my life miserable because I wouldn't lower my standards to his."

"Yeah, well it's funny that even your *former* best friend backs up everything Jared has said about you," Kathleen snarled.

That did it. Now I was really mad. Too angry to make small talk with the cheerleaders, I stomped out of the restroom. It didn't take long to find Jared. Surrounded by an elite crowd, Jared was entertaining everyone with his sharp wit. I noticed Terrence and Roz were standing nearby, laughing at the clever remark he had just made. Caught up in laughing at his own joke, Jared didn't see me coming. Roz did, and for once, I saw fear in my former friend's eyes.

I didn't say a word. I simply marched up in front of Jared and slapped his face as hard as I could. Then I turned to glower at Roz and Terrence. Looking shocked, Roz stood her ground, but Terrence eased behind her for protection.

"That's what I should've done Saturday night after the three of you ruined my dress and hair," I exclaimed, hoping my words would carry down the hall. "Instead, I hid in the bathroom while you deserted me, leaving me stranded in Salt Lake City while you three went to the dance."

Jared held the side of his face. "You can't do this," he mumbled, using his tongue to check to see if his teeth were still attached.

"I just did, and I'm great at instant replays," I threatened, raising my hand. Jared backed off, still holding his cheek. I focused on my former friend. "Roz, I can understand Jared and Terrence spreading nasty rumors around—rumors that aren't true," I stated clearly, glancing around at the crowd that had gathered. "That's how they get a thrill out of life, making other people miserable. But you, Roz . . . why?" I asked, my voice finally breaking. Unable to meet my gaze, Roz stared down at the floor.

Sensing I was losing the edge my temper had inspired, Jared tried to reestablish his coolness by calling me the "B" word. Fortunately, the principal happened to walk by just then, and he doesn't take kindly to words of that nature. Jared was marched into the office for a little chat while I continued to stare at Roz. Made uncomfortable by the showdown, most of the crowd wandered away. Now it was just Roz, Terrence, and me.

"Roz?" I repeated, tears making an appearance. I noticed Roz was fighting the same battle.

"Leave me alone, all right," Roz said, running down the hall.

Terrence, careful to stay out of my reach, called me the same name Jared had used, then hurried after Roz. I stood alone, crying. I suppose it was a victory of sorts—not one I would ever celebrate. Turning, I walked out of the school and went for a long drive, too upset to attend my afternoon classes.

* * *

My drive took me up a portion of Ogden Canyon. I usually love seeing the fall colors. Now I came to the canyon for a different reason. Pulling into a picnic area, I left my car to sit on a nearby table. There I sobbed where only the wind and the colored leaves could hear me. Sympathizing, the breeze had increased, tangling my hair as I wept.

Unable to think, I sat for over an hour, too numb to feel the temperature drop. By the time I returned to my car, my body was pretty much frozen, but the sensation refused to penetrate my heart. In agony, I drove toward home, questions plaguing me on the way. How could things get any worse? How would I ever fix what had happened? My life was ruined, and I was certain I would never be able to return to school again.

As I drove past the Ogden temple grounds, I felt drawn toward the peace I knew existed in that sacred place. Turning the car around, I parked nearby and walked through the metal gate onto the sidewalk. I stared at the beautiful building. "Father, why is it so hard?" I whispered, gazing from the spire into the blue sky. "Why do I feel so alone?" A solitary tear wandered down the side of my face. I stood in place for several long seconds, and although clear answers did not come to mind, I did feel slightly better. Maybe I wasn't as alone as I thought.

I continued to stand there, pondering the mess that was my life. Images of the Savior came to mind, a reminder that I wasn't the only one who had walked a difficult path. He, too, had been mocked and scorned for standing up for the truth. He had been left alone when He had needed others the most. And He had suffered more than I could ever comprehend. Fresh tears filled my eyes as I experienced an inner warmth, a witness of the great love our Elder Brother feels for each one of us.

I'm not sure how long I remained in front of the temple. Several people walked past, probably thinking I had lost my mind as I stood transfixed by the comfort I was experiencing. Finally, I realized I needed to go home, knowing my mother would be worried. I walked back to my car, still shaken by what had taken place at school but sensing I would get through it somehow.

* * *

When I walked in the door, I struggled through a coughing fit—my outing had made my cold worse. Mom stood waiting in the kitchen. I was sure the school had called to report my absence. I expected a lecture but received a hug instead.

She asked one question, "Are you okay?" Wouldn't you know it was the question that always triggers tears.

For several minutes, I grieved over what I had lost. When the emotional storm passed, Mom led me into the living room and tried to help me sort through the pieces of my life. We agreed I could no longer count on Roz for any kind of friendship. Mom also stressed that I needed to keep my distance from Jared and Terrence. It hurt to see the look in her eyes when I told her what those two had called me. It was worse when I revealed the story that had been spreading throughout the school, one Roz had helped to create.

Suddenly, I could see where I had inherited my spunk as my mother made plans to call three sets of parents as well as to visit the school the next day and straighten everyone out. I pleaded with her to stay out of it, certain her help would only make things worse.

"Mom, I have to work through this myself," I stressed.

"You shouldn't have to deal with any of this," Mom exclaimed.

"No, I shouldn't," I replied, "but I don't have a choice."

"Are you sure?" Mom asked, reaching to brush my hair out of my eyes. "We could make arrangements to get you into a different school."

"I can't let these guys win," I countered. "If I stay away, then people will believe everything Roz, Jared, and Terrence tell them. If I'm there, day after day, maybe the others will realize what I stand for. Besides, maybe I can write an editorial about how quick people are to jump to the wrong conclusions. You know, the evils of gossip."

Joey began to cry, a signal he had awakened from his afternoon nap. Rising, Mom gazed down at me. "When did you get to be so grown up?"

Certain I wasn't, I was touched Mom felt that way. I almost smiled, but the memory of what I had endured at school clouded everything. How was I going to handle this disaster? The only thing I knew for sure was that I couldn't give up. I recalled a seminary lesson we had been taught not long ago. Brother Baker had commented that whenever something is important, it's stressed in the scriptures repeatedly. If it's in there at least three times, that means it's a precept we'd better heed. Then he had pointed out how often the scriptures tell us to endure to the end.

Thinking about this, I wandered down the hall to the bathroom and glanced at my reflection. The wind had snarled my hair into quite a mess. It took patience, but after several minutes of careful brushing, my hair settled into place. I gazed at the improvement and had an analogy come to mind. In my honors English class, we'd been learning about analogies and our teacher had asked us to watch for these kinds of things in everyday life. Standing there, I thought about how my life had been snarled into a mess. It would take a lot of patience, but maybe someday I would be able to work out the painful knots until everything fell into place.

Cheered a tiny bit by that thought, I shut off the bathroom light and went to help my mom fix dinner.

* * *

Hi Ed.

I'm sorry I haven't written for a few days. Things have been pretty crazy here. The homecoming dance was a disaster. Long story short—the guy I went out with was a real jerk. I never should have gone, but Roz talked me into it. I didn't really want to go, but I kept thinking I could keep her out of trouble. Only it turned out the other way—I'm the one who ended up in a whole mess of trouble. You see, we went to this restaurant called the Mayan . . .

Chapter 19

I wasn't feeling the greatest, but I decided that since I had missed church on Sunday, I had better make an appearance at Young Women Tuesday night so people in our ward didn't start thinking the Relief Society president's daughter had gone inactive. Besides, I wanted to see if the younger girls had heard any of the gossip that was going around school about me. I hoped they didn't believe a word of it, and I was in just the mood to kick their pants if they did.

Roz and I were the oldest Laurels in our ward. During girls' camp this summer, our Laurel leader, Kaye Dunning, had pulled the two of us aside to tell us how proud she was of the fine example we were setting for the younger girls. Kaye had then stressed how much it would mean if the two of us would share our testimonies that night around the fire. I had dutifully followed through on Kaye's request, but Roz had balked, telling me later that she wouldn't be forced into sharing anything. Even then, Roz had shown signs of rebellion, and I had missed it, passing it off as one of her mood swings.

I've heard my mom say that hindsight is always better. I never understood what she had tried to say until now. Now I could look back and remember several incidents when Roz had said or done something questionable; her change of heart hadn't occurred overnight. All those seeming-jokes Roz had been making about the Church, Young Women, Sunday School, and seminary lessons had been warning signs. Guilt descended upon me with a fury. I had been so caught up in my own concerns—mostly silly things, now that I thought about it—that I had been blind to the danger Roz had been in. Some friend I had been.

After opening exercises, as I continued to brood over the mistakes I had made, the young women of our ward were gathered into the gym. That night we were decorating cakes. I didn't feel much like participating. As I edged toward one of the gym doors to leave, Kaye caught me.

"Laurie, could we talk?"

I have a lot of respect for Sister Dunning, which is probably why I didn't bolt from the gym. Instead, I turned to face my Laurel leader. Kaye is not much taller than me, quite slender, and has medium-length brunette hair. She blends in with us so well, there are times when people think she's one of the girls she teaches.

"Since we've combined tonight with the other Young Women classes, there will be enough adult supervision going on in here," Kaye said, pointing to one of her counselors. "Let's head down the hall and find an empty classroom." Pushing the gym door open, she waited until I moved through before she followed me down the carpeted hall.

No doubt Kaye had heard the rumors that were circulating. I fervently hoped she wouldn't believe what was being said. It's not good if your Young Women president thinks you're being immoral. Not only would our class be subjected to yet another chastity chat, but I could count on meeting with the bishop in the near future too. Groaning, I entered an empty classroom and flipped on a light. Kaye stepped in behind me and closed the door. She pulled out a couple of chairs and motioned for me to choose one. Then she pulled her chair around to face me and sat down.

"Laurie, there are some stories going around," she began, and my heart sank. Surely Kaye would know me well enough to know those things weren't true. "I caught bits and pieces on Sunday. I've heard more details tonight from some of the younger girls."

Shaking my head, I couldn't look at her.

"I want you to know I understand what happened. Your mother talked to me after church on Sunday and told me what took place Saturday night."

I breathed a sigh of relief, grateful I wouldn't have to explain it all myself. For once I was glad Mom had interfered.

"I'm sorry things went so badly for you."

Kaye paused, and I straightened in my chair to look at her. At first, I thought she was trying not to cry. Then I caught on that she was fighting an urge to grin. "Did you really slap Jared Moulton across the face today like the girls told me?" she asked.

I shyly nodded.

"He had it coming," Kaye continued, still smiling. "I understand he's . . . not a very nice young man," she said, choosing her words carefully. "Normally I don't endorse violence, but between you and me—good job," she said, her brown eyes twinkling. "What did your dad think about what you did today?"

"That I stole all his fun," I admitted. "He really wants to get his hands on Jared."

"I'll bet," Kaye sympathized. "I could see my husband feeling the same way if we had daughters." Then she paused. "Laurie, I know you're going through a rough time, and it breaks my heart to see how you're suffering," she said, her smile drooping into a worried frown. "It also breaks my heart to think about Roz." At the mention of my former friend's name, Kaye teared up. "I've sensed for quite a while that Roz has been struggling. That's why I've tried to gear a few lessons around topics I thought would help, like the importance of maintaining our testimonies. It's also why I've stressed the standards in the Especially for Youth pamphlet lately, and why I didn't hold back anything during our last lesson on chastity."

I nodded, agreeing. Kaye's last lesson on that particular subject had rivaled my mother's when it came to being blunt and to the point. We had all exited the classroom looking as mortified as Kaye had been throughout the awkward lesson. It hadn't helped when a member of the bishopric had chosen that day to visit our class. I think he was more embarrassed than anyone else in the room.

"I noticed at girls' camp this year that Roz had brought along some interesting books to read," Kaye stated, gazing at me for confirmation. "She left one lying on her sleeping bag. When I poked my head inside the tent, I didn't like the looks of it."

I nodded, blushing as I thought about the suggestive covers on some of Roz's books.

"A while back, when I touched on the importance of avoiding inappropriate books, music—"

"Movies," I murmured, opening my eyes to meet Kaye's concerned expression.

"Movies too, huh?" Kaye repeated, folding her arms. "During that lesson, Roz had a defiant look on her face. I had a feeling then she was into some questionable stuff."

"It started this summer. She would rent movies that had some graphic scenes. I thought at first it was by mistake, that she didn't know what was in them. We always fast-forwarded through those parts."

"But they were still there," Kaye pointed out.

I slowly nodded. "We did walk out of a movie we went to see in a theater this summer," I said in our defense. Then I thought about the night Reese had tried to warn me—he had seen the danger of what was going on. No wonder he kept leaving messages for me in his letters. He was afraid I would slip into the same trap Roz had fallen into.

"How many times didn't you walk out?" Kaye asked.

I flushed again, thinking about the pay-per-view movie Roz had insisted that we watch before school had started. True, I had looked away during the scenes that had given it an R rating, but I should've stood up and gone home. Instead, I had sat there until Regina had come home and Roz had been forced to switch it off.

"Here's a good rule of thumb. I've shared it with you girls before. If you wouldn't feel comfortable having the Savior look over your shoulder whenever you read a book or watch a movie or surf the web, then leave it alone."

Kaye had told us that repeatedly. Isn't it funny how you shrug things off your leaders and parents stress, thinking they're being silly or overprotective? Now I cried, wishing I had listened.

"Laurie, I didn't want to make you feel worse," Kaye said, unfolding her arms. "I want you to know how proud I am of you for taking a stand for what's right. I know it's not an easy thing to do. It takes a lot of courage."

"But I should've done more. I should've stopped Roz," I tearfully exclaimed. "I never dreamed it would turn out like this."

"Roz has made her own decisions. You can't blame yourself for what's happened."

"But if I'd been a better friend—"

"You tried. You're not perfect—none of us is. But you have tried to be a good friend to Roz. I've seen that."

"She's always been there for me during times when most friends would've walked away. That's why this hurts so bad," I sniffed.

"I know," Kaye sympathized. "Do you think you can be there for her now? I know you have a lot to overlook and forgive, but someday she's going to need you. It may take her a while to realize it, but that day will come."

"Like when Stacy was there for Reese," I said quietly, understanding part of what those two had been through. Thanks to Stacy, Reese was now part of our family again. Thanks to Mom,

Reese had hung in there. Thanks to them both, he was currently serving a mission. Could I do the same for Roz?

"Until then, continue being a good example. Pray about it, and do the things that come to mind. You may be the only one who can reach Roz right now."

The realization of what Kaye was saying hit hard. I couldn't wallow in self-pity and nourish the anger I felt toward Roz. I had to let it go to help her.

"Tonight when you go home, if he hasn't already given you one, ask your dad for a father's blessing."

Dad and I had both been too upset to think about that option. I'm surprised Mom hadn't mentioned it on Sunday. Maybe she had been waiting for everyone to calm down.

"Laurie, you aren't alone in this trial," Kaye continued. "There are a lot of people in your corner, including me. I'm hitting a temple session tomorrow, and I plan to put both your names on the prayer roll while I'm there." Rising, Kaye drew me up into a brief hug. Then, making me promise to keep in touch regarding how things were going, she left me alone to think about the task that lay ahead.

* * *

Dad was really good about giving me a priesthood blessing later that night. He was glad that we had finally hit on something he could do to help. We waited until Mom had put Joey to bed, then the three of us gathered in the living room. Dad had me sit in one of the recliners, and when we were ready, he gave me a wonderful blessing that made all of us cry. Among other things, I was promised that if I would stand firm in my current path, I would be the means of helping those around me who were struggling. In my mind I saw an impression of Roz's beautiful face, and I felt certain she would be among those I might be able to help. Strengthened by this promise, I was able to sleep well through the night, too exhausted to dream.

* * *

Laurie, wow—you're really going through a bad time. I wish we lived closer. Not only would I try to cheer you up, but I'd teach Jared Moulton a lesson he wouldn't forget any time soon. And you're right. He's a total jerk. Stay away from him and from guys like him. They're no good. The bad thing is, they're every-where. There are guys like that on my football team and in our school here. And if any jerk ever treats my sisters like you were treated over the weekend . . . it'll get real ugly.

I'm sorry about Roz. It must hurt a lot to lose your best friend that way. Do you think she'll realize how wrong she is to turn her back on you?

You know, when I read your last e-mail, I couldn't help but compare you to Nephi. (Don't fall out of your chair. Yes, I'm finally reading that book you sent. It's actually pretty interesting.) Anyway, that must've been tough for Nephi to have to continuously fight against his big brothers. And like Roz, Laman and Lemuel should've known better. I mean, an angel appeared to them. What more did they need?

Do they ever figure things out? No, don't tell me. I want to read it for myself.

My dad saw me reading the Book of Mormon the other night. I don't think he was very happy about it.

He asked me where I got it, and I told him you had sent it to me. He didn't say much after that. He has a pretty high opinion of you—I told him how neat your family is and that you're always trying to stand up for the right thing. I've even shown him the editorials you've been writing for your school newspaper. That reminds me, thanks for sending me copies. I've enjoyed reading them. I think my favorite one was the first one you wrote about helping those in need. You did a great job with it.

Hey, maybe you can write something about what's going on in your high school right now. If anyone can make people think twice about it, you can.

Well, I'd better sign off. It's late, and I still have a trig assignment to finish up.

Write soon.
Ed

Chapter 20

School the next day was as bad as the day before. Actually, it was worse. The cheerleaders were more obnoxious, saying things they hoped would hurt my feelings. I tried to ignore them, but their cutting remarks still found their target. The football players were even more graphic with their crude exclamations and gestures whenever I walked by. To escape them, I entered classrooms and saw chalkboard messages that had been left for me by some of Jared's friends. I erased the vulgar words, but not before comments were made by those who had either written them or read what was there.

The final straw was my locker, which had once again been filled with pornographic pictures after my first-hour class. Fighting tears, I shredded the obscene images and threw them away, deciding this was the battle I would fight that day. Gathering my courage, I took my complaint to the vice principal.

A woman about my mother's age, Mrs. Vance was shocked by what I told her during lunch break. I had brought the only picture I hadn't torn up as evidence of what I was finding inside my locker. When I handed it to her, the tall, blonde woman turned pale, then looked like she was going to be sick before she tore the offending picture into pieces and threw it into the wastebasket beside her desk. When I asked to be reassigned to a different locker and that the combination be kept secret to prevent this harassment from continuing, she agreed. She also stated she would like to catch whoever was doing this, that it went against school policy, and that these students should be punished. I knew who the guilty parties were, but I also knew it would only make things worse if I pushed the issue. I had purposely not used anyone's names, knowing it would have hurt Roz. I wouldn't have had a problem turning in Jared and Terrence, two people I knew were behind the pictures, but revealing their names would have led to trouble for Roz, and I figured she was in over her head as it was. As I pondered her dilemma, my near-drowning experience in San Diego came to mind. When the current had dragged me along, I had been unable to resist the crushing waves. Was Roz feeling like that now? In a way, I hoped she was—it meant there was still hope. It meant she could still feel remorse.

While I silently contemplated the mess Roz had dragged us into, Mrs. Vance looked through the computer files and found a locker that wasn't being used. It was located between the junior and sophomore lockers, but I didn't care. The inconvenience was worth the peace of mind I would gain from moving.

When I went back to my locker with the empty box Mrs. Vance had given me to load my books into, I wasn't amused to find that it had been filled with gross pictures again. Hopefully this was the last time I would have to shred and discard pictures of this nature.

"Hey, Laurie, don't be greedy, girl. Share some of those with us."

I turned to glare at one of Jared's football friends. That was my only response. There were no words to convey how I actually felt, at least not words I would choose to use. Ignoring him as he continued to mock me, I emptied the locker of the obscene computer printouts, then began stuffing my books and binders into the box Mrs. Vance had given me to use.

"Knock it off," I heard someone say to the football player who was still giving me a bad time.

I glanced over my shoulder and saw that my defender was none other than Todd Napier, the quarterback for our football team. I didn't know Todd very well. He was cute but shy. His hair was coal black, and while he wasn't overly tall, he was very muscular.

His teammate protested Todd's involvement. "What's your problem, dude? I was just—"

"I know what you were doing. Cool it," Todd threatened. He wasn't as big as my tormenter, but the other guy backed off and walked away. "Could you use some help?" Todd asked, gesturing to the box I had nearly filled.

"Sure," I stammered, wondering why Todd was being nice to me.

"I feel bad about yesterday," he said, stepping closer.

Todd had been one of those to see me slap Jared. Still uncertain of the quarterback's motives, I handed him a book to set inside the box.

"It took a lot of courage to stand up to Jared," Todd continued, looking uncomfortable. I figured it was because he was standing beside me. People who used to talk to me were currently keeping their distance, fearing the fallout would affect them.

"That's it," I said, glancing at the empty locker. Someone had already removed my favorite quotes and the picture of the Savior. In a way I was glad. It didn't seem right to have the Savior's picture next to the filth that had been invading my locker lately. I secretly hoped Roz had been the one to take those items. Maybe they would eventually have an influence on her.

"Laurie, I should've said something yesterday," Todd continued.

Rising to my feet, I gazed at him. What was he getting at? Was he really trying to apologize?

"Jared was wrong to say those things about you. I knew it couldn't be true. You're not that kind of girl."

He caught me so off guard, I almost burst into tears.

"Jared's a self-centered jerk," Todd said, picking up my box. I knew it was heavy, but when I offered to help him carry it, he refused. Maybe he thought this was his penance for not sticking up for me yesterday. "You're not leaving the school?" he asked as we walked along.

"No, I'm switching lockers. Someone's been putting some awful things in that one."

"Let me guess . . . Jared?"

"Hey, Todd, tryin' to get in good with Jared's girl?" one of Jared's friends crowed.

"These guys are pushing it," Todd growled. "It's time we turned this around."

"I feel the same way," I agreed. "But I'm afraid we're outnumbered."

"That hasn't stopped you from striking back," he said, smiling. Todd had a nice smile. It reminded me of Ed's.

"Yeah, well—I heard what was going around, and it made me furious. Especially after what happened Saturday night—"

"What did happen?" Todd asked. "I heard Jared's version. I'd like to hear what really took place."

By then, we had reached my new locker. I motioned for Todd to set the box down and thanked him for helping me. Then I glanced at the paper Mrs. Vance had given me, and after my second try at the combination, I popped it open. Still debating over the wisdom of telling Todd the details of Saturday night, I glanced at him again. Was he setting me up, or was he being sincere? There was only one way to find out. So as he helped me organize my new locker, I told him what had taken place during my Mayan adventure. When I finished, he shook his head.

"That figures. Only Jared would be that cruel."

"He wasn't alone. Terrence was right there with him. And Roz certainly didn't do anything to stop them."

Todd frowned. "I always thought Roz was like you—you were two girls who weren't afraid to stand up for what was right."

Biting my lip to keep it from trembling, I couldn't answer for several pain-filled seconds. "The Roz I used to know was just like that."

"What changed?" he asked, a sympathetic look on his face.

"A lot of things," I managed to say. "But I'm not giving up. Somehow I'll get through to Roz—even if I have to tear Terrence and Jared into tiny pieces to get to her."

"If you need extra help with that, let me know," Todd said as the bell rang. "I'd love to deflate those two idiots." He glanced at his watch and winced. "And now I'd better hurry. I have strength-training this hour, and it's on the other side of the school."

"Thanks again," I said as he hurried down the hall. A tiny surge of hope warmed my heart. Smiling, I reached for my English book and hurried to class before the tardy bell rang.

* * *

When I got home, Mom asked about my day. I left out most of what had taken place, knowing it would just upset her. Avoiding what I had been subjected to, I told her about Todd and how nice he had been to me. Brightening, Mom asked me to babysit Joey, stressing she had a Relief Society errand to run. I didn't ask any questions, figuring it was none of my business. I should have asked.

The errand she set out on was to go see Regina, Roz's mother. Mom counted it as a Relief Society errand because she's in our ward. Unfortunately, the visit didn't go well. I know this because of the way my mother was fuming about it nearly two hours later when she returned home. I caught a couple of snatches, and I knew exactly what Mom had been up to. I demanded an explanation, and this is what she told me.

She began by emphasizing she'd had the best of intentions. Mom had figured if she talked to Regina about what was going on, it would help smooth things between Roz and me. Mom also said that if the tables were turned, she would want Regina to tell her if I were heading for trouble. Evidently Regina hadn't felt the same way. It took some persuasion on my part, but Mom finally told me everything.

I about died when she admitted she had gone to Regina's office. Now remember, Regina is a busy, successful lawyer. She works as an associate in an Ogden law firm. Choosing that setting for this conversation probably wasn't the best idea, but in my mother's defense, she didn't want to bother Regina at home, and she didn't want Roz to overhear anything that was said. So she bothered Regina at the office instead. Not good.

Now Regina was obviously aware there were problems between Roz and me. Most parents will side with their children, and Regina was no exception to this rule. So when Mom commented that she wished Roz and I could talk things out, Regina let my mother know there was nothing more for Roz to say. I could tell Mom was toning down what had actually been said, but I gathered Regina hadn't been very complimentary toward me.

Again, I haven't been a perfect teen. After Allison's death, I'll admit I was kind of self-centered. Sometimes I tended to be negative. I know Roz put up with a lot. But I've changed. So has Roz. It's almost like we've switched places, and now I'm the strong one. Weird, huh?

Back to Mom's story. Regina managed to tick off my mother, so Mom told her that Roz and I weren't getting along because Roz was hanging out with a wild crowd. That went over big. Regina let Mom know she had met Terrence, and in her opinion, he was a nice young man. When Mom told me that part, I wondered what Regina's response would have been if she had witnessed what I had seen the night of the homecoming dance.

Anyway, Regina got in a snit and informed my mother that I was jealous of Roz's popularity. Then, before she escorted my mother from her office, Regina exclaimed that I needed intense therapy. I don't think Mom meant to blurt that out in front of me, but she got caught up in the story and shared it anyway. Bottom line, now Regina and Mom are feuding. A big help.

"Honey, I'm sorry," Mom apologized when she finished telling me what had taken place. "I'm afraid I made things worse."

I agreed but knew it wouldn't be a good idea to say that out loud. I murmured that it would be all right, then I wandered into the study to check my e-mail. I sat down in front of the computer and connected to the internet. While I waited, I gazed at the picture I was now using for my personal wallpaper, the one of Ed and me in San Diego—definitely a happier time.

It made my day to find I had an e-mail from Ed waiting to be read. I also perked up over how far he had read in the Book of Mormon I had sent him. Shivers raced up my spine as I contemplated where this could lead. Surely Ed would embrace the truthfulness of the gospel. And he would make such a good Mormon. Of course, his parents might not feel that way.

Sighing, I reread Ed's message, then wrote one to him.

Dear Ed,

Your e-mail was a welcome relief after today's adventures. Did I tell you what I keep finding in my locker? Some people are so crude. So here's what I did to stop it . . .

* * *

After I sent off my e-mail message to Ed, I checked my inbox again to see if I had received anything from Reese. I was disappointed to see he hadn't sent anything yet. His e-mails had become a lifeline for me. Like Ed's. They both seem to know exactly what I need to hear.

Frowning, I noticed that I had received four e-mails from people I didn't know. I've learned to be cautious about e-mails like that—Roz's new friends have been sending me garbage since Sunday, thinking it's funny. And that's exactly what those e-mails were, disgusting items I deleted as soon as I saw what they were. Just as I sent them to die in cyberspace, a new e-mail popped into my box. This time it was from Roz. I was hesitant to open it, certain it wouldn't be a positive boost like Ed's. It wasn't.

Laurie,

Getting your mother to yell at mine is probably the stupidest thing you've ever done, and you've done plenty of other stupid things—I should know! Back off and keep your nose where it belongs, in the center of your pathetic face.

Nice. Just what I needed, another friendly pep talk, compliments of Roz. Shaking my head, I closed out of my e-mail account, walked out of the study, and headed into my bedroom to work on my homework.

Chapter 21

LAURIE'S VIEW

Over two hundred years ago, a tyrant overstepped his bounds. When our forefathers saw that their freedom was at stake, they banded together, and though their numbers were small in comparison to their foes, they fought back and achieved victory when most believed they would face defeat. And because of the effort they made, a new country was born.

Now here we are, facing our own time when we must have the courage and honor to take a stand. Are we as brave as our ancestors? Can we band together against a plague that is destroying the spirit of this school? Things are far from well within the walls of Roy High. A handful of people are running it into the ground, and most of us are standing idly by, watching it happen.

Is it right that a few people dictate how the rest of us act? That we live in fear of what they may do or say? They destroy others' lives with their pointed acts of cruelty and gossip. It has become an out-of-control fire. It started with a tiny spark, and because most of us ignored it, it is roaring into a raging inferno, consuming everything in sight.

I doubt that is what most of us truly want. None of us wishes to be burned. But how many of us are heaping fuel on the fire? How many are standing idly by, too apathetic to care? It's time to take a courageous stand and work together to squelch the flames that are threatening our school.

You may think I'm being overdramatic. You may think this doesn't affect you. And maybe it doesn't now. But how long before it does? How long before people snicker at you as you walk down the hall? How long before those you once thought were your friends talk about you behind your back?

The choice is ours. We must all become part of the solution. We can no longer allow one small group to control how we behave and what we believe. We must take back our school.

* * *

The following Monday, as I walked from the parking lot to the school, I spotted Roz coming from the other direction. She hadn't been coming to church lately, so school was about the only chance I got to see her. For once, Terrence wasn't hanging on her. I decided it was worth trying to talk to her. "Roz," I called out. Roz looked up at me, then hurried faster toward the school. Hurt by this deliberate action, I slowed to kick at the dried leaves that were scattered across the browning lawn.

Glancing up, I watched as Roz entered the school. Being ignored by her was bad enough. The stories I had been hearing about her hurt more. I had tried to refute them, but most people laughed and told me I didn't know what I was talking about. It stung to realize they were right—I didn't know Roz anymore. For years we had shared secrets and giggles, plans for the future, and hidden sorrows. Now we were separated by an emotional canyon that threatened to engulf us both.

"Hey, Laurie," a deep male voice called out.

Startled, I jumped, dismayed to see Jared coming up behind me. "What do you want?"

"I think you know," he said, grinning as his eyes wandered over my body.

Shuddering, I glared at him. "Leave me alone."

"You don't want to be left alone or you never would've written that stupid editorial," Jared replied. "It was like sending me an open invitation."

"Jared, it must be nice to live in your own little world where everything revolves around you." From the blank look on his face, I doubted he understood what I was saying. Sighing, I turned back around and headed toward the school.

"I'm not as bad as you think," he said, following me onto the sidewalk. "In fact, most girls would give anything to go out with me."

"I'm not most girls," I replied.

"I know. That's why I like you and why I'm willing to give you another chance."

"Look, Jared, you're not getting what I'm saying—"

"No, you're not getting what I'm saying," he countered. "I'm having a party Friday night after the game. My house. No parents. They'll be gone for the weekend. It'll be a good time. Lots of people will be there, including you."

"I'm not interested—"

"Roz will be there."

"Roz?"

"Yeah. She told Terrence that if you came to this party, she'd start speaking to you again."

"Right," I said dryly.

"Your loss," Jared replied. "But if you care about your friend, you might want to come."

"Why?"

"Terrence is making his move on Friday night."

Something inside me snapped. Jared didn't care about Roz. And as for Roz, she had made it next to impossible for me to help her out of the pit she had fallen into. "Well, I heard Terrence has already made his move, so why should it matter if I'm there or not?"

"She's your friend. I thought you might want to know. We LDS types have to stick together," Jared added as he walked away. "Friday night. My place. 10 P.M. Be there."

"Dream on," I exclaimed before I stormed inside the school. Who did this guy think he was? *We LDS types?* Since when had being LDS meant anything to him? And what made him think I would have anything to do with him—ever?

As I walked down the hall, I tried to calm down. Turning Jared down—again—was asking for more trouble. But what choice did I have? Envisioning continued persecution, I groaned. Last week had been an adventure in humility as it was. The letters that had been directed toward my fiery editorial had been less than supportive. Jared's elite friends were still doing their best to make my life miserable. For now, they couldn't get into my new locker. But that hadn't stopped them from taping pictures of refrigerators and ice cubes all over the outside of it, as well as several suggestive words that had been cut and pasted into place on my locker door. A nice touch I removed every day. That wasn't all I had endured lately.

Todd had told me about what had been etched into the doors of the stalls in the boys' restroom last Friday. I'm sure Roz had given my phone number to whoever had written the message. As a result, we had received several obscene phone calls over the weekend. After the first two calls, made from pay phones to avoid detection, I had quit answering the phone. Mom had taken the next call, which hadn't been good. The caller (I'm betting it was Jared) had assumed it was me since our voices are similar. So Mom caught an earful of gross obscenities before she slammed the phone down. She immediately called the police to report it, but since we couldn't give them a personal phone number to trace, nothing could be done. We began looking carefully at the caller ID before answering.

Dad had been furious about the phone calls. After he had returned home that night, he had waited until the caller ID had revealed that it was another call from a payphone. Picking it up, he had blown a whistle into the phone, effectively ending the problem. Dad had grinned, pleased with himself over his retaliation. Even though Mom had scolded him about his behavior, I could tell her heart hadn't been in it. She had been secretly pleased we had struck back.

When I told Todd what had been going on, he had offered to paint over what had been carved into the old paint of the bathroom stalls. I told him it wouldn't matter; a new message would appear in spite of his efforts.

It was nice to know I had at least one friend. Todd had been making it a point to watch for me when I entered the school so he could escort me through the halls. He also started sitting with me during lunch so I wouldn't have to eat alone. Todd assured me there were others who were just as upset as he was over what was going on, but as far as I could see, he was the only one brave enough to take a public stand.

Unfortunately, he paid dearly for trying to help me. During our next home football game that Friday night, it soon became apparent the offensive line was out to teach Todd a lesson, no doubt under Jared's supervision. I noticed that instead of getting clear to receive the ball from Todd, Jared made himself scarce. While Todd frantically looked around for someone else to take the ball, the other team repeatedly broke through to sack him, plowing through our line with ease. Each time Todd was hit, a part of me died. I was glad when the coach finally called a time-out to lecture the team. I'm not sure what was said in that heated huddle, but it didn't make any difference. The next time Todd went out to play quarterback, a defensive lineman from the other squad broke through without any trouble and hit him hard in the chest. I heard someone holler that Todd had been speared and the refs called an illegal procedure on the other team. They should have called it on ours. It was their fault Todd had been hurt.

Todd didn't get back up to acknowledge the yards that had been gained for our team. The coaches ran out onto the field and soon an ambulance drove down. I moved as close as I could get to the field, crying. A woman standing next to me looked even more upset than I felt. From the color of her raven hair, I figured it was Todd's mother. She pushed her way past where I was standing to run onto the field, and a man I assumed was her husband was right behind her.

That's when I saw Roz. She looked sick. Turning, she saw me and, for a moment, acted like she wanted to say something. Bursting into tears, she disappeared into the crowd. I probably should have gone after her, but I was too concerned about Todd.

I glanced around and saw that the other team had had the decency to kneel with their helmets removed as the EMTs worked on Todd. I was ashamed to see that only half of our football players paid Todd a similar tribute. Among those who remained standing was Jared. Still wearing his helmet, the number on his shirt stood out, number 1, an ironic symbol.

Todd was loaded into the ambulance and his mother was allowed to ride with him. I watched as his dad climbed up front with one of the EMTs. Then the ambulance flashed on its lights and drove away.

"That makes me so mad," I heard someone remark. Turning, I saw the head cheerleader of our school, Susie Hansen. The petite brunette was crying, pointing toward our football team. "You bunch of jerks," she exclaimed. "You don't deserve cheers," she continued. She glanced at me. I expected her to say this was my fault. Instead, she moved to where I was crying and gave me a hug. "C'mon, Laurie. Let's get out of here."

She led me through the crowd. What neither of us realized was that half the crowd was following us away from the football field, disgusted by the poor sportsmanship our team had shown. Susie guided me to her car and said that she would drive us both to the hospital to see how Todd was doing. On the way to McKay-Dee, Susie cranked up the heat to warm us up. I was shivering, but it had more to do with what I was feeling than how cold it was.

"Laurie, I'm sorry I haven't talked to you before. I've wanted to . . . I should've. I knew what was going on—I think a lot of us did."

Susie spoke haltingly, as though what she was saying was difficult. I soon learned why when she said these words. "I went out with Jared once . . . last year. There's a reason his nickname is Handsy, and it has nothing to do with how well he catches the football when Todd throws it to him."

Numb, I nodded. All I could focus on was the knowledge that Todd had been hurt because of me.

"A couple of weeks ago, when I walked down the hall and saw you slap Jared, well, I really wanted to cheer. And I loved your editorial last week. I should've told you that before now."

"You only went out with him once," I murmured, about three sentences behind Susie.

"Yeah, that was enough for me. And trust me—things didn't go as far as he wanted everyone to believe then, either."

"Why does he do this?"

"I don't know. He's a real piece of work. But I think most of us have had it with him. And after tonight, he's the one who had better watch his step. The rest of us are through watching ours."

We drove in silence the rest of the way to the new hospital. Driving past what was left of the old McKay-Dee, Susie turned into the new IHC facility and drove quickly into the visitors' parking lot. We found a place to park and hurried out of Susie's car.

"At least I'm wearing the sweat-suit version of this outfit," Susie said, looking down at her cheerleader apparel.

"You look fine," I mumbled as we walked toward the hospital.

"You don't," Susie commented. "Are you feeling okay?"

"No," I replied. "But I won't until I know Todd's all right."

"Todd's a great guy," Susie said. "We've dated a few times—he's nothing like Jared."

Nodding, I shouldn't have been surprised. Someone as nice and good-looking as Todd would obviously have a girlfriend. It hit me like a ton of bricks, however, as did the realization that I was only a charity case to them both—someone to be pitied and taken care of like a stray puppy.

"C'mon, let's go find out how Todd's doing," Susie encouraged as we walked through the automated doors into the hospital.

It took some doing, but we finally located Todd's parents on the first floor near the ER.

"How's Todd?" Susie asked Todd's mother.

"It's his sternum," the woman replied. "It's probably broken. They're getting ready to take an X-ray to see how bad it is. They may have to do a CT scan to get a clearer picture." She looked at me curiously.

"Oh . . . uh . . . Mrs. Napier, this is Laurie Clark. One of Todd's friends."

"I keep telling you to call me Nancy," Todd's mother said to Susie. "It's nice to meet you, Laurie."

Unable to express myself coherently, I merely nodded. Worry over Todd and the feeling that I was intruding on a private family moment clashed. But I did want to know if Todd was going to be okay.

At that moment, Todd was wheeled out of the ER by a couple of nurses. Pale, his eyes were closed, and he quietly moaned, causing me more distress. His parents quickly moved to his side and walked with their son as he was wheeled down the hall on his way to radiology.

"Laurie, Nancy said for us to wait in the lobby. She'll come talk to us after they know what's going on with Todd."

Again I followed Susie. When we reached the lobby, I think we were both surprised to see how many kids from our school had gathered there. Nearly forty students were milling around, waiting for news.

"Susie, how's Todd?" someone called out.

"He's in a lot of pain. They think his sternum is broken," Susie replied.

"Man," a deep male voice exclaimed, "he's the only decent quarterback on our team."

"Yeah, well, you can thank Jared Moulton for what's happened," Susie said, her temper flaring again.

"He's not the one responsible for this." Kathleen Tracy stepped forward. Certain I knew what the redheaded cheerleader was going to say next, I squared my shoulders for the impact.

Susie must've thought the same thing. She moved in front of me and glowered at Kathleen. "Laurie had nothing to do with this, and if any of you are thinking that, you should be ashamed of yourselves."

"But she—" Kathleen stammered, pointing at me.

"Laurie is a wonderful person, and she hasn't deserved how some of you have been treating her. You all know how Jared lies about everything, how he's always trying to make himself look better at the expense of someone else. I should know—look what he put me through last year. I know exactly what Laurie is going through, and it needs to stop. Just like Laurie said in her editorial."

I blinked rapidly. Susie had been through this same kind of treatment? Where had I been? Who had helped Susie? Lowering my head, I chided myself again for being so caught up in my own life I had blocked out what was going on around me. I suspect a lot of us are guilty of that offense.

I moved out from behind my protector and faced my peers. "I'm sure Todd was hurt tonight because he's been trying to help me," I said, trying to control the tremor in my voice. "No one knows how bad I feel about that—" As hard as I tried, I couldn't stop the tears from flowing freely down my face. "But you were there tonight . . . You saw what happened out on that field."

"Todd was hurt because of you," Kathleen hissed.

Before I could react, Susie shoved Kathleen hard in the chest. "Back off," she said sharply. "Todd was hurt because we've let Jared and his group control our school for far too long. It stops now." Her brown eyes flashed with rage as she openly defied Kathleen and anyone who challenged her. "If you're truly concerned about Todd, you're welcome to stay. If you just stopped off on your way to Jared's party, you can leave. We don't need you here."

I heard several mutterings, and someone called Susie the same name Jared had called me a couple of weeks ago. Then, with Kathleen leading the way, about half of those who had gathered left the hospital. The rest stayed, which to my way of thinking was a small victory. These were people who were siding with Susie, and possibly with me. I glanced around at the twenty or so students who remained. Among them was the perky blonde cheerleader who had taken part in the restroom drama a couple of weeks ago. A sophomore, it was good to see she was going to follow Susie's example instead of Kathleen's.

The perky blonde approached me, acting timid. "Laurie, I'm sorry about the other day. Kathleen told me some stuff. I didn't know she was lying. Susie straightened me out about it last week," she apologized.

Susie had been sticking up for me before tonight? Then I remembered what Todd had said earlier this week—that there were others who were upset over what Jared had been doing. I glanced at Susie, who was now talking with some of the students who had stayed. Swallowing a lump in my throat, I refocused on the blonde cheerleader and told her not to worry about what had happened. I endured an awkward hug from her, then sat in a nearby chair to wait for word on Todd.

Chapter 22

Mom went with me to the hospital the next day. Todd's sternum had been fractured in half, and it would require surgery to pin it back together. I felt I owed it to him to at least wait at the hospital until I knew the surgery had gone well. When Mom and I arrived, we found that Susie Hansen was already there, sitting with Todd's parents. I still felt awkward around Susie, not to mention Todd's parents, but they warmly welcomed Mom and me and invited us to join them in the waiting room. Introductions were made. We asked about Todd and learned that despite everything he was going through, he was in good spirits. Mom smiled tearfully at Nancy and Kyle Napier and thanked them for raising such a valiant young man.

"You'll never know how much it has meant to Laurie, and to her father and me, that someone like Todd would try to help her."

"After Todd saw what Jared put Susie through last year, he said he would never just stand idly by if it happened to someone else," Nancy replied.

"Todd helped me more than he thinks," Susie contributed. "He was my friend when no one else would be seen with me."

I nodded. Todd had done that for me too. I found my thoughts wandering to Ed. Ed would've done the same thing—he was that kind of guy. It was good to know there were still decent young men in the world like Todd and Ed. The others like Jared tended to hog the limelight, but there were still quiet, good works taking place in the world. That knowledge gave me a warm feeling inside.

It didn't take long for my mother to feel right at home visiting with the Napiers. While they chatted, Susie moved to sit closer to me and tried to strike up a conversation. It felt weird at first—a word here and there as we each struggled for something to say. Then Susie asked me about the night of the homecoming dance. As I explained the events of that evening, she sympathized, especially over what had transpired between Roz and me.

"You two have been so close," she observed. "This must be killing you."

I nodded. That particular pain went too deep to share. Instead, I forced a smile and said, "You mentioned last night that Jared had been awful to you last year."

"Oh, yeah," Susie replied. "Mostly nasty items I found stuffed inside my locker," she said, flushing. "Gross comments from the basketball team—the team Jared was playing with at the time."

"So this is how he always acts," I mused.

"Only to those of us who turn him down," Susie responded. "Why do you think he gets his way so much of the time? People live in fear of what he tries to do."

I thought of Roz. Was she trapped by that fear? I felt sick as I thought about the poor choices my friend had made.

"That's why we need to put Jared in his place. He and his goons have gotten away with too much the past couple of years. Like I said last night, it needs to stop."

I nodded. "I just wish Todd hadn't been hurt."

Susie gazed steadily at me. "Quit blaming yourself. Jared did this, and Jared will answer for it. I've already heard he'll be suspended from school for what he pulled last night. A couple of the football players told the coach Jared had asked the team to let Todd get hurt. The coach was so upset, he took it to the principal, who in turn called the school board."

"Really?"

"Uh-huh. I know cuz my dad's on the school board." Susie grinned, and it was contagious. "I think a lot of things are going to come out during the next few days that will make Jared's life as miserable as he ever made anyone else's."

Liking that plan, I leaned back in my chair and listened as Susie listed the grievances she knew would be thrown at Jared.

* * *

That night, I returned to the hospital with Susie. The surgery had gone well, and Todd would eventually make a full recovery. When I heard that news, I was so relieved, I started to cry. Todd's mother gave me a hug and told me to quit worrying, assuring me that they didn't hold me responsible for his injury. I suspected Susie had told them how bad I felt, but it was good to hear that Todd's parents didn't blame me.

The night before, Dad had a long talk with me, reminding me that we aren't responsible for what others choose to do. I knew he was not only talking about the football game, but also about Roz. He stressed that we can't control the choices other people make—we can only control ourselves. I couldn't have stopped what happened Friday night. Jared was the one who had chosen to hurt Todd, something I would've never wished on anyone.

As Susie and I rode in the elevator that would lead us to the floor where Todd's room was, I felt a mixture of excitement to finally talk to him and a stab of anxiety over how he would feel about me after all of this. I appreciated Susie's invitation to come with her. It would have been difficult coming on my own. On our way to the hospital, we had stopped to pick up some balloons for Todd that wished him a speedy recovery. We had also selected humorous get-well cards. In mine, I thanked him for being so willing to stand by my side during this difficult time, and I promised to always be there for him.

When we walked into Todd's room, his parents as well as his two younger brothers were already keeping him entertained. Nancy Napier smiled when she saw the two of us and motioned for us to come in.

"Hi, girls," Todd said, still looking pale. He grinned, gesturing to the balloons. "Look what they brought me."

"Hey, big guy," Susie said, as she tied the balloons to the head of his hospital bed. She reached to take his hand, and only a dolt would've missed the chemistry that fired between them.

Shortly after that, Todd's parents kissed their son good-bye, then made an exit, dragging their two younger sons with them. I was tempted to make my escape with them, but Susie and Todd asked me to sit in a chair near his bed. Susie sat on a chair on the other side of his bed, still holding his hand.

So I sat, looking as uncomfortable as I felt. "Todd," I stammered, "I'm sorry about this."

"Like it's your fault," Todd said, laughing as he tucked his free hand behind his head. "Laurie, we all know who to blame for this, and it isn't you."

"Still, this never would've happened—"

"Don't sweat it," he advised. "Friends stick together, right?"

Biting my bottom lip, I nodded.

"And we're friends," he emphasized. "Now, catch me up on what's going on. Mom and Dad told me a few things, but I was kind of groggy earlier."

Smiling, Susie told Todd what she had shared with me earlier that day, and Todd laughed when he heard that Jared was in big trouble.

"Couldn't happen to a nicer guy." Todd glanced at me. "What do you think, Laurie?"

"I agree," I answered. "But I would still like to see him humiliated in a very public way."

"Ditto," Susie agreed.

"Hey, you two, that's stooping to his level," Todd cautioned.

"So what's your plan?" Susie asked, laughing.

The rest of the visit was light and fun, and I was glad I had come. When it was time to go, I stepped out into the hall to give Todd and Susie some privacy. Grateful for the way they had fellowshipped me, I found my thoughts wandering to Roz. Would I ever be able to rebuild that friendship? I understood now that despite my best efforts, a lot of that would depend on her.

* * *

Laurie, I can't believe everything you're going through right now. It's like the more you try to do the right thing, the worse it gets. Kind of like here. I've read through the entire Book of Mormon, and I know it's true. But my parents don't want to hear it.

I drove up to check out Nauvoo, like you suggested. What a cool place. And you're right, there's a special feeling in that area. I wish you could come see it with me.

I even drove over to Carthage to take a look at the jail, and after I saw the actual room where Joseph Smith was shot and killed, I felt overwhelmed. I'm not sure I can put it into words, but it's an experience I will never forget.

Laurie, I want to take the missionary discussions, but I'm not sure how to do it without upsetting my parents more than they already are. This is so hard. Then I

read about what you're enduring and I feel ashamed. I
wish I were as brave as you . . . and Todd. I hope he'll
be okay. Know I'm saying prayers for both of you.
Hang in there, and thank you for being such a source
of inspiration in my life.

Ed

* * *

When I returned home, I walked into Dad's study, determined to catch up on my e-mail. I reread the latest e-mail from
Ed—pleased that his testimony of the gospel was growing, but
saddened that his parents weren't being very supportive. I began
typing an e-mail to him, telling him how neat I thought it was
that he was trying so hard to gain a testimony. I also stressed
that sometimes, even when we're trying to do the right thing,
we can be hit with all kinds of challenges, emphasizing that it's
part of the test of this life. Then I bore my testimony that I
knew, despite everything, that we are beloved children of God
and that we are always watched over. I also stated that eventually all things can work for our good, if we'll let them.

I reread the last e-mail Reese had sent me. I knew Mom and
Dad had kept him updated concerning my current situation.
That was obvious from the way Reese offered me advice on how
to deal with people like Jared. His suggestion to have Dad box
Jared up to send to the St. Louis Zoo still made me smile. I
typed my brother a quick e-mail to let him know things were
improving. Then I shared the events of the past two days. I sent
it off, then looked at my inbox. There were three new e-mails. I
deleted two without giving them another thought. Evidently
Jared was still up to his old tricks.

The third e-mail was from Roz. I debated over it for a few
seconds, then finally opened it to see what she wanted.

Laurie,

I want you to know that I had nothing to do with what happened Friday night. Terrence had said that they were going to get even with Todd because of how he's tried to stick up for you. I didn't know it would be something like this.

I know you probably won't believe me—but I am sorry Todd was hurt.

Roz

I sat and stared at the computer screen. Then I cried for several minutes as I tried to sort through how I felt. Confused, I finally shut off the computer and went to bed, but it was hours before I could finally fall asleep.

Chapter 23

After Young Women the next morning, my Laurel leader called to me before I left our classroom.

"How are things going?" Kaye asked as she finished erasing the chalkboard.

"You probably heard about Todd," I replied.

She nodded. "It was so unnecessary." Setting the eraser on the tray in front of the blackboard, she dusted off her hands and gazed at me.

"Yeah. Not only is Todd through with football, but he told me last night he probably won't get to wrestle this year either."

"I hope Jared's proud of himself."

I told her what Susie had said about Jared's possible suspension from school, and Kaye was glad to hear it.

"It's the very least that should happen to that young man," Kaye responded. "Are Todd's parents going to press charges?"

"I doubt it. They're upset, but they said they'd let the school board handle things."

"I hope the school board throws the book at him," Kaye commented.

I half smiled. If Susie's father knew everything Jared had pulled on her last year, it was a guarantee.

"I noticed Roz didn't come to church again today."

"Yeah," I said quietly. Then I told her about the e-mail Roz had sent last night. "It's a start."

"Maybe a cry for help," Kaye mused. "All those prayers on her behalf have got to start kicking in eventually." She smiled at me. "I'm proud of you for hanging in there. I know you've had a rough month."

"Things are going better," I said, thinking of my new friends. Susie had invited me to come over to her house after school the next day to work on a science project that was due this week. I was looking forward to it.

I promised Kaye I would keep in touch, then, certain my parents would be waiting for me, I left the classroom. I wandered out into the hall and saw Mom talking to Regina Whiting.

Frowning, I wondered if they were arguing again. I hesitantly took a step forward, then paused when Regina totally lost it. Mom embraced her, holding her tight for several seconds before she guided Roz's mother into a classroom for privacy.

Had Regina finally caught on to what Roz had been doing? Was it as bad as I feared? I leaned against the wall and closed my eyes.

Bouncing Joey in his arms, Dad found me a few minutes later. He usually tends Joey during Relief Society, calling it his male-bonding time with my younger brother. "Hey, where's your mother?" he asked, holding Joey out to me.

I gave Joey a quick hug, and he slobbered all over my cheek. Wiping it off, I told Dad that Mom was busy and we should go home and finish getting dinner ready. He liked that idea, but he was worried about leaving Mom stranded at the church as we had all ridden to church together that morning. I figured Regina had probably driven herself to church, as I had noticed earlier she had come alone for sacrament meeting. I told Dad I was sure Mom would be able to catch a ride home, and we started walking down the hall. Then I heard Mom calling my name. I turned, and she motioned for me to come down to where she was. Not sure if she was ready to leave yet, I handed Joey back to Dad. I knew the minute Joey saw Mom he wouldn't go to anyone else.

"Go see if she's ready to head home," Dad encouraged as he pulled his tie out of Joey's mouth.

I walked toward my mother with a heavy heart. Unsure of what she wanted, I hoped I wouldn't have to talk to Regina. I was certain I knew things Roz's mother didn't want to hear, and I didn't want to know why Regina was crying.

"Laurie, tell your dad to take Joey and go home without us. Then come back down . . . Regina wants to talk to you." Absorbing this news, I must have looked scared. Mom gave my shoulder a reassuring squeeze. "It'll be all right. I'll be here with you."

Sighing, I walked back to relay her message to Dad.

* * *

Regina wiped at her eyes with the tissue Mom must have retrieved from the restroom around the corner. In all the years I'd known Roz and her family, I'd never seen Regina cry. My heart went out to her as she repeated the story she had already shared with my mom.

"Like I told your mother, when I opened this month's bill for the TV satellite, I couldn't believe it. We subscribe to the basic channels that come with the cheaper package, so it runs about thirty dollars a month. Last month's bill had been higher than that, but we had selected a couple of pay-per-view movies. This month, our bill was outrageous. I almost called the company to complain. Then I looked at the list of pay-per-view movies that had been selected during the month." Regina paused, trying to keep herself under control. "Suddenly I understood why our bill had increased," she sniffed.

Heartsick, I gazed down at the carpeted floor. Regina knew, and this was not going to be pleasant.

"Friday night, I accused my son of watching those movies. Most were R-rated. I pulled up the menu on the TV to check things out. Steve and I have always believed in trusting our children. When we subscribed to the satellite company, Steve and I talked it over, and we agreed we didn't need to set the ratings control on our TV, thinking our children would use common sense. We've taught them what is and isn't acceptable. Then I saw that list, and I thought it was Tyrone." Regina shook her head. "It never dawned on me that it would be Roselyn. And that daughter of mine stood there and watched me ground her brother for something he didn't do, and she never said a word. Tyrone kept denying it, and I was so angry, I sent him to his room without supper. And Roz never said a word."

Regina wiped at her nose, and I focused on my hands, wishing I had gone home with Dad.

"It wasn't until yesterday that I realized my mistake. I stumbled onto something on the computer. Something surfaced under documents when I was looking for a paper I had typed up the other day. I scanned through the document titles, and there it was, a file Roz had saved. It was full of e-mails from Terrence. I was going to leave it alone, but something nagged at me to look through it." Fresh tears rolled down Regina's face. "Almost every e-mail was filled with lewd jokes and suggestions that Terrence had sent her. I can't believe she saved any of it." She wiped at her face with the damp piece of tissue in her hands.

It wasn't until I felt the tears slide down my own face that I realized I was crying.

"Then I decided to check the history stored on our computer." Pausing, Regina took a deep breath. "I couldn't believe how many times someone had been into chat rooms. And some of the room titles made me sick." She took a deep breath, as if she was still fighting that nausea. "I was able to pull up some of the archives, and it wasn't until I began checking the dates that I realized there was no way it could've been Tyrone.

He hadn't been at home when these items were accessed . . . but Roz had been home, obviously chatting away. My own daughter was online flirting dangerously with anyone who would pay attention, using vulgar language I had no idea she knew." Regina shook her head. "That's when I remembered seeing a book several weeks ago, lying on the couch in the family room. The cover was atrocious."

Please don't make me say it, I silently pleaded as Regina gazed at me. I didn't want to confirm what Regina had already figured out.

"Laurie, tell me what you know about this. That book wasn't yours, was it? Roz told me it was when I asked her about it. She claimed you were into reading sleazy romance novels and that you'd left this one with her, telling her to read it."

"What?" I exclaimed, my temper flaring. Roz had blamed her stupid books on me? "I don't read those kind of books. Or watch those kind of shows—"

"I know, Laurie. Roz was the one . . ." She closed her eyes in pain, unable to finish the sentence.

The anguished look on her face tore at my heart. "Sister Whiting . . ." I began.

Her dark eyes opened. "You've always called me Regina, please don't start calling me Sister Whiting now. I know I said some harsh things to your mother a while back—I regret every one of them, and I'm sorry for what I said about you." She wiped at her nose again. "Laurie, I'm asking a lot. I'm asking you to forgive me and to help me understand why this happened."

I gathered my courage and tried again. "Regina . . . during the summer, Roz began reading those books. She thought they were great, and she tried to get me to read them," I added, enduring my mother's searching gaze. "We got into a big argument over it. I told her they weren't good, and I wasn't interested in reading any of them."

"And how did she respond to that?"

"She told me to grow up and quit being such a baby," I admitted.

"What about the movies?" The look on Regina's face rivaled the one my mother always uses to get me to talk.

"Yes, she's had a problem with R-rated movies," I said, my voice barely above a whisper. Fresh tears made an appearance as I revealed everything I knew, including the night Roz had invited me over to watch that stupid pay-per-view movie. Just when I thought I was finished with the inquisition, Regina asked me to tell her everything that had happened the night of the homecoming dance. I glanced at Mom, and she nodded, letting me know this was something I had to do. So I told Regina everything that had taken place, hating the parts I had to share about Terrence and Roz. As I described the way his hands had wandered all over Roz that night, Regina winced, and from the stricken expression on her face, I'm sure she blamed herself, thinking about the dress Roz had worn.

After we covered the Mayan adventure in minute detail, Regina quizzed me over what had been going on at school. You could tell she was a fantastic lawyer as she led me into saying things I wouldn't have revealed otherwise. I did avoid the gossip that was spreading and only shared what I knew for myself to be true, including the fact that pornographic pictures had been stuffed inside my locker. I also told her about the nasty e-mails I had been receiving from Jared and Terrence with Roz's knowledge. It was the only way they would have had access to my e-mail address.

When I'd said all there was to say, Mom did her best to comfort Regina. I sat and grieved for my friend and for her mother. Regina called herself a failure as she sobbed against my mother, and I knew it wasn't true. She had tried to teach Roz right from wrong. She wasn't a perfect parent—I don't think there are any in this world. But I knew Regina loved Roz, and I hated how this was tearing her apart.

I remembered what my mother had endured when Reese had been in his rebellion mode. There were many nights when I had heard her cry herself to sleep. I had made myself a promise then that I would never do that to her. I'm sure her hair has turned grayer over some of the things I've done, but I don't think I've ever shattered her heart. It's a goal of mine to never go there. As I witnessed what Regina was suffering, it renewed my resolve. I also vowed to make a few things clear to Joey when he got older. Breaking Mom's heart was off limits or he would answer to me.

I glanced at Regina, heartache evident in her face. She was calmer now, talking quietly to Mom in the corner of the room. I shook my head, wondering if Roz had a clue about what her mother was going through. Then it hit me—Roz needed to see this. That's how Regina could reach her. I was certain it would work. Rising from my chair, I shared my idea, stressing that what I had seen Mom suffer with Reese had been an influence on the choices I had made.

Regina gave me a look like I'd lost my mind, but Mom smiled and agreed with what I was saying.

"It might be a way to get through to Roz," Mom added. "Let her know you're hurting."

"And what if she doesn't care," Regina replied, pacing the small area in the classroom.

"When you talked to her last night, you were angry," Mom tried again.

"Furious," Regina emphasized.

Mom ran a hand through the front of her short hair. "And I'll bet Roz was embarrassed and enraged herself."

"It wasn't pretty," Regina admitted. "There was a lot of yelling. She had such a cold look on her face when she caught on that her secret was out. She didn't shed a tear. That's why I finally grounded her until she's thirty and slammed out of her room. When I tried to talk to her this morning, her door was locked. So I came to church . . . alone. Steve decided to spend the day with Tyrone, trying to undo the damage I've done." She wiped at her eyes with one of her hands. "I've certainly made a mess of things. I hope it's not too late."

"Roz sent me an apology Friday night," I blurted out, remembering the e-mail that had shown up in my inbox.

"She what?" Regina asked, refocusing on me.

"Roz sent me a short e-mail saying how sorry she was about Todd. She told me she had nothing to do with it, but she did mention something about Terrence being involved."

Regina's eyes narrowed, and I had a pretty good idea of what she would like to do to that young man. It was the same look Dad had on his face whenever he thought about Jared.

"Don't you see?" I said excitedly. "I saw Roz Friday night after Todd was hurt. She was upset, and the e-mail she sent shows she was feeling pretty bad about it."

Regina looked confused. "What does that have to do with this?"

"You're afraid she doesn't feel remorse for what she's done," I tried to explain. Regina nodded. "That e-mail proves she does regret some things. She wouldn't have sent that note if it wasn't bothering her."

Mom moved to my side. "Laurie's right. It sounds like Roz is thinking through a few things. This would be a good time to talk to her."

Looking uncertain, Regina stared at the frosted window. I glanced at it myself and had another analogy hit. My English teacher would be proud. Roz was like that frosted window. She wouldn't let anyone see what was going on inside her. But if you could get her to open up, it could change everyone's view. Wow, I'd have to write that one down when I got home.

"Regina, I feel impressed to tell you that Roz needs to hear how much you love her," Mom said. "Under the circumstances, she may be afraid she's lost that love."

Regina bit her bottom lip. She finally uttered one word. "Never," she hoarsely whispered.

"Trust me, I know," Mom agreed. She glanced at her watch. "Should we go home?"

Nodding, Regina reached for her purse. "I'll drop you two off on the way," she offered. "It's the least I can do to thank you for everything."

"No, we only live a couple of blocks away. We'll walk," Mom countered as she followed Regina out of the room. "You need to hurry home to Roz. We'll be fine."

It was cold outside. What was my mother thinking? I stepped out into the hall and was about to ask her when I saw the determined expression on her face and knew better than to argue. Mom had something on her mind, and she obviously wanted to talk to me before we arrived home. Sighing, I zipped up the thin, hooded sweater I was wearing over my blouse and resigned myself to freezing to death on the way home. I guess it was my turn to become a frosted window.

* * *

I decided it was in my best interest to allow Mom to control the conversation on the way home. I had no idea what she was after, and I figured it wouldn't help if I started spouting apologies until I knew what she was up to. I figured out one thing— fashion doesn't matter to my mother. She had bundled me up in a green men's ski coat someone had left at the church, informing me that she would bring it back later so whoever owned it could claim it. In the meantime, she wanted me to use it, commenting that my sweater wouldn't keep a fly warm. Then she wiggled into her warm wool dress coat and we set off for home.

We actually live about three and a half blocks from the church, but who was counting?

After walking in silence for about five minutes, our breath visible as we moved forward on the sidewalk, Mom cleared her throat and spoke.

"Why didn't you tell me about the pornographic e-mail Jared and Terrence have been sending you? Or the pictures they stashed in your locker?"

I winced, knowing exactly where this chat was heading. "I was embarrassed," I admitted.

"We could've bought a filter to put on the computer," Mom pointed out. "Or you could've changed your e-mail address."

Great, now I was feeling guilty, and I hadn't done anything wrong. "I deleted most of it without even looking at it," I said in my defense.

"But you still saw some of it, right?"

I slowly nodded.

"I recently attended a special stake meeting. They had invited a local LDS psychologist to give the Relief Society presidencies in our stake a presentation on the danger of pornography—information that will eventually be shared with the individual wards."

I braced myself. This was going to be worse than the chastity chats we'd had in the past.

"Did you know it's an addiction, like alcohol or drugs?" Mom continued. "Good people can get sucked in so easy, it's scary. We were told in that meeting that just one time can hook a person. And have you noticed once those images are planted inside your head, it's almost impossible to get rid of them?"

That part was true. There were some items I was afraid I would never be able to forget, compliments of Roz and her new friends. I know my cheeks were as red as my cold nose, and it wasn't from the walk. "How do you stop it?"

"Never start is a good rule of thumb," Mom exclaimed.

"But like with me, because of Jared and Terrence, I saw some terrible things. It made me sick. It still does when I think about it."

"Good. Hopefully that's how it will always affect you. Laurie, I'm not saying you have a problem. I'm saying because of what you've been through, some unwanted images may be planted in your mind."

"What do I do?"

"Use other images to block them out. Whenever one of those pictures come to mind, try blocking it out with a positive image."

This was something similar to what our seminary teacher had recently advised us. He had challenged us to pick a favorite hymn or Primary song and to think of the lyrics whenever bad thoughts came to mind. Understanding what Mom was trying to teach me, I said, "An image like the sunsets in San Diego."

"Yes, or one of the beautiful temples you've seen. An image of the Savior or our family. Anything that will jar you out of the negative image. You have to retrain your brain and then screen what you permit yourself to come in contact with."

Shivering, I shoved my hands deep inside the pockets of the green coat I was borrowing. Deep in thought, I didn't see the car that drove up behind us.

"Janell, Laurie, I need your help," Regina said, sticking her head out the window.

Mom and I hurried back to Regina's SUV and climbed inside, Mom up front and me in the backseat. Instantly I appreciated how warm the car was.

"It's Roz. She's missing."

My eyes widened.

"Steve's looked everywhere. We even tried calling Terrence's house, but his mother said she's not there." Regina looked over the seat at me. "Laurie, do you have any idea where Roz would go?"

Stressed, I couldn't think clearly. I was glad when Mom suggested that Regina take us home, and then we'd split up three ways to search.

Chapter 24

As I drove around in my red Honda Civic, I frantically searched the parks and other places where Roz and I used to go, but there was no sign of her. *Not like Reese,* I found myself chanting. *Not like Reese.* Reese had disappeared for about a year and a half. Despite everything, it would kill me to not hear from Roz for an extended amount of time. I banged my fist on the steering wheel. This wasn't good. Where could she have gone?

I finally pulled into a church parking lot near Clinton. Figuring I could use some guidance, I offered a quick prayer for help. Opening my eyes, I stared at the brick building in front of me. I'm not sure how long I sat there, but finally a memory came to mind, a place where I had gone seeking solitude last year after Reese had come home. Hoping I was right, I turned my car around and drove to Antelope Island.

* * *

Antelope Island is the largest of the ten islands in the Great Salt Lake. It's full of different kinds of animals, including bison. A lot of people like to explore it—go hiking, picnicking, that kind of thing. The road that leads to the island is near Layton. There's a causeway that you drive across to get to the island, a road built up over the wet, marshy ground.

Dad had said that the original causeway was submerged under water for about ten years. Then in 1992, things dried up and the road was repaired. Now people can drive across without any trouble at all. Unless it's Sunday and you left your purse at home. Then you have to park clear out in the north forty and walk. They charge eight dollars to drive into the island, but it only costs four dollars to walk. I was able to find that much money stuffed in my car, most of it loose change from tips I had received at Harold's Burgers. I still didn't like that I had to pay for something on Sunday, but I hoped Heavenly Father understood this was going for a good cause.

Fortunately for me, I had taken the time to change into jeans and a sweater and my own winter coat before I left to search for Roz. I was also wearing my favorite pair of Nikes, which added to my comfort as I walked into the park. I knew it wouldn't take long to walk down to the isolated spot I had found last year.

I thought about what Regina had told Mom and me earlier when she had driven us to our house. There had been no note. Roz's purse was gone. Steve Whiting's Volvo was missing too. I suspected Roz had taken it. But it wasn't parked with the other vehicles in the parking lot where I had left my car. Hurrying forward, I scanned the horizon for a white car, but there weren't any to be seen.

Last year, Roz had come looking for me, knowing how upset I was. At that time, I'd decided it wasn't fair that everyone treated Reese like royalty after the mistakes he had made. I know—I had a lot of growing up to do. Anyway, after blowing up at my parents, I had gone for a bike ride. I hadn't meant to ride out so far, but I wanted a water moment. It's something Roz and I have talked about. When life crashes in on you, it helps to go where you're surrounded by beauty. Sometimes a forest scene can provide a lift. But when I'm really upset, I like looking at water.

How Roz found me that day, I'll never know. She just smiled and sat down next to me to stare out at the lake until I was ready to come home. We didn't even talk. We didn't have to then.

As a familiar ache rose in my throat, I choked it off. Crying would not help me find Roz. Instead, I increased my pace and found the spot where I had enjoyed last year's water moment. But I was the only one standing there, staring out at the water. Disappointed, I shoved my hands inside my coat and sat down on a nearby rock. It was ice cold, but I didn't care. I would sit here and think until I could find Roz.

"What are you doing here?" a familiar voice asked about five minutes later. I nearly jumped out of my skin, she startled me so bad. I slid off the large rock and turned around to face Roz.

"I came to look for you," I replied.

"How did you know I was here?" she asked, looking puzzled.

"How did you know last year?" I retorted. I was relieved to see that Roz had dressed warm.

Shrugging, Roz moved past me to sit closer to the water. I had brought Mom's cell phone with me, and I used it now to let my mother know I had found Roz. I moved to where Roz couldn't overhear. Then I told Mom I wasn't sure how long this would take, but I would bring Roz home. She promised to call Regina and let her know so she wouldn't worry. Clicking off the phone, I returned it to my coat pocket. Then I walked down to Roz's side and sat on another cold rock. We sat like that for ten or fifteen minutes. Then Roz broke the silence.

"You didn't have to come."

"I wanted to," I replied.

"Why?"

I leaned down to pick up a nearby pebble to hurl into the water. I watched the ripples until they disappeared. "You were always there for me," I finally said.

"You don't owe me anything," Roz replied.

She was keeping her back to me, but I could tell she was crying. Taking that as a good sign, I stayed put.

"I've been awful to you," Roz stammered about five minutes later.

"Yes, you have," I agreed, and for a few seconds, I was tempted to shove her off her rock and into the frigid water—a payback for the Mayan catastrophe. Taking a deep breath, I ran my hands through my hair and tried to control myself.

"You'll never be able to forgive me."

"It'll take time," I said, careful to keep my voice steady. I didn't want Roz to know how much this was tearing me up inside. I was glad I had found her, but I was still furious over what she had put me through. Thanks to her—and Jared and Terrence—I had a lot of negative images floating around in my head. Plus my life had been a living Hades. Right now, a part of me wanted to scream at Roz and then shake her until her teeth rattled.

Instead, I kept reminding myself of the look on Regina's face after church today. I felt the weight of Regina's tears and knew that how I handled this conversation could go a long way toward bringing Roz back home.

"I meant what I said in the e-mail I sent you Friday night," Roz mumbled.

"I know," I said softly, gazing out across the water. *That's right,* I told myself. *Be one with the water. Be at peace. Don't shove Roz's face into the mud.*

"Is Todd going to be okay?"

"You heard he had to have surgery," I said, still trying to gauge her mood.

Roz nodded. "Some kids showed up at Jared's house Friday night. They'd come from the hospital for a party . . ." her voice faltered.

"I'd heard about that party." I decided it wasn't a good idea to share that Jared had invited me to attend, or that he had announced Terrence's plans for her.

Rising, Roz picked up a handful of pebbles and flung them into the water.

Sliding off my rock, I stood beside Roz. To shove or not to shove, that was the question. My conscience won the battle. Sighing, I tucked my hands into the pockets of my coat and tried again to be one with the water.

"I was so mad at Terrence for what he and Jared pulled during the game. They went too far. They always go too far." Lowering her hands, she clenched them into fists. "I just wanted to be popular . . . to be loved. Was that asking too much?"

Sensing Roz wasn't seeking answers from me, I remained silent.

"Laurie, what happened? I've asked myself that question so many times. Why? Why did I agree to go to the dance with Terrence? Why did I buy that stupid dress? I knew it was wrong. But it was so pretty—and there you were shoving what I knew was right in my face. It made me mad. So mad, I wouldn't let myself see how hurt you were. I kept reminding myself about the times you had upset me. And Jared said we were just being funny. That it was all a big joke. It would teach you a lesson. But it only made things worse."

Roz rambled on for several minutes, then she covered her face with her hands and cried. The anger I was feeling helped me remain in control. Roz had messed up big-time, and she needed to know how badly she had hurt herself and me. But as she continued to cry, I softened. I found myself wondering what Mom, Regina, and Kaye would want me to do. How would the Savior handle something like this? Uncertain, I remained in place, with my hands in my pockets and bold accusations in my head. Unspoken, they faded into whispers. And bit by bit, Roz began pouring out her heart.

I learned Terrence had pushed her into doing things that weren't good. Liking his attention, she had given in, but it wasn't as bad as I had feared. Unlike the rumors going around, Roz had drawn a line in the sand. Saddened by what she had allowed, I was still proud of how she had repeatedly pushed Terrence away whenever things had started getting out of control.

Then, Friday night, Terrence had tried to force himself beyond that line, and Roz had walked away. Salvaging what was left of her pride, she had come home to hear her brother being raked over the coals for something she had done.

"Why does everything always hit at the same time?" Roz agonized. "I couldn't deal with that right then, not after what I'd been through with Terrence. I didn't tell you, but Terrence was drunk Friday night. He was so drunk, that's the only reason I was able to get away," Roz stammered. "If he'd had his full strength . . ." Roz couldn't say it, but I knew what she was implying. "Mom has no idea what I went through that night. She was standing there yelling at Tyrone . . . and I needed her so much."

This time when Roz burst into tears, my hands came out of my pockets, and I drew her into a hug. She cried for quite a while, and so did I. And while our friendship would never be the same, we were still friends.

I'm not sure how long we stayed on the island sharing tears and tender secrets. Roz did most of the talking, and I tried to understand. Toward the end, she began asking me how I felt, and I hesitantly told her. I think we both knew it was the only way to tear down the wall between us. Roz faced it with quiet grace, reminding me of her mother.

When it started getting dark, we walked down to where Roz had parked her dad's car, and she drove me to where I had parked mine. We parted at the causeway, taking different routes home. And yes, another analogy came to mind as I pondered the fact that we all walk separate journeys in our quest to find our way.

Chapter 25

Roz told me later that when she walked into her house, both parents hugged her until she couldn't breathe. Then her mother led her upstairs to her bedroom for a lengthy heart-to-heart that took most of the night.

Sunday night after I returned home, I typed an e-mail to Ed, telling him about what had happened, sharing that I thought Roz and I were friends again. Then I pasted most of that letter into an e-mail for my brother. When I was satisfied with both e-mails, I sent them off into cyberspace, marveling that with the touch of a button, you can communicate with people all over the world. Yawning, I stretched, then decided to call it a day and went to bed.

I wasn't surprised when Roz didn't show up at school the next day. I learned later that Regina had taken the day off to spend with her. It was great to know that Roz and her mother were back on good terms. I was worried about how Roz would be treated when she did return to school. It would be a different battle than the one Susie and I had fought. In some ways, it would be harder. First, Roz would have to convince people she was no longer part of Jared's crowd and no longer Terrence's girl. She would be hit with taunts from both sides. Unfortunately, some of the goody-goodies could be as cruel with their comments as those who ran with Jared.

I talked things over with Susie during lunch Monday after-noon and asked if she had any ideas. All she could think of was to surround Roz with people like us who were determined to help her regain her self-esteem. That wouldn't prevent others from treating her badly, but hopefully we could be there to boost her back up when someone had knocked her spirits to sea level. I also decided to write an editorial about how we tend to judge people, hoping I could get my point across. I was learning that my editorials were making a difference out there, even if most of the letters to the editor were negative. For some reason, people only like to send in letters when they want to complain. You hardly ever hear from those who agree with what has been written. Kind of a sad commentary on our times, actually. Too much criticism and not enough praise.

There was a bright spot to the day. Earlier, during the first-hour class, Jared and Terrence had both been escorted from the school, suspended for the stunt they had pulled during Friday's football game. They would miss an entire week of school, and they were kicked off the football team for the rest of the season. It was also rumored that Jared's parents had returned home Friday night instead of Saturday night as they had originally planned. They had been shocked to walk in on what can best be referred to as a den of iniquity. When I heard about their reaction, I felt sorry for Jared's parents. How could you ever explain having a kid like Jared? On the other hand, Lehi and Sariah had endured Laman and Lemuel. I'm sure that wasn't a good time either.

With Jared and Terrence out of circulation for a while, I thought it would give Roz a better chance at starting over without their interference. I should've known Terrence wouldn't give up that easily. For a week, he couldn't talk to Roz at school, but he kept calling her at home. Roz's father finally answered, picking up the phone to tell Terrence to stay away from his daughter or there would be serious consequences. It gave Roz some breathing room, but I sensed it wasn't over.

* * *

Hi, Laurie.

Man, what a week you've had. I'm sorry Roz's mother was so upset, but I'm glad you were able to help her. And talk about saving the day—how did you know where to find Roz when she disappeared? I know, you keep telling me that the Holy Ghost is a wonderful guide. And you know what, that's really true. Which is why I'm now taking the missionary discussions. I couldn't ignore the promptings I was receiving . . . even if I made my mother cry. And two of my sisters aren't speaking to me because I made Mom cry. And Sarah thinks I've lost my mind. She hung up on me the other day when I tried to call and talk to her about why I'm doing this.

Dad took my decision better. He's still upset over it, but he told me that he's raised me to do my own thinking and that if this is what I really want, he won't fight me. But he doesn't want me to have the discussions in our home. I guess it looks kind of bad to have Mormon missionaries showing up at a Baptist preacher's house to teach the gospel. So I'll be meeting them at a neighbor's house down the street. Turns out this lady is LDS and thrilled to be part of my discussion adventure. I'll let you know how it turns out.

Well, I guess I'd better wrap this up. I can't believe how late it is already. Hang in there—you're doing good things. Look at the influence you're having on me.

Write soon.
Ed

* * *

I was ecstatic over Ed's news that he was taking the missionary discussions. After reading his latest e-mail, I sent him one that gushed with happiness and support. Then I sent one off to Reese, telling him that I was having a missionary experience too. Actually, more than one, considering how hard Roz was now trying to turn things around. The two of us had been having a series of long discussions about the gospel, standards, things of that nature. When Roz told me that she was meeting with the bishop to work through the repentance process, I felt like doing the dance of joy. I refrained, but inside, I was dancing away.

I was also happy when Todd was able to return to school. He was still in a lot of pain, but that was to be expected considering the extent of his injury. Every time he breathed in, he winced. But Susie and I did our best to clear a path for him when he walked slowly to each class, and we took turns carrying his backpack for him. Roz helped out when she could, but I had noticed she didn't feel comfortable around my new friends and usually kept a low profile. As I had feared, there were a lot of rumors circulating about Roz, but Susie and I did our best to quell them, and I hoped Roz wouldn't hear any of the gossip.

On Todd's second day back in school, Jared surfaced to complicate things.

Also recently back in school, Jared must have figured that he owed Todd for the trouble he'd been in. Jared got this huge grin on his face, walked over, and before anyone could stop him, he smacked Todd in the chest, pretending to welcome him back.

Todd dropped to his knees in pain, and Jared was escorted to the office. A teacher had watched the whole thing from across the hall and reported Jared's actions to the principal. We weren't surprised to learn that Jared had been suspended again. Rumor had it that he might be sent to a correctional facility if his behavior didn't improve. I didn't like the guy, but that sounded pretty harsh. On the other hand, what a relief it would be to never have to worry about him again—something that made graduation day very appealing.

Todd was in so much pain after Jared's welcome that he called his mother to pick him up from school early. Nancy Napier wasn't a very happy camper when she arrived at the school a few minutes later. Susie and I had stayed with Todd in the office until his mother came, unwilling to leave him alone or unprotected.

"How did this happen?" Nancy demanded of the principal when she entered the school office.

"We can't keep an eye on all the students all the time," Mr. Nedry replied, pulling nervously at his shirt collar. "We try, but it just isn't possible. But know that we've suspended Jared Moulton for his violent actions against your son."

"Well, I should hope so," Nancy fumed. "Todd has been through enough because of Jared. If this happens again . . ."

Mr. Nedry continued to do his best to soothe Nancy. "Rest assured, we'll do what we can to prevent it from being a continued problem."

Right. Like they were able to stop Jared and his pals from decorating my locker every other day, I thought silently. Or how Susie was protected last year from the same treatment. I didn't even want to think about what was ahead for Roz. For her it would be worse because, for a little while, she had been one of them.

With Susie's assistance, Nancy helped Todd out of the office and then out of the school. I heard Nancy muttering that she'd have to take him back to the doctor to make sure he hadn't been seriously injured. Hoping Todd was still in one piece, I held the front door open for them when they walked out, then stayed behind, not wanting to be a third wheel. Or a fourth. Something like that. As I turned to walk back to class, I heard someone hiss my name. I glanced off to the side and saw Roz peeking around the corner. Curious, I walked over to where she was hiding.

"What's up?"

"Where's Terrence?" Roz asked.

I glanced around, but I didn't see any sign of her former boyfriend. "Has he been bugging you today?"

Roz nodded. "Why did I ever go out with that moron?" she moaned.

I knew the answer, but I wasn't going to say it out loud and especially not to Roz. "What did he do now?"

"This," Roz replied, holding up an 8" x 10" poster. It was a picture of Roz wearing an extremely revealing two-piece swimming suit with a caption that read, *Roz knows how to treat a man.*

I snatched the paper from Roz and was about to tear it into pieces when she pulled it away from me.

"Laurie, they're being passed out all over school. Tearing up one isn't going to make the rest of them go away."

"Okay, let's go show this one to Mrs. Vance," I suggested. Maybe it was time for Terrence to be transferred to a correctional facility too.

Roz protested, but I dragged her with me into the office. Unfortunately, Mrs. Vance was otherwise occupied. Mr. Nedry offered to help us, but I assured him that we needed Mrs. Vance. Roz was embarrassed enough as it was—talking things over with Mr. Nedry wouldn't help.

While we sat waiting for Mrs. Vance to return, I glanced at the picture Roz was trying to hide. "How did he get that picture of you?"

"It's only my face," Roz explained. "He scanned in my face and added the body from another file. You can do anything on a computer these days."

I moved her hand for a closer look at the poster and now saw that the body in question did not belong to my friend. Not only was the upper body more endowed, but to the best of my knowledge, Roz didn't have a tattoo on her upper thigh. Roz turned the poster over, anxious to keep it hidden.

About five minutes later, Mrs. Vance appeared. "Hello, girls. Mr. Nedry said you needed to talk to me."

We followed her inside her small office, and I closed the door. We sat down on the hard plastic chairs in front of her desk. Roz was fidgeting nervously, and I could see she was going to need some help with this.

"Mrs. Vance, do you remember what I kept finding in my locker about a month ago?"

She frowned. "Yes, Laurie. Is it happening again?"

"Something similar—only worse."

"How could it be worse?" Mrs. Vance asked.

I nudged Roz, but she wouldn't let go of the paper in her hands. Instead she stood and tried to leave the room. Rising, I blocked her path.

"Girls, what's going on?"

"Show her, Roz. That's the only way to stop this."

"Roselyn, what's in your hand?" Mrs. Vance asked. I've noticed she uses students' full names when she wants their complete attention.

Trembling, Roz turned and handed the paper to Mrs. Vance. Then, closing her eyes, she sank back down in her chair.

Mrs. Vance gaped at the offending paper, her eyes widening as she glanced from it to Roz. "Oh, my . . . this is horrible. Who did this?"

I glanced at Roz to see if she would say his name, but she didn't.

"Do you know who's doing this?" Mrs. Vance repeated.

I decided to change the subject for now. "The worst part is, copies of that are spreading all over the school."

"Did you pose for this picture?" Mrs. Vance asked, still looking appalled.

"No," Roz exclaimed. "It's only my face. He used computer graphics for the rest. That's not my body." Roz started to cry. I didn't blame her—I would've cried too. I thought about how upset I had been a month ago. Only then, Roz had been partially responsible for my suffering. If I had been one to hold a grudge, I might have secretly enjoyed what was going on now. A tiny part of me did. But most of me felt terrible for Roz. This was far worse than what I had endured.

Mrs. Vance reached into her desk and pulled out a box of Kleenex. I wondered if she was used to girls falling apart in her office. "You say these are circulating throughout the school?" she asked as Roz tried to compose herself.

"Yeah," I answered.

"I don't suppose Jared Moulton had anything to do with it?"

I tried to keep a blank expression on my face, but Mrs. Vance must have seen something. Terrence may have been the one passing the poster around, but I suspected Jared had designed it. Roz had already told me that Jared was the mastermind behind most of the pranks that were pulled on people. Wasn't that cute? Jared called them pranks. I don't think that's what Todd would call them.

I sat up in my chair. Roz's mother was an attorney. This personal attack against Roz would surely qualify as a court case. "Mrs. Vance, don't you think this is a form of sexual harassment?"

Mrs. Vance peered over her glasses at me. "What are you getting at, Laurie?"

"We could take these boys to court, right?"

Sliding her glasses back in place, the vice principal gazed at the poster in her hands. Then she removed her glasses and rubbed at her forehead as if she were getting a headache. "I don't think we want to take that extreme measure."

"Why not?" I asked. "Do you know there are students in this school who live in fear because of people like Jared and Terrence?"

"I knew it," said Mrs. Vance, writing down the two names.

"I didn't say that's who did the poster," I pointed out.

"Are they the ones responsible?"

Last month when Mrs. Vance had asked me that question, I had refused to answer, trying to protect Roz. Now whom was I trying to protect? It came to me in an instant. Myself. And Roz. If we told who the guilty parties were, they would make our lives miserable the rest of the school year. *But weren't they doing that already?* The question popped into my head in an annoying fashion.

"Look, girls, unless you tell me who did this, my hands are tied. Like last time, Laurie," she said, giving me an exasperated glare.

"You've talked to Mrs. Vance before?" Roz said, just putting that one together.

"How do you think I got my locker changed?" I responded.

"It was the same two boys, right?" Mrs. Vance prompted.

My silent debate continued.

"It was," Roz said, making the decision for me. She chewed her bottom lip. "Laurie didn't tell you who it was before because I was involved too."

Mrs. Vance dropped her pencil over that confession. She put her glasses back on and stared at Roz. "Do you mean to tell me that you were behind those horrid pictures Laurie found in her locker?"

I had to give Roz credit for taking it on the chin. She sat there and told Mrs. Vance everything. How Jared had furnished the porn pictures, bringing them from home. How she had opened my locker for him, and how Terrence had helped Jared tape the posters in place.

"And you're still speaking to her?" Mrs. Vance asked me, leaning back in her chair.

"Yeah," I replied. "We've worked things out." *For the most part,* I added silently. There were still moments when I felt resentful over what had been said and done, but it was getting better.

"I see," Mrs. Vance said, scribbling something on the notepad on her desk. "So, I'm gathering that you, Roz, are no longer hanging out with Terrence and Jared."

Roz nodded.

"Wise decision." She turned to me. "And you've decided to forgive Roz for what she did."

Now it was my turn to nod.

"And you're both upset over this new poster."

This time Roz and I nodded in unison.

"A poster that was designed by Jared and Terrence."

She almost tricked us with that one. Roz and I sat very still and contemplated the consequences before we silently agreed to give in.

"It was Jared and Terrence," I said, taking the lead.

"Thank you. Now, here's what I propose. Roz, what you did to your friend is abominable. It was tasteless, juvenile, and will not go unpunished."

"But . . . I—"

Mrs. Vance cut me off. "Laurie, I appreciate the fact that you're mature enough to let this go. But we've been trying to crack down on this kind of thing for quite some time. As you said yourself, acts of this nature make coming to school miserable for our students, and we can't have that."

Why had I brought Roz in here? This wasn't going to help. As my temper began to flare, I glanced at one of the posters hanging on the wall. *"I have one nerve left, and you just stepped on it."* Truer words were never spoken.

"Mrs. Vance, punishing Roz isn't going to change what happened. I think she's suffered enough."

Mrs. Vance silenced me with her infamous look, the one that made it clear she was running out of patience. "That's for me to decide, not you." She studied the notes she had been making and gazed severely at Roz, who was slumping down in her chair. "Here is my decision. We have a tutoring program going on after school." She pushed a few buttons on her keyboard and studied the computer screen in front of her. "I see that you are an excellent math student," she said to Roz. "For the next six weeks, you are to report to Mr. O'Brien each day after school, and you will spend approximately one hour each day of the school week working with students who need extra help in their math classes."

Roz didn't look very thrilled, but I felt she got off easy. It could have been much worse.

"As for Jared and Terrence, I will be talking things over with Mr. Nedry. Their actions are more serious and will require further thought."

"What about the posters of Roz?" I asked.

"We'll probably never find them all," Mrs. Vance said. "But we will make it clear that if anyone is caught with one in their possession, they will face detention." She rose from her desk, an indication that it was time for Roz and me to leave. As I opened the door, she had one final piece of advice for Roz. "I hope you realize how lucky you are to have someone like Laurie for a friend."

I don't know how that comment made Roz feel, but it did quite a bit for my self-esteem.

Smiling, I left the office and attended what was left of my third-hour class.

Chapter 26

Somehow we survived that first semester of our senior year. What a roller-coaster ride it turned out to be. But some good things had come out of it, like the new friends I had made. Plus, there was even a stronger bond between Roz and me. We had both discovered important things about ourselves. I learned I was stronger than I ever imagined. Roz found out why we've been given standards and that they actually do mean quite a bit to her. She also enjoyed being a math tutor. After her six-week punishment was over, she continued staying after school to help struggling students. From this experience, she learned that she wanted to go into teaching. She decided that if BYU-Idaho would have her, she would apply to go there to college next fall.

I don't think Terrence or Jared learned anything the first part of our senior year. No one seemed overly sad when the school finally expelled them for varied infractions that had included the lewd poster of Roz. The final straw was a poster they had made up of Mrs. Vance. This time it was only one poster, similar to the one they had done of Roz, but with a picture of Mrs. Vance they had obviously scanned from last year's yearbook. It was found hanging in the boys' locker room. Bad move on their part. They were no longer welcome at Roy High School.

Around Christmastime, I received the best gift of my life. Ed called to let me know he was getting baptized. As you'll recall, his parents weren't happy with him for investigating the LDS

Church. But Ed's parents are tolerant, kind-hearted people, and they finally told Ed that if this was what he really wanted, then he could be baptized. So he set a date. I wish I could've been there to see it. Instead, I had to make do with what Ed told me about that special day, and I treasure the picture of him dressed in white, which he e-mailed me. You can probably guess what became my wallpaper on my computer settings at home.

Sighing as I gazed at how handsome Ed looked in white, I pulled up my word-processing program and started to type this week's newspaper editorial. This time *Laurie's View* would tout the advantages of group dating, the beginning of a series I planned to do that would call for a return to old-fashioned values. I knew it would stir up some controversy, but I didn't care. After all, it was my view.

About the Author

Cheri J. Crane is a former resident of Ashton, Idaho. She attended Ricks College where she obtained an associate's degree in English. Shortly thereafter, she met and married a returned missionary named Kennon Crane. They made their home in Bennington, Idaho, and began the task of raising three sons.

Cheri enjoys numerous hobbies, which include cooking, gardening, and music. She also loves spending time with family and friends. A Type 1 diabetic, she heads a local chapter of the American Diabetes Association. Cheri has spent most of her married life serving in the Primary and Young Women organizations. Currently, she is serving as the first counselor in the stake Relief Society presidency, as ward camp director, and as ward teacher improvement coordinator.

Cheri is the author of eight other books, the most recent being *The Long Road Home*. She can be reached at info@covenant-lds.com.

EXCERPT FROM *The Long Road Home*

CHAPTER 1

Seventeen-year-old Reese Clark's blue eyes widened with delight when Stacy Jardine walked into the small kitchen of her home in Roy, Utah. Reese self-consciously ran a hand down the back of his thick black hair, wishing he had spent more time with his own appearance. He had lost track of the time playing basketball at a friend's house as they celebrated their high school football team's homecoming victory earlier that afternoon. Reese's mother had finally called to remind him that he needed to shower and change before picking Stacy up for the homecoming dance. There had barely been time for that when he arrived home.

"I told you Stacy had dolled herself up for this dance," Ann Jardine beamed.

Nodding in agreement with Stacy's mother, Reese continued to gaze at his date for the evening. Wearing a maroon prom dress he knew she had borrowed from a friend, Stacy was gorgeous. The floor length dress had a high neck and long, lacy sleeves. Modest but elegant, the gown accentuated Stacy's slender waistline. Reese's eyes traveled to Stacy's face. Naturally beautiful, she hadn't used much makeup, only a hint of base to cover two small blemishes on her chin, a touch of rouge on her cheeks, and a trace of eyeshadow and mascara to accent her dark brown eyes. Her long, brown hair had been swept up in the back with pearl-draped barrettes. The sides of her face were framed by loose curls.

"Wow," Reese whispered as he pulled at the snug maroon tie he wore with the black tuxedo he had rented for the evening.

"Go stand next to Reese and I'll take your picture," Ann insisted, grabbing her camera from the kitchen table. "Now turn sideways.

Stacy, turn your face toward me. Reese, quit looking so stiff," Ann laughed. "Relax, and put your hands around her waist. There, that looks more natural. Good. Smile," she encouraged, taking another shot with her camera.

"Mom," Stacy said, glancing at the clock, "we're going to be late."

"Maybe if you hadn't spent so long in the bathroom, you'd have more time now," Stacy's younger brother teased.

Stacy stuck her tongue out at the sixteen year old. "Behave, Brad."

"I could say the same thing to you two," Brad countered.

"Now, Brad, that's enough," Ann said, reaching for a lacy white shawl that had been draped over a kitchen chair.

"Don't worry, Mrs. Jardine, I'll be a perfect gentleman all evening and have her home at midnight," Reese promised.

Ann smiled at Reese, then pointed to the plastic box he had left on the kitchen table. "Aren't you forgetting something?" she asked.

He followed her gaze to the table. "The corsage," he exclaimed. He carefully pulled the arrangement of tiny white roses, accented by baby's breath and green fern, from its transparent container and held it out to Ann. "Could you pin this on Stacy? I'm terrible at this sort of thing."

"I'll do it!" Brad volunteered.

"I don't think so," Stacy refused. "You'd probably skewer me on purpose. If you wanted to pin a corsage on a girl, then you should've asked someone to the dance yourself," she added.

"Maybe some of us think it's silly to waste that kind of money on a girl," Brad said, grinning.

Reese winked at Brad. "When the right girl comes along, it's worth all the money in the world."

Ann began a coughing fit that lasted several seconds. Reese glanced at the concerned look on Stacy's face. He knew how worried she was about her mother's health. Ann had smoked for years and now endured a persistent cough.

"Are you all right?" Stacy asked in a subdued voice.

Nodding, Ann retreated to the kitchen sink, grabbed a plastic tumbler, and filled it with water. She took a long sip, breathed deeply, then set the glass on the counter and hurried to the fridge. "Don't forget his boutonniere," she said, pulling out the small plastic box.

Stacy slipped an arm around her mother's slender shoulders and gave her a quick squeeze. Reese overheard the whispered thanks that passed between the two and smiled. Ann and Stacy were close, bonded through shared trials that had nearly torn their family apart. Stacy's father had been an abusive alcoholic, so Ann, Stacy, and Brad had learned to depend on each other for comfort and support. Larry Jardine's costly habits grew progressively worse until Ann had given him an ultimatum. His disappearance from their lives a short time later had almost come as a relief, though it left tender wounds that never seemed to fully heal.

After the divorce, Ann had moved the three of them into a small house they could afford to rent. She worked two jobs—as a clerk in a local grocery store during the day, and at a video store at night—to keep them afloat financially. Stacy spent three afternoons a week cooking at a nearby drive-in after school. Brad did his part by working part-time at a local garage and helped Stacy straighten things at home. Pulling together, they were surviving this latest chapter in their lives. Reese admired their determination and envied their close relationship.

Ann returned her daughter's squeeze. "You two have a good time tonight," she said, handing the rose boutonniere to Stacy.

Stacy nodded, then walked to where Reese was waiting and pinned on his flower.

"Did she stick you, Reese?" Brad inquired.

"Nope," Reese replied, shaking his head at Stacy's brother.

"You guys aren't very entertaining," Brad complained.

"That'll come later," Reese said, invoking a look of dismay from Stacy and Ann. "I didn't mean it like it sounded," he stammered, turning a deep shade of red. "I meant when we get out on the dance floor."

"I think I'll be watching out the window tonight when you bring Stacy home," Brad laughed.

"I don't think so," Ann said as she helped Stacy with the shawl. She tied it in place, draping the knot down the front of her daughter's borrowed dress. "Have fun," she said as Reese walked Stacy to the door.

"We will," Reese called back.

"I'll bet," Brad sang out, wiggling his eyebrows.

"Mom!" Stacy complained.

"Already taken care of," Ann said, signaling that Brad had gone far enough.

"Sorry about that," Stacy apologized as Reese helped her onto the porch. He closed the screen door, then escorted her to the green sedan he had borrowed from his parents.

"Wait until my family has their turn," Reese sympathized. "This will seem mild."

"We're going to your house?" she asked excitedly.

Reese nodded, enjoying the sudden sparkle in her dark eyes. "That's where we'll end up for dessert," he explained. "Since there are six couples in our group, we decided to have a progressive dinner. We'll have one course at each guy's house."

"This sounds like fun," Stacy commented as Reese helped her into the car.

"Better than a fancy restaurant?"

"Much," Stacy replied.

"All righty then, let's be on our way," he said, making sure Stacy's dress was tucked inside the car before closing the door.

* * *

"Here you are—finally," Janell Clark sang out as the six couples invaded her home later that evening. "I thought you said you'd be here around seven," the attractive blonde added, directing her gaze toward her son, Reese. Truthfully, she was relieved they were late arriving. It had given her a chance to thoroughly clean the house after a crazy day of running errands. It had also given her enough time to change into a dark pair of dress pants, a cream-colored blouse, and a matching sweater. Her short hair had been styled in a flattering fashion, swept back at the sides and curled on top. Her bright blue eyes sparkled with delight as she studied the becoming but modest gowns the six girls had chosen for this special night. With today's fashions, that was a major accomplishment.

"We were beginning to wonder if we needed to send the search and rescue out to look for you," Will Clark added, glancing at their son.

Janell laughed at the look of mock indignation on Reese's face. With that expression he looked so much like Will. Nearly the same height, father and son were close to six feet tall. Their hair was the same color, though there was a difference in the amount of hair they had. Reese's short hair was dark and thick, unlike Will's hair that was thinning on top and greying at the sides.

"We're only an hour late," Reese teased, leaning to kiss his mother's cheek. "It took us longer at each place than we had figured."

"I see," Janell said, closing the front door. She turned for another look at the dressed-up teens. "You all look great."

"I'll say," Will agreed. "I'll go grab the video camera. We need to preserve this rare occasion—it's the first time I've ever seen Reese in a tux," he said, hurrying from the room.

A chorus of dismay echoed in the entry way as Reese began leading everyone into the dining room for dessert. Janell slipped an arm around Stacy's waist as they followed behind the small crowd. "You look beautiful."

"Thank you," Stacy replied in a hushed voice.

"Are you having fun?"

Stacy nodded. "Reese's friends are so funny."

"Reese thinks he's quite a comedian himself," Janell replied, releasing Stacy as they approached the table.

"I know," Stacy whispered.

"Know what?" Reese asked.

"Never mind," Janell responded. "Now, who's ready for dessert?"

"Bring it on," one of Reese's friends encouraged. "What are we having?"

"Strawberry cheesecake," Janell announced, enjoying the delighted murmurs that circulated the polished oak table. Turning, she stepped back into the kitchen.

Stacy followed. "I'll help you," she offered.

"I'd appreciate that," Janell said, opening the fridge. She placed the large cheesecake onto the counter and motioned for Stacy to grab the small paper plates she had set out earlier. "Just don't get any of this on that gorgeous dress," she cautioned. "I'd feel terrible."

"So would I," Stacy agreed.

"Tell you what, I'll dish it up and you can hand it out, how's that?"

"Sounds like a plan."

"I found the camera! It was buried under a pile of clothes in the laundry room—something I suspect Reese knew all along," Will announced as he walked into the dining room with the camcorder.

Reese shook his head in protest, but the mischievous look in his blue eyes revealed the truth.

"Now, everyone, act natural," Will encouraged. "Where's Stacy?"

"I'm helping your wife," Stacy replied from the kitchen.

"Hurry. I'm not sure how long this battery will hold out," Will said, moving around the table for a better shot.

"I can't believe he's filming this," Stacy whispered to Janell.

Janell smiled at the young woman her son had been friends with for nearly a year. "I can. We have a collection of interesting footage from every event this family has participated in since he bought that camera three years ago. Some tapes I've threatened to burn."

Stacy giggled. "Mom's the same way . . . I mean . . . we don't have a camcorder, but she's always taking pictures of me and Brad. She took several tonight before Reese and I left."

"I'd like a copy of those," Janell said as she began cutting the cheesecake into small, squared sections.

"Sure. Mom always gets double prints."

"I'd be willing to pay for reprints if you want to keep the extra shots," Janell replied. She glanced at Stacy. "So, how are things going?"

"Tonight?"

"In general," Janell responded. "I haven't had a chance to visit with you for a couple of weeks."

"I know," Stacy said as she set the plates near the cheesecake, spreading them out on the counter. "It seems like all I do anymore is go to school, work at the drive-in, and stay up late doing homework."

"Are you keeping up okay?" Janell asked, concerned.

Stacy nodded. "Who needs sleep?"

"We all do," Janell counseled. "Are you still taking those honors classes?"

"Sad but true."

"Is it worth it?"

"I think so. I'm hoping to get a scholarship. That's the only way I'll be able to go to college."

"Where's that cake?" Reese hollered from the dining room. "The crowd is getting ugly in here!"

"It's coming," Janell called back, her blue eyes twinkling with suppressed humor. "Well, so much for small talk. Guess we'd better feed the starving masses." She placed slices of cheesecake onto the small paper plates as Stacy took them into the dining room. When Stacy came back into the kitchen for the final serving, Janell handed it to her. "What would you think about coming over for dinner tomorrow after church?"

"Sure," Stacy accepted.

"Great. I assume Reese is picking you up for church in the morning?"

"He said it depends on what time we get home tonight," Stacy said, laughing at the look of mock horror on Janell's face.

"So help me, if he doesn't get you home by midnight—"

"He promised my mother that he would," Stacy interrupted.

"Well, he'd better," Janell exclaimed. "I don't know, though. You look like a goddess tonight, so I'm a little concerned."

"Don't worry, I'll keep Reese in line," Stacy promised.

"Good girl," Janell replied.

"Stacy? Did you lose your way?" Reese hollered.

An amused look passed between Janell and Stacy. "I'll be right there," she called back. "Persistent little thing, isn't he?" Janell observed. "You'll have to watch out for that."

"I know," Stacy agreed before moving into the dining room to join the other teens.

* * *

Dancing in Reese's strong arms across the crepe-papered gym, Stacy wished the evening would last forever. Twisted strands of blue and white hung from wires that crossed the dimly lit room, giving it an ethereal quality. After enjoying several slow songs, Reese led her to the refreshment table for a glass of punch. Making their way through the crowd, they spied two vacant chairs and sat down.

"I thought maybe we could use a break," Reese said, sipping the fruit punch.

Stacy nodded. She returned a wave from one of her friends, then smiled at Reese.

"Are you having fun?"

"Yes," she bubbled. "Are you?"

"Let's see, I recently consumed the best meal I've had in a long time and I'm with the most beautiful girl in the world. Yeah, I'd say I'm having a good time. I do have a confession to make, though," he added.

"What's that?"

"This monkey suit is the most uncomfortable thing I've ever worn in my life!"

Stacy laughed. "But you look so good in it."

"Really?" he replied, puffing up. "Well, as Dad always says, maybe we'd better preserve this moment for our future posterity. I don't think the line for pictures is getting any smaller, so we might as well get this over with."

"*What* future posterity?" Stacy pointedly asked as Reese reached for her empty paper cup.

Reese wiggled his eyebrows. "Time will tell," was his only reply before he helped her to her feet and led her across the large room.

* * *